THE HARRY HOUDINI MYSTERIES

THE DIME MUSEUM MURDERS

DANIEL STASHOWER

TITAN BOOKS

THE HARRY HOUDINI MYSTERIES: THE DIME MUSEUM MURDERS

PRINT EDITION ISBN: 9780857682840

E-BOOK ISBN: 9780857686190

Published by Titan Books
A division of Titan Publishing Group Ltd
144 Southwark St, London SE1 0UP

First edition: February 2012

2 4 6 8 10 9 7 5 3 1

Visit our website: www.titanbooks.com

A CIP catalogue record for this title is available from the British Library.

Printed and bound in the USA.

What did you think of this book? We love to hear from our readers. Please email us at: readerfeedback@titanemail.com, or write to us at the above address.

To receive advance information, news, competitions, and exclusive offers online, please sign up for the Titan newsletter on our website: www.titanbooks.com

THE
DIME MUSEUM
MURDERS

∼ 1 ∼

THE BALLY

COULD IT REALLY BE THAT TIME OF THE YEAR AGAIN? ANOTHER Halloween, already? It must be, the old man told himself. There were reporters in the downstairs parlor, and that only happened at Halloween.

How long had it been now? Twenty-seven years? Twenty-eight? Yes, twenty-eight. It hardly seemed possible. Harry had been dead for nearly three decades.

Even now, the old man was particular in matters of dress. He had spent fifty-three minutes polishing his black Riderstone wing-tips that morning, applying a second coat of EverBlack with an oil-soaked chamois, and buffing the stitch-work with his late wife's eyebrow pencil. His best suit, the double-breasted tick-weave, got a vigorous brushing, and his black onyx shirt studs received a last-minute spit-shine. A brisk dousing with Jenkinson's Lime Pomade completed his toilette. On his way downstairs, he paused at the mirror. Not bad for a man of eighty-four. In the old days, they called him "Dash."

Seated in the parlor, he waited quietly for the interview to begin. The photographer, a man named Parker, fussed and clucked over his light meter while the reporter glanced at his notes. Matthews, he said his name was. Call me Jack.

Very little changed about this ritual from year to year. The cameras seemed to get smaller, and the reporters younger, but each interview crept along in the same weary way. One year, there had been a man with a moving picture camera, crouching beneath a black cloth while his hand turned a crank. Another year there had been a recording device with two large spools of silver wire. Matthews, a plump-faced youth with thinning ginger hair, seemed content with the traditional pad of paper and a well-chewed pencil.

Always the same questions, though. *Tell us what you remember about your brother, Mr. Hardeen. If your brother were alive today, Mr. Hardeen, what sorts of escapes do you suppose he would be performing? Can you tell us how he made that elephant vanish, Mr. Hardeen?*

And every year, come what may, the big wrap-up question: *Do you suppose, Mr. Hardeen, that your brother will ever make good on his promise to send a message from the spirit world?*

He had not yet made up his mind how to play the interview this year. For a few moments he considered reprising his Wily Codger routine from the year before. This entailed a great deal of thigh-slapping and many repetitions of the phrase "I kid you not, Sonny Boy..." It played well and traveled wide, bringing a harvest of clips from all over the map—Louisville's *Courier-Journal*, Toledo's *Evening Bee*. He couldn't remember them all, but they were in the press book.

Or perhaps he would give them the Wistful Trouper. This involved lengthy patches of misty-eyed reminiscence about gaslit stages, Bertrand's Alum Face Paint, and the great days of the sideshows and dime museums. He had a heartwarming anecdote about Emma Shaller, the Ossified Girl, that could always be counted on for three or four column inches.

Parker, the photographer, was now frowning over a troublesome shadow. The old man folded his legs and ran his hand across his shirt front, checking the red silk handkerchief in his breast pocket. There had been a time, the winter season of 1931–32, when his show traveled with 612 props. Today, he needed only one. *Tell me, Mr. Hardeen*, the reporter would ask, *were you and your brother close at the time of his death?* At this, the old man would sit back in his chair as if surprised by the question, and impressed by the reporter's insight. Clearing his throat, he would begin to answer but then stop himself, as though seized by a sudden rush of feeling. He would smile faintly and shake his head at this—such emotion! After so many years!—and clutch at his handkerchief to dab his moistening eyes.

And here was the beauty of the thing. As he plucked the red silk from his pocket, a small metallic object would fall heavily to the floor, perhaps rolling to the reporter's feet. *I'm sorry, at my age it's difficult to bend—would you… ?* The reporter would pick it up. A heavy gold medallion with a strange insignia. *Did this belong to your brother, Mr. Hardeen?* And the Great Hardeen would fold his hands and allow a wry smile to play across his lips. *In a sense, young man.*

You see, it's a memento from the very first time that Harry Houdini ever died.

I'm sorry? Well, Mr. Matthews, it's a long story, and I know that you and young Parker want to get back to the city. Maybe some other—?

No? You want to hear it? Well, let's see how much of it I remember. I've never told this story before. In fact, they made us swear an oath on the Wintour family Bible, which was a bit of a laugh, if you must know. The Brothers Houdini, sons of Rabbi Mayer Samuel Weiss, taking a solemn vow on a Bible. But we gave our word and I've held to it. I know Harry did, too. Never even told Bess, so far as I know. Still, there's been a lot of water under the Williamsburg Bridge since then. I read the other day—in the *Herald*, you'll be gratified to hear—that Lady Wycliffe has finally passed. The last great society hostess. Folded her last napkin, you might say. I've kept my mouth shut all these years out of respect for her. She was a fine woman, and she deserved better than that goggle-eyed bastard she—

But I suppose I'm getting ahead of myself. Would you mind drawing those blinds just a bit? My cataracts. The light, it troubles me a bit.

Thank you. Now, gentlemen, you're certain that you'd like to hear about this? You don't—? Very well.

It must have been September, or perhaps October, of 1897. I turned twenty-one that year. Harry would have been twenty-three. My brother was going through a rough time. He'd worked like a dog, but try as he might, he couldn't quite break out of the small time. He was strictly a novelty act—traveling circuses, the midway, that sort of thing. He and I had done an act together from the time we were kids, but that changed when he married Bess. From that point on, she did the act with him and I did the booking and advance work. Truth be told, the duties were pretty light. There wasn't a tremendous demand for appearances by the Great Houdini at that stage, but I was always on hand, behind the scenes. Nowadays you would call me a theatrical agent and pay me a fat commission. Back then, we literally worked for food.

We'd been traveling quite a bit that year—sometimes with the Welsh Brothers Circus, sometimes with the Marco Company. We did all right trailing through such places as Cherokee, Kansas and Woonsocket, Rhode Island, where people seemed grateful for most any form of entertainment. Harry's escape act hadn't quite taken shape yet, but he did a passable magic routine. He fancied himself a master manipulator, and billed himself as the "King of Kards." Bess worked as his assistant, and also pulled an occasional spot as a singer. "The Melodious Little Songster," we called her. She had a wonderful voice and—I don't mind telling you—she was easy on the eyes.

In a traveling show just about everyone takes a turn on stage, and I did my share as a juggler and an acrobat. I also worked as a spotter for the trapeze team, and occasionally I put on a gorilla suit for the "Beasts of All Nations" tableau. I liked circus life. The work suited me and I enjoyed the travel and the small towns, which reminded me of my boyhood in Wisconsin. If not for my brother, I might well have spent the rest of my working life touring the sticks. Even my modest talents were sufficient to earn a living. Nobody ever got famous working town fairs and medicine shows, but nobody ever worked himself into an early grave either.

In those days, you could make a living without ever setting foot in a big city. For that matter, you could do well without ever touring America. Carter the Great, one of the best magic acts of all time, spent years overseas, just to stay out of Kellar's way. You've never heard of Kellar? He was king back then. But the road show wasn't enough for Harry. He had to make it big. And to do that, he had to conquer New York.

New York didn't want to know from Harry Houdini. I was with him when he went calling on a booking agent named Arthur Berg, who was a big fish in those days. They called him "Snaps," because he could make or break a career with a click of his fingers. Harry had been sending him stacks of clippings from small town newspapers, most of which had been planted—and sometimes even written—by yours truly. "Houdini Astounds Residents of Kennesaw." "Houdini A Delight, Say Audiences in Lynchburg." Personally, I didn't put a whole lot of stock in the good opinion of papers like the Brattleboro *Gazette*, but Harry did. He preserved each clipping as though it were edged in gold. Gathered them all up in a shiny leather binder, which he proudly laid out in front of Mr. Berg when we finally got in to see him. Snaps barely looked up from his desk. "Very nice, Mr. Houdini," he said. "But what have you done *locally*?"

It just about killed Harry. It was too late to hook up with another traveling show that season, and the small cash reserves we'd managed to build up on the road were draining rapidly. I finally got him a job at Huber's Fourteenth Street Museum. The dime museum. The ten-in-one.

You're too young to remember the ten-in-one. Some people called it the freak show, but it wasn't a freak show—not really. Human curiosities, they called them. Marvels of the natural world. Peerless prodigies of physical phenomena. You paid a dime, you got to see ten different acts. They say Barnum himself got it going. Gather 'round, all—the show is about to begin.

Just about every circus in America had a show like that on its midway. You paid a little extra, they lifted up the flap and let you in. It was supposed to make you feel sort of daring. The whole point was to turn the tip as quickly as possible. Sorry? The tip. That's the crowd. "Turning the tip" meant getting the crowd gathered, taking their money, and herding them through the tent as quick as you could. The acts were lined up on a platform, one after the other, and the talker would hustle the audience from one to the next as though pushing them with a broom.

Harry worked dozens of these places. In fact, they used to call him "Dime Museum Harry," and even after he'd made it big, he was always afraid that he might have to go back. It was no kind of life for Bess, I'll say that. She used to sell toothpaste to the other performers on the road, just to keep us fed.

Dime museums in New York were a whole lot different from dime museums on the road. For one thing, there were enough people in New York to keep the show running year round. On the road, stopping in the burgs and backwaters, pretty much everyone within twenty miles who had a dime would have seen the show after three days. In New York, with its constant supply of fresh marks, the shows tended to set up in storefronts and theater lobbies, rather than in tents or circus wagons. It made for more pleasant working conditions, and there was always a chance that a real live booker might catch your act. Or so we hoped.

There was only one spot open at Huber's Museum, so Harry and Bess did the act while I beat the bushes. I called on agents and managers with Harry's beloved press book, and talked a good line about his fabulous drawing power in central Illinois. I guess we'd been back in New York for about three weeks by then, and I had worked my way pretty much to the bottom of the pecking order. I seem to recall showing the book to a guy behind the screens of a Punch and Judy show. He didn't even bother to take the puppets off his hands, he just had me turn the pages for him. Even he couldn't use us.

It must have been around six in the evening when I caught the elevated train to Huber's. It was raining, and I can remember cradling the press book under my coat to protect the leather. I wasn't especially looking forward to seeing Harry. He'd just about reached the end of his tether, and I had no good news for him.

I left the train at Fourteenth Street and walked east toward Union Square. When I got to Huber's I found Albert Sandor leaning against the wall outside with a cigar clamped between his teeth, cleaning his nails with a toothpick. Albert was the outside talker at Huber's, the guy who kept up a fast-running patter to attract a crowd and move them through the "Hall of Curiosities." It was a rare thing to see Albert with his mouth shut, and I guessed that the talent was taking a doniker break.

Albert looked me up and down and gave a two-tone whistle. "Hot date?" he asked.

I was wearing a double-breasted wool suit that a tailor in Kansas City had assured me was the latest European fashion. A banker's gray with a windowpane check if you looked real close, wide lapels, and a nipped-in waist. I also had a cream-colored shirt with a fresh collar and cuffs, and a wide pukka silk tie which, if I'd unbuttoned my jacket, would have displayed a portrait of the late General Gordon. The haberdasher made me a deal. For good measure, I also had on a good pair of brown leather oxfords that still held their shine, though they no longer kept out water.

"Who's the lucky girl?" Albert asked.

"There's no girl," I said. "I wear my best suit when I go calling on bookers. It doesn't show the wear at the knees." I jerked my head toward the platform. "How's the draw?"

"Running at about three-quarter capacity," he said. "Not bad for a Tuesday."

"A tribute to the drawing power of the Great Houdinis, wouldn't you say? Might be time for Mr. Beckman to move them up to the main stage." Mr. Beckman was the guy who managed Huber's at that time. He also happened to do the booking for a big variety palace called Thornton's across the street, a fact that was not lost on my brother.

Albert grinned and knocked the ash from his cigar. "Dancing girls, Dash. That's what brings the crowds, and that's what Mr. Beckman wants. 'Charming young ladies in revealing fashions.' That's what it says out front. The crowd at Thornton's wouldn't know what to make of an escapodontist."

"Escapologist."

"Whatever. Your brother is better off on the platform."

"We'll see," I said. "What sort of a mood is the justly celebrated self-liberator in this evening?"

Albert grinned and continued grooming his fingernails. "He was in a lovely humor when he came off after the three o'clock. Came up to me and demanded I deliver hot water and fresh towels to his dressing room after each performance."

"He has a dressing room?"

"Seems he's marked out some territory at the back. Near the boiler."

"Imagine that."

"So now he wants fresh towels, seeing as how he has a fancy dressing room."

"I'm sorry, Albert, he can be—"

He waved his toothpick. "Not a problem. I told him to take it up with the wardrobe mistress."

"Since when do we have a wardrobe mistress?"

"We don't."

I shifted the clipping book under my arm. "I'll talk to him."

"Do that."

"Any chance of giving him the extra time he wants? He wants to try out a new bit. Two audience members come up and tie his hands, then Harry—"

"I know, Dash. He told me all about it. He gets three minutes, just like everybody else."

"It could be a great act. He gets out of the ropes, and also a bag and a trunk. But the kicker is that—"

"—when it's all over, Bess is inside the trunk. I know, Dash. They've switched places. In the twinkling of an eye. But he still only gets three minutes. Just like everybody else."

I turned and gazed across the street at the marquee of Thornton's Theater, which was emblazoned with the name of Miss Annie Cummings, the Songbird from Savannah. "You know," I said, "my brother really is as good as he says he is."

"Sure, Dash. And one day it'll be his name up there in tall letters. And shortly after that, I'll be elected president of the United States."

"What a gruff and crusty fellow you are, Albert."

"I'm a realist, Dash. I know your brother is talented, but it's not enough. His timing stinks. His delivery stinks. His patter stinks. His—"

"All of those things will get better. I'm telling you, he's a natural showman. He has a real instinct for drama. I've seen people literally holding their breath waiting to see if he'll find a way to escape from an old nailed-up packing crate. All he needs is a chance to show what he can do. Now, if Mr. Beckman should give him one of the warm-up spots at Thornton's, just a few minutes at the top of the show, I know Harry could—"

"Dash. It's a dance hall. Burleycue."

"Harry's worked burlesque halls before."

"Really? I wouldn't have thought he had the legs for it." Albert looked at his watch and tossed away the stump of his cigar. "Do me a favor, wouldja? Run the bally for me? Chester's down with the grippe."

The bally, I should probably explain, is an act performed outside the tent or the theater to lure the marks inside. A crowd gathers to see the act—whatever it is—and the talker launches into an elaborate spiel, describing the many miracles and marvels to be found just beyond the ticket window. If the talker is any good—and Albert was one of the best—the marks will just about knock him over in their haste to get inside. Sometimes the bally would be a sword-swallower; sometimes a fire-eater. The absent Chester was an accomplished blockhead—meaning that he could drive three-inch spikes into his nose with a hammer.

Happily, Albert didn't expect anything quite that exotic from me. There was a set of heavy wooden Indian clubs sitting by the entrance. I picked them up and started juggling—an easy overhand pass routine—while Albert delivered his grind. I don't remember exactly how the patter went, but I do recall that it began with the words "Step right up, folks," and that it promised "a world of wonders such as mortal eyes have never beheld."

Between Albert's grind and my juggling, it wasn't long before we'd gathered a crowd of perhaps fourteen or fifteen people, about as many as could be expected on a chilly Tuesday evening. Albert collected a handful of coins, issued paper tickets, and ushered our small audience through the door.

The so-called Palace of Wonders had been established on the ruins of a failed butcher's shop, and the smell of salty meats still hung about the room. Mr. Beckman had used red and gold hanging banners to cover the walls and display windows, but otherwise the space was much as it had been—a long, dingy room with high windows along the left-hand wall. No one had even bothered to sweep the sawdust from the floor.

A narrow platform ran along the left wall beneath the windows, creating a performance ramp that Albert described as his "Arcade of Miracles." It was perhaps two feet high and no more than four feet deep, and the performers stood there in plain view waiting for the show to start. They all snapped to attention as the crowd filtered in, and bustled around the platform trying to make themselves look interesting.

Albert's job was to herd the crowd from one edge of the platform to the other, allowing them the requisite 180 seconds to enjoy each of the acts. He did this with uncommon skill. "Hurry along, folks!" he would cry, with a slight edge of alarm to his voice. "You won't want to miss our next Oddity of Nature!"

The Oddities of Nature, it must be said, were looking a little haggard, since this was their tenth show of the day. Nevertheless, they managed to rouse themselves as Albert urged the crowd forward. It started with Miss Missy, the Armless Wonder, who sat drinking tea from a China cup daintily clutched between her toes, and moved on to the Human Skye Terrier, whose shaggy dog head benefited greatly from artfully placed chin and chop pieces. Next came the Tattooed Lady and the Moss-Haired Girl, followed by the Sword-Swallower and the Double-Bodied Wonder, who had a pair of tiny legs—meant to be the remnants of a Siamese twin—poking out of his mid-section. The Living Skeleton, the Human Telescope, and Vranko the Glass-Eater rounded out the entertainments.

As each act finished in turn, the performers were given thirty seconds to hawk a souvenir item for a nickel or a dime, which gave them the chance to augment the meager salary they drew from Mr. Beckman. For the most part, these items took the form of a booklet or a keepsake scroll that related the performer's brave and heart-rending struggle against the cruel hand of nature. Miss Missy's story, I recall, was especially touching. It was a miniature volume entitled "My Blessed Life," with her portrait on the front in all her armless glory. It began with the words, "I am never too busy to lend a helping foot."

Other performers went for cheap wooden novelties. Harmi, the Sword-Swallower, offered little wooden sabers, and Benny, the Human Skye Terrier, did a brisk business in personalized grooming supplies. I can't remember what my brother was selling that year—it was either his "Teach Yourself Magic" booklet or "Professor Houdini's Ten Steps to Perfect Health."

When all the novelties were bought, Albert herded the audience toward the last act—Harry Houdini of Appleton, Wisconsin, performing as "The King of Kards and Konjuring." My brother never got a lot of credit for it, but he was a pretty fair card mechanic in his day. While he waited for the crowd to shift down to his end of the room, he stood at the front edge of the platform plucking card fans from thin air. He was dressed in a black suit with a string tie and a straw boater hat, and had his sleeves pushed back to show off his muscular forearms. As the crowd circled, Harry went into some flashy hand-to-hand cascades while Albert introduced him.

"Kidnapped by gypsies at the tender age of six months, the infant Harry was soon earning his keep by plucking coins and wallets from the pockets of unwary passers-by. By the age of five, the pint-sized prodigy was apprenticed to Signor Blitz, the greatest of all the magicians in the world, and by his twelfth year, the precocious prestidigitator was the favorite of the sultans and sheiks of far-away lands. He appears today by kind permission of the czar of Russia, to whom he serves as court conjurer. Ladies and gentlemen, I give you, the one, the only—Harry Houdini!"

It was a stirring intro, and I could feel a building sense of anticipation from the small crowd as they awaited this extraordinary young man's first miracle. Then Harry spoiled it. He talked.

I was reading my brother's biography the other day. It had many kind things to say about Harry's "mesmerizing stage presence" and "compelling natural charisma." Clearly the author had never been to Huber's Museum. The truth is, Harry didn't have a lot of natural charisma at that time. He was only beginning to learn to relax onstage. In a few years' time he became a lot breezier, and learned to treat the audience as if they were all in on a big secret. In those early days, he came across like some sort of German physics professor. He lectured the audience, and directed them on the proper manner in which to appreciate the genius of Houdini. It might have played well in Europe, where they still dressed up their magic acts as "philosophical experiments," but in New York, they just wanted entertainment.

"Ladies and gentlemen," my brother said from the platform, "I am the Great Houdini, the justly celebrated self-liberator and eclipsing sensation of Europe. I will now entertain you."

My sister-in-law Bess stepped from behind a makeshift curtain, carrying a velvet-trimmed prop table. She was wearing what I always thought of as her "sugarplum fairy" costume. It was all gauze and puffs that made her look like a Christmas ornament with legs. Her legs were her best feature, and even though she wore tights, I never understood how she got away with that outfit in those days.

"And now," said Harry, "if it will please the ladies and the gentlemen, I urge you to direct your attention toward the glass bowl that I am holding. It is enormous, as you see, and very heavy, because to the brim it is filled with water."

He stepped forward, holding the bowl stiffly at arm's length. "Observe closely, and you will see the little fishes swimming merrily in the water. Do you see them? They are very jolly little fellows, swimming back and forth."

Albert caught my gaze and rolled his eyes. *Faster, Harry*, I said under my breath. *There's a guy in the back who's still awake.*

"I command your attention as I place the bowl onto this lacquered tray that my lovely wife Bess is holding. Now I display for you a large black foulard. You see it? There is nothing unusual about this cloth. Here is one side—here is the other. Now I cover the bowl and lift it high in the air. At this point, you must prepare yourselves for a miracle. It is really quite an astonishing shock, so I would ask that you steel your nerves for the amazement which I now present."

Just do the trick, Harry, I muttered. *And for God's sake, don't mention the traveling circus.*

"Long ago, when I was a boy in Appleton, in the fine state of Wisconsin, the traveling circus came to town. It was a wondrous sight for a small American boy like myself. Jugglers they had, and clowns, and an elephant, and many tigers. But of all the wonders I saw that day, none amazed me so much as the magician who caused a bowl of goldfish—a bowl much like the very one I hold here—to vanish as if into thin air."

From the platform, Bess caught my eye and flinched slightly.

She still held the black lacquered tray, waiting for her cue to leave the stage. She never lost her frozen smile, but her eyes were haunted.

"On that day," Harry continued, "I promised myself that I would grow up to perform that trick just as well as that man in the circus. And because this is America, I knew that a boy with a dream in his heart could grow up to become whatever he wished. A doctor, a lawyer, a politician... even a magician! And so, ladies and gentlemen, behold the miracle of the vanishing goldfish! I throw the foulard heavenward—and voila!—the enormous bowl has vanished!"

Let me tell you three things about the goldfish trick. One, it's the best stand-alone vanish in the history of magic. Two, it needs to be done fast, without a lot of anecdotes about the circus. Three, my sister-in-law Bess is quite a bit stronger than she looks.

It's a brilliant trick when it's done right, but you wouldn't have known it by the six-thirty crowd at Huber's Museum. Their reaction, as Harry flicked the cloth heavenward, left much to be desired. One might have called it a respectful silence. I suppose there must have been some scattered applause, and perhaps a bit of it was done by someone other than myself. Most of the others simply shuffled their feet and coughed politely.

When I think back on it, I remember something that Will Rogers once said about my brother. This was years later, of course. Rogers was watching from backstage while Harry worked on a particularly difficult handcuff challenge. The thing about it was that Harry had gone into a little curtained cabinet while he worked on the handcuffs, so the crowd couldn't actually see him. There wasn't a thing going on, but the whole audience was happy just to sit there and wait for my brother to finish. It took him an hour and a half, and the crowd never took its eyes off the cabinet. When Harry finally emerged, holding the handcuffs high over his head, they jumped to their feet. Will Rogers said he couldn't possibly follow an act like that.

He said, "I might just as well have gotten on my little pony and ridden back to the livery stable as to have ridden out on that stage." It was a fine compliment, but I can't help thinking what Rogers might have thought if he'd ever seen Harry at the dime museum. In those days, Harry couldn't hold the audience even when he was standing right in front of them. It was so quiet you could actually hear the floorboards creak.

Albert was just about to move the crowd off when I caught him by the elbow. "Let him do the new bit," I said. "The trunk trick."

"Aw, knock it off, Dash," he said. "We've been over this again and again."

I pulled out my most prized possession, a gold Elgin pocket watch. "Let him try it," I said. "I promise you, each one of these people will be cheering at the end. If the crowd doesn't go wild, I'll give you the watch."

Albert looked at my face and saw that I was serious. He glanced at his own watch, a tin conductor's chrono, and looked back at me again. "Sorry, Dash," he said, not without regret. "You know the rules. He's already had his three minutes. If I let Harry pad his slot, then Harmi's going to be after me to make time for that ridiculous 'Dance of the Seven Sabers.' Everything'll get longer and before you know it we'll be down to five shows a day."

"Come on, Albert. Just this—"

He held up his hand. "Sorry. I'm going to the blow-off."

I turned away and shoved my watch back into my vest pocket. Albert stepped forward and asked the crowd to gather round for a "very special added amusement."

Every sideshow worth its salt had a blow-off—an extra act tacked on at the end to lure an extra nickel from the marks. This was always staged in a special annex—a small extra tent or a back room of some kind—or, in this case, an abandoned meat locker. Most of the time the blow-off would be a creepy, scary sort of illusion, like the old Headless Lady effect. In that one, you walked into the room and saw the body of a young woman sitting in a chair. She appeared normal in every respect, but for the fact that she had no head. There would be a bunch of wires and tubes filled with gurgling liquid sprouting out of her neck. The talker would explain her predicament in a low, quavery voice. "Decapitated in a tragic railway accident, this brave young lady is kept alive by a miraculous combination of modern medicine and American know-how…"

The blow-off was always especially good at Huber's, but Albert had an uphill climb trying to work up any enthusiasm from the crowd. My brother Harry had left them in an unhappy stupor, and no one seemed terribly eager to cough up an extra nickel for whatever awaited them in the so-called "Chamber of Chills."

"This attraction is not for the faint of heart," Albert warned. "This hideous freak of nature is the only one of its kind in the entire world, an unholy coupling of man and insect, a poignant hybrid of beauty and terror. I must caution you, ladies and gentlemen, the mere sight of what lies just beyond this room has made women faint and strong men buckle at the knees. Who among you has the courage, indeed, the fortitude to venture past this fateful portal?"

By the time Albert finished, nearly all of them had summoned the necessary fortitude. Albert collected a handful of nickels and shepherded the crowd through the door into a small, candle-lit room. There, sitting on a small wooden pedestal, was the most beautiful Spider-girl I ever saw. She had a furry, dark thorax with a bright yellow hour-glass shape on the back, meant to suggest the markings of a black widow. There were eight hairy, segmented legs—two of which were moving slowly up and down—and it had the head of my sister-in-law, Bess Houdini, with a bright ribbon in her hair and red polish on her lips. "Howdy, folks!" she called, waving one of the furry legs.

"Be careful, ladies and gentlemen," Albert warned. "Whatever you do, don't make any loud noises! I know she looks calm and friendly, but we had a fellow in here last week who—well, let's just say it wasn't a pretty sight."

Bess cocked her head and wiggled her thorax as Albert continued. "Folks, I'm sure you're all wondering how this hideous conjoining came to be. How did such an angelic face come to be transplanted onto that eight-legged horror? Only seven years ago, Alice Anders was the daughter of a world-renowned explorer, joining her father on a dangerous journey along the Amazon River. One night, while the explorers lay asleep in their tents, a sinister creature stole into the camp, lured by the sweet smell of young Alice's perfume. When the party awoke in the morning, they found a spectacle so ghastly that they were driven mad by the mere sight of it. There before them lay—"

We never discovered what the explorers saw, because at that moment Albert was interrupted by a loud crashing noise which, if you really stopped to think about it, sounded an awful lot like a pair of cymbals.

"Heaven help us!" Albert shouted. "The Spider-girl is attacking! Run for your lives!" At this, Bess pulled her lips back in a snarl, revealing a pair of gleaming fangs. As she edged forward just slightly, a thin stream of red liquid dribbled from her bottom lip. Not a lot of people were there to see that. Most of them had already run screaming for the exit door, which Albert held open in an obliging manner.

No sooner had the last of the marks bolted through the door than the Spider-girl broke off her attack.

"Very nice, Mrs. Houdini," said Albert, dusting off his hands. "I doubt if Miss Bernhardt could have done better."

"And the costume suits you," I added, gesturing at the bobbing thorax, "but don't you think you're showing a bit too much leg?"

"Very funny, Dash," she answered. "I hear Weber and Fields might be looking for a third comic. Why don't you run on down to the Palace?"

"I just came from there," I said. "They don't need comics, but there's a spot for a dancing girl, so long as she has eight legs. Say, you don't suppose… ?"

"Just help me out of this thing, would you, Dash?"

I walked behind the pedestal and helped to disengage her from the apparatus. Bess stood up and stretched to work out the kinks. "Tell me you've found us another booking, Dash," she said. "Please tell me you've found us another booking."

"Nothing yet," I said.

"Father preserve us," she said. "Have you told him yet? Have you told the man whom the Milwaukee *Sentinel* called the 'most captivating entertainer in living memory'?"

"Not yet."

"I wish you luck," she said, dabbing at some blood on her chin.

I could hear Harry in the main room, shouting something about towels, clean water, and performers of a certain "exalted magnitude." Then the door banged open and my brother hurtled into the room, chin first, looking like a boxer coming out of his corner. I knew that if Harry followed his normal pattern, he would need about three minutes to blow off steam. The steam usually blew in my direction.

"Dash!" he called, barreling toward me. "See what has become of the Great Houdini! Have I not proved myself? Have I not created a unique, exceptional act as the justly celebrated self-liberator, renowned for his death-defying acts of bravery?"

"You have indeed, Harry," I said.

"Am I not the man whom the Milwaukee *Sentinel* called the 'most captivating entertainer in living memory'?"

Bess and I exchanged a look. "You are indeed, Harry," I said.

"Europe is rich with opportunity for a talented man such as myself, but I am determined to succeed in America, the land of my birth. And yet, here in the city of New York, the place I love above all others, I am regarded as a simple conjurer. A mere magician! It is madness, is it not?"

"It is indeed, Harry," I said.

"Intolerable," he said. "You may walk with me to my dressing room."

You may wonder why I put up with him. To be frank, I'd long since learned to lower the volume on him when he launched one of his tirades. Had I actually been listening, I might have pointed out to him that America was not, in fact, the land of his birth. Hungary was the land of his birth. Budapest, to be specific. America was the land of *my* birth, which explained many of the differences between us.

He led me into the dank back room of the butcher shop, toward a small equipment closet that he had commandeered as a dressing area. His mirror and makeup kit were neatly laid out on a block table that—judging by the ragged grooves on its surface—had once been used to saw carcasses. Harry sat down on a rickety stool and faced the mirror.

"Why won't they let me do the trunk trick, Dash?" he asked. "It was such a hit on the road. I could be the finest escape artist who ever lived. You see that, don't you?"

"As far as we know, Harry, you're the *only* escape artist who ever lived. So there isn't a whole lot of demand for it just yet. Everybody knows what a magician does. Nobody's ever heard of an escape artist."

He looked at himself in the mirror. For some reason, he insisted on wearing full stage makeup on the sideshow platform, and spent half an hour troweling on heavy foundation each morning. The dark penciling on his eyebrows and the orange tint of his cheeks made him look like a stern carrot. He dipped his fingers into a wooden tub and began slathering his face with butterfat, which was what we used for makeup remover in those days.

"Why don't we have some posters made up?" he asked. "That might help. We could show me struggling with chains and handcuffs. 'Will He Escape?' It would be very dramatic."

"Posters cost money, Harry."

He sighed and rubbed his face with a scrap of coarse wool.

"What about Sing-Sing? That would be free."

Harry had come up with the idea of breaking out of a cell at Sing-Sing prison, figuring that such a stunt would grab a fair number of headlines. "I've spoken to the warden three times," I said. "He doesn't want you anywhere near the place." Actually, the warden's exact words had been somewhat more explicit, and involved many repetitions of the phrase "brass-plated nut case." I saw no reason why Harry needed to hear that.

"They are afraid of Houdini," he said. "It will make them look bad if Houdini breaks free of their brand-new jail."

Bess crept past me and squeezed onto the stool next to Harry. "I asked Albert about doing the trunk trick," she announced.

"You did?" Harry looked at her in the mirror. "What did he say?"

She reached down and began untying the ballet slippers she wore on stage. "You won't like it, Harry."

He laid his hands on the table. "Tell me."

Bess pulled off her slippers and began winding the ribbons. "Albert says that watching you is only slightly more interesting than watching a cigar store Indian. He says that your patter stinks. I believe he had much the same conversation with Dash."

Harry turned to me. "Is this true?"

"He may have mentioned something of the sort."

He looked into the mirror and fell silent, his face a study in dejection. Bess stood behind him and placed her hands on his shoulders. "Well," he said after a time. "I don't suppose I've ever heard—"

"Mr. Houdini?" We heard a voice coming from the main room.

"In here, Jack," Harry called, turning toward the door.

Jack Hawkins, the errand boy from Thornton's across the street, poked his head through the doorway. He wore the red and gold uniform of a theater usher, complete with a round chin-strap hat that concealed most of his bright red hair. Alert and eager to please, Jack must have been all of eleven years old at the time. Harry and I took an interest in him because we'd both also worked as bellhops at his age, and like Jack, we'd always been willing to jump through hoops for a nickel tip.

"Evening, Mrs. Houdini," Jack said, tugging at his cap. He thrust an envelope at Harry. "Telegram came for you at the box office, sir."

"Good lad," said Harry. He was always saying things like "Good lad" and "There's a good fellow" to Jack. He also liked to tousle the boy's hair, which Jack endured with ill-concealed annoyance.

Harry unfolded the telegram and scanned the contents. "It seems that I am moving up in the world, Dash," he said, raising his eyebrows. "I've been invited to the home of Branford Wintour. On Fifth Avenue, no less."

I whistled. "Branford Wintour? What's he want with you?"

"Who's Branford Wintour?" Jack asked.

"They call him the King of Toys," I explained. "There's hardly a boy in America who hasn't played with one of his whirly tops. He has a big factory in New Jersey—wooden soldiers, paper novelties, train sets. Anything you can imagine."

"I don't have much time for wooden soldiers," Jack said in a husky voice.

"What's he want with you, Harry?" I repeated. "Some sort of society wing ding?"

"I think not," Harry said. "It seems that Mr. Wintour has been murdered, and only Houdini can tell the police how it was done."

Bess and I looked at each other. Harry's patter—Albert's opinion notwithstanding—was getting better by the minute.

2

THE HUMAN PIN-CUSHION

"HARRY," I SAID, AS WE TROTTED UP TOWARD FIFTH AVENUE. "YOU really need to fill me in on the details. How was he murdered? Why do they need you there?"

He pulled the collar of his shaggy astrakhan cloak up around his ears, pretending not to have heard.

"Who sent the telegram? Why won't you tell me anything?"

My brother closed his eyes and lowered his chin to his chest, apparently lost in thought.

We were riding in a horse-drawn calash, jostling hard as the driver maneuvered around the evening theater traffic. Harry had said little since we'd left the theater—nothing, in fact, apart from a single line: "It is a case for the Great Houdini!" He delivered this sentiment while throwing his cloak around his shoulders.

Now, sitting back against the leather seat with his brow furrowed and his fingers steepled at his chin, he looked for all the world like the hero of some stage melodrama.

"Harry—" I began again.

"Dash," he said impatiently, "you cannot expect me to divulge the particulars. It is traditional that the detective remain tight-lipped until he reaches the scene of the crime."

Ah. Suddenly it made sense. "Harry," I said, "you're thinking of detective *stories,* not real detective work. And anyway, you're a performer, not a detective."

"Performer!" he snorted. "I am no mere performer! I am Houdini! I have talents and knowledge that other men do not! At least our New York City police seem to appreciate this, if the theatrical community does not."

We rode in silence for a moment. "At least let me see the telegram," I said.

Wordlessly, he passed it over. It read: "Need Houdini Urgent Home Branford Wintour Stop Murder Investigation Stop Lt. Murray."

"Harry, this doesn't tell us much. Apart from the fact that this Lieutenant Murray is careful with his pocket change. Ten words exactly."

"It tells us a great deal," he said.

"Such as?"

He gave me a corner-of-the-eye look. "It is a capital mistake to theorize in advance of the facts."

"Harry," I said. "For God's sake."

I should explain something. My brother was not a great reader, but he dearly loved his detective stories. He would read them on trains, backstage, in the bath—virtually anywhere. His favorite was Sherlock Holmes, whose adventures he followed religiously in *Harper's Weekly* until the detective's tragic death at the hands of Professor Moriarty, an event that left him despondent for some weeks. Harry read the Sherlock Holmes stories many times over. Our late father could jab a pin into a random passage of the family Talmud and call out each word it had pierced on the subsequent pages. Harry could do the same with *The Adventures of Sherlock Holmes.*

"Harry," I said, starting again, "this is a police investigation. You can't barge in there and expect to lead them around by their noses. There's no Inspector Lestrade in the New York Police Department."

"I will merely give them the benefit of my acknowledged expertise."

I muttered something under my breath.

29

"Pardon me?" Harry said. "Would you please repeat that?"

"I didn't say anything."

"No one will be dropping *me* over a waterfall anytime soon, Dash," he said. "And anyway, it was the Reichenbach Falls, not Rickenstoff."

I folded my arms and fell silent until we pulled up to the Wintour mansion.

Branford Wintour's home had always been something of an architectural curiosity. I remember that when they had built the place a few years earlier there were jokes about whether Manhattan would sink under its weight. It took up a good chunk of land and was lousy with gables and mansards and spires and all sorts of other features that you don't see much on Fifth Avenue these days, including a three-story aviary. Wintour had chosen a spot directly across the avenue from the Vanderbilt pile, and for a time it seemed as if he might put his neighbor in the shade.

Harry and I scrambled out of the calash and faced a brilliant white expanse of marble that might have given Nansen and Peary some uneasy moments. We crossed the vast forecourt and had just finished climbing the steps when the front door swung open. I had expected a butler but instead we found a uniformed patrolman in a blue greatcoat and leather helmet.

"Which one of you is this Houdini character?" he asked.

"I am Houdini," my brother answered, puffing himself up to an impressive five-foot-four.

"The lieutenant wants you to wait here."

We followed him into a vaulted two-story entry hall. "Harry," I whispered. "This room is bigger than the last theater I worked." Sad to say, I wasn't joking.

A pair of mahogany double doors opened and a big, beefy man in a rumpled brown suit stepped toward us. "Name's Patrick Murray," he said in a voice not long out of Dublin. "I'm the detective in charge of this case. Appreciate your answering my wire."

"Hmm," said Harry, stepping back to appraise our new acquaintance. "Patrick Murray. You are Irish, I perceive."

Strange to say, Harry wasn't kidding either. Murray looked at me and raised his eyebrows. I shrugged. "I can see you're going to be a big help to us, Mr. Houdini," he said.

"I shall certainly do my best to assist in whatever way possible," said my brother, who was a bit tone deaf when it came to irony. "Now, perhaps it would help if you showed me to the murder scene. I trust your men haven't been tramping about in their muddy boots, obscuring clues, damaging valuable—"

"My men are doing their jobs as instructed," Murray said firmly. "And I believe we'll be able to manage the murder investigation on our own. We've asked you here because there's an aspect of the crime that seems to fall under your area of expertise."

"Oh?"

"The murder weapon."

"The murder weapon? That is most gratifying. In what way does the murder weapon fall under my area of expertise?"

Murray sighed. "Branford Wintour seems to have been murdered by a magic trick."

Harry glanced at me with shining eyes, struggling to conceal his pleasure at this news. "Please continue," he said.

Lieutenant Murray motioned to a very tall, somewhat stooped elderly gentleman who had been standing quietly by the mahogany doors. "This is Phillips, Mr. Wintour's butler," Murray said as the old man stepped forward. "I wonder if I might ask you to repeat what you've just told me for these gentlemen?"

"Of course, sir," the butler said, clearing his throat. He turned to us and began to speak in a flat, toneless manner, as though instructing a new member of the staff on the placement of finger bowls. "It is Mr. Wintour's habit of an evening to spend an hour or so answering correspondence in his study. He customarily takes a glass of Irish whiskey at five-thirty, but there was no response when I knocked at the door this evening."

"Did you break down the door?" Harry asked.

"Certainly not."

"What did you do?"

"I did nothing. I assumed that Mr. Wintour did not wish to be disturbed. It was only when he failed to appear for dinner that I grew concerned. He had arranged a small dinner party for this evening. When the guests began to assemble at six o'clock, Mr. Wintour had still not emerged."

"So you broke down the door?"

A pained expression crossed the old butler's face. "I saw no need to break down the door. I decided to telephone, in the event that he might have fallen asleep on the settee. It would not have been the first time. There is only one telephone in the house and that is in Mr. Wintour's study. I stepped across to a neighboring house to telephone."

Harry nodded. "But he didn't answer?"

"No, sir. By now I had begun to grow alarmed. On the advice of Mrs. Wintour, I telephoned a nearby locksmith, a Mr.—"

"Featherstone," Harry said. "A reliable, but unimaginative craftsman."

Lieutenant Murray's eyebrows went up at this, but he said nothing. Phillips carried on as if he hadn't heard. "Mr. Featherstone arrived some moments later and managed to open the door using a skeleton key."

"Is that the study over there?" Harry asked, gesturing at the heavy mahogany doors.

"It is."

"It's a routine Selkirk dead-bolt with a three-wheel ratchet. My sainted Mama could open that lock with her darning needle."

Phillips dipped his chin and peered at Harry over his half-glasses. "We had not known that your mother was available, sir," he said.

"Please continue, Phillips," said Lieutenant Murray.

"Once Mr. Featherstone had opened the door, I found Mr. Wintour at his desk."

"Dead?" Harry asked.

"I still believed he was asleep, but I could not rouse him. That was when I summoned the police."

"That'll do, Phillips," Lieutenant Murray said. "Gentlemen, if you'll follow me." He led us across the foyer to the study doors. There were a number of uniformed officers milling around, and to my surprise Harry appeared to know most of them. He nodded at a stocky young man sitting by the doors, and received a casual salute in return.

"Harry," I whispered, "how do you know—"

"Later," he answered.

One of the doors to the study was partially open, and I could see the bustle of plain-clothes men as they examined, measured, traced, and sketched along the edges of the scene. Then Murray pushed open the door and we saw the rest.

The study reeked of culture and old money, though I knew perfectly well that Wintour had made his loot within the past decade. Shelves of books with leather spines stretched across the left side of the room, broken only by a tall marble fireplace. Ancestral portraits and richly colored tapestries covered the other walls, and there were a number of marble busts sprouting up on alabaster pedestals throughout the room, creating a museum effect. A pair of club chairs, a settee, and a couple of Chesterfields were positioned just so in front of a flat-top, marble-inlay desk, the surface of which could easily have accommodated six or seven of the performers from Huber's Museum.

Though the furnishings imparted a certain baronial splendor to the room, it was clear that the occupant, who had made his fortune in the manufacture of children's toys, had never entirely put aside the playthings of youth. In one corner, the head of an outsize jack-in-the-box bobbed back and forth. A spectacular collection of wind-up animals, clockwork figures, and tin soldiers littered the surface of a library table, and a tall cylindrical zoetrope stood on a special display stand nearby. Most impressive of all, an enormous two-tiered model train set was arrayed on an oblong slab of polished wood. The track ran in a cloverleaf pattern perhaps five feet in each direction, with a web of heavy cording leading to a black control panel on the floor.

I confess that I might have spent the entire evening admiring that wondrous train set, but there were more urgent calls on our attention. "Gentlemen?" said Lieutenant Murray. "If I could ask you to step this way." A set of white hospital screens had been erected behind the desk. Three of Wintour's dinner guests— two men and a woman—were arranged on the Chesterfields, and I guessed that the screens had been placed to shield them from an unseemly spectacle. The lieutenant motioned us to step behind the partition. Although I had prepared myself, the sight of the dead man caught me by the throat.

Wintour lay on his back, stretched out upon a deep red Oriental rug. He wore a gray brushed flannel suit, a white cotton cambric shirt, a wide boating club tie, and the face of a man in torment. His eyes bulged and his tongue jutted, and patches of dark purple were spreading across his cheeks. I don't know what Mr. Wintour's views on the afterlife may have been, but he had the look of a man who had seen his destination and didn't much care for it.

"How old was he?" Harry asked softly.

"Fifty-three," Lieutenant Murray answered. He waited another moment while my brother and I recovered ourselves, then led us out from behind the screens. "You'll notice that this is an interior room," he said. "No windows. No other entrance apart from the doors we used. Those doors were locked from the inside and show no sign of tampering. Mr. Wintour seems to have been alone in his study at the time of his death. No one in the household heard anything unusual, nor had there been any unexpected visitors this afternoon. We expect that—"

"The fireplace," Harry said.

"What about it?"

"Has the fire been burning all day?"

"The butler laid it one hour before Mr. Wintour entered the room."

"I only ask because in a story by Mr. Edgar Allan Poe, the murderer was found to have entered by means of—"

"The chimney. Yes, Mr. Houdini. 'Murders in the Rue Morgue.'" Lieutenant Murray scratched his chin. "Our investigation is as yet in its earliest stages, but we've managed to rule out homicidal orangutans."

Harry colored slightly. "It's just that—"

"If I could ask you to direct your attention to the murdered man's desk, Mr. Houdini. That's why I've asked you here this evening."

A thick white cloth was spread over the center of the murdered man's desk. We could see the outlines of a squat, lumpy object beneath it. Murray motioned to an officer standing to the side. "Carter, mind showing our guests the, uh, device?"

With an anxious expression, the young officer stepped to the desk and gingerly pinched the edges of the cloth. Cautiously, as though a sleeping snake might be coiled underneath, he lifted the cloth and eased it to one side.

Harry sprang forward. "*Le Fantôme!*" he cried, thrusting his chin forward across the desk. "Do you see it, Dash? It's magnificent!"

The object was a small wooden figure, perhaps twelve inches high, draped in a Chinese silk kimono. It sat cross-legged on a square wooden pedestal, gazing intently at five ivory tiles at its feet, each bearing the image of a green dragon. In one hand, the figure held a tiny flute; the other clutched at the folds of its robe. A black, braided pigtail ran down the figure's back, and its face was painted with Kabuki markings.

"I would not have believed that it still existed," Harry said. "Look at the articulation of the joints! See the pinpoint mechanism of the jaw hinge?"

At the front of the pedestal was a set of small lacquered doors. Extending his index finger, Harry poked at the tiny latch. A uniformed officer moved forward to stop him, but Lieutenant Murray waved him off. Harry flicked the latch and the doors swung outward to expose an array of ancient cogwheels and drive bands.

"Astonishing!" he declared. "Look at the gears! They are made of—of—" He leaned in close and sniffed at the workings. "Yes! The gears are made of cork! And the shafts, they are hollow bamboo! How extraordinary that they should have survived all this time. And see the weights and counterweights? They are nothing more than tiny bags of silk, each one filled with sand. The craftsman who created this device can only have been a genius! It is even more beautiful than I imagined!"

"I'm glad you think so," said Lieutenant Murray. "But can you tell us what it is?"

"It's an automaton," Harry said, keeping his eyes fixed on the small figure. "One of the most exquisite ever made."

"An automaton," Lieutenant Murray said. "A little doll that moves and does tricks. Like a child's toy. We knew that much. And it's supposed to be worth a fortune because it's from the collection of some French guy with the same name as you. That's one reason we called you."

Harry straightened and set his mouth in a tight line. "Dash," he said, "perhaps you'd better enlighten them about the 'French guy.'"

The lieutenant folded his arms. "Just tell me about automatons," he said to me. "I've never seen one before tonight. What are they? What do they do?"

There must have been a dozen people in the room—police officers, medical workers, and a small knot of people in evening dress who appeared to be the dead man's dinner guests. All of them stopped what they were doing to listen to me. I was momentarily stage-struck. "Well," I began. "Um, let me see…"

"Begin with Jacob Philadelphia," Harry said.

"Well," I said again, "there was a magician named Jacob Philadelphia who was active in the eighteenth century, and he—"

"Born in 1734," my brother said.

"Thank you, Harry, that was very illuminating. This magician liked to display automatons—or automata, if you will. Little clockwork figures like this one. These figures, which resembled ordinary dolls, could move and perform in amazingly lifelike ways. At the magician's command, they did tricks for the audience. One changed water into wine; another gave answers to mathematical problems. Sometimes these figures were designed to look like animals. There was a very famous peacock that strutted around the stage, spread its feathers, and even gave a nice little screech."

I paused and surveyed the room. People appeared to be listening, so I continued. "Bear in mind, many of the people who came to see these devices had never seen a mechanical device more sophisticated than a clock. So a little doll that could play cards, or a monkey that could smoke cigarettes, would have seemed quite miraculous. Jacob Philadelphia made a good living with his automatons, and they didn't require a whole lot of effort from him. He basically turned a key, set the machines going, and collected his money."

I glanced around again to take the crowd's pulse. There was a regal-looking lady sitting on one of the Chesterfields who kept nodding and smiling, as though giving encouragement to a clumsy piano student. I took a deep breath. "Sometimes these devices weren't all they seemed," I continued. "There was a German magician named Herr Alexander who had a magic bell. You asked it a question—for instance: 'What's two plus two?'— and the bell would chime out the answer. Samuel Morse, the inventor of the telegraph, came to believe that Alexander had devised some new telegraphic system. Actually, the bell was rung by a bird hidden inside the workings."

This drew an appreciative smile from the Chesterfield, so I persevered. "Then there was the Kempelen Chess Player, from

Austria. It looked like a much larger version of our friend here," I pointed at the device on the desk, "but it had Turkish robes and a turban. There was a chess board on top of the gear cabinet, and the figure sat behind it. At the turn of a key the figure not only pushed its own chess pieces across the board, but also moved its head to follow the play of opponents. Benjamin Franklin played it twice—and lost. Edgar Allen Poe was so impressed that he wrote a long article trying to explain how it worked. Poe guessed wrong on some of the finer points, but his basic theory was correct—a human chess player, hidden inside the cabinet, controlled the movements."

Lieutenant Murray looked at his watch. "This is all very edifying, young man, but we have a body decomposing here, and I'd really like—"

"You must forgive my brother," Harry said, breaking in. "Sometimes he forgets himself." He turned to me as if reprimanding a schoolboy. "Dash, tell them about the Frenchman."

I shrugged. "Jean Eugène Robert-Houdin was a French magician—"

"Born in 1805," said Harry.

"—born in 1805—who started out as a clock maker. He was a genius with mechanical apparatus, and his effects made use of electricity and modern innovations in a way no one had ever seen before. At the time, magicians tended to wear long Merlin robes and conical hats, as though they were sorcerers of some kind. Robert-Houdin appeared in normal dress clothes, and presented himself as a man of science, rather than superstition. Over the course of his career he amassed an enormous collection of automatons. He was fascinated by them and studied their workings to help create his own mysteries."

I could see Lieutenant Murray's eyes glazing over, so I tried a different tack. "Imagine if Thomas Edison had a big warehouse and he gathered up historical inventions like Alexander Graham Bell's telephone and Samuel Morse's telegraph. The objects would be important and valuable for their own sake, but all the more so because Edison had taken inspiration from them. That's what Robert-Houdin's collection was like, and that's why people are so fascinated by it."

Lieutenant Murray glanced at the little Japanese figure on the dead man's desk. "So where is this collection now?"

"That's just it. It's supposed to have been destroyed. Near the end of his life, Robert-Houdin's workshop burned down. It's believed that the entire collection was lost."

"Or so they say," Harry added.

"There were rumors at the time that the fire had been set by a jealous rival, who stole the collection and set the fire to cover his tracks. Any time an automaton turns up that's known to have belonged to Robert-Houdin, it sends up those rumors all over again."

"And this one belonged to him?" Murray asked.

"Absolutely," said Harry. "It's called *Le Fantôme*. One of Robert-Houdin's jewels. *Le Fantôme* in French means—"

"The phantom," Murray said, bending over the little figure. "Strange thing to call it. It looks Oriental to me. Japanese."

"But Robert-Houdin was French."

"Ah. And was he a relation of yours, Mr. Houdini?"

Harry bristled at the suggestion. "He was perhaps the greatest charlatan in all of—"

"No relation," I said, quickly. It had been a touchy point for some little while. Robert-Houdin had, in fact, been my brother's boyhood idol, ever since the fateful day when a copy of the Frenchman's memoirs fell into Harry's hands. But as he got older, and his ego reached its maturity, he came to regret having chosen his stage name to appear "like Houdin." In time he would write a book about Robert-Houdin intended to expose the Frenchman as "a mere pretender, a man who waxed great on the brain work of others, a mechanician who had boldly filched the inventions of the master craftsmen among his predecessors." These sorts of things mattered very deeply to Harry, if not to anyone else.

"Tell me something," Lieutenant Murray continued. "Are

these things really so valuable? If this French guy's collection still exists, what would it be worth to-day?"

Harry considered for a moment. "Possibly as much as ten or twelve thousand dollars."

A respectful silence fell over the room.

"Perhaps that was the motivation for his murder," Harry said.

Lieutenant Murray looked at Harry with amused delight. "I don't know, Mr. Houdini. If I were the murderer, it would seem a waste of effort to kill Mr. Wintour over the phantom doll here, and then leave it behind when I made my escape."

My curiosity got the better of me. "How was he killed, Lieutenant?"

"That's why I asked you here. He was killed with this. With the doll."

Harry's eyes widened. "Killed with *Le Fantôme*? How is it possible?"

"Somebody hit him over the head with it?" I asked.

"No, the doll itself—I'll get the doc to explain. Dr. Peterson?"

A short, stocky man with an impressive mane of white hair had been busying himself near the white hospital screens, jotting notes with a gold pencil in a leather notebook. He turned toward us and withdrew a folded handkerchief from his breast pocket. "He was killed with this," he said, unfolding the white cloth.

"With a handkerchief?" Harry asked.

"Look closer," Peterson said.

"It's nothing. A splinter."

"A splinter tipped with poison, unless I'm very much mistaken. I took it from the dead man's neck."

"How did it get there?"

Lieutenant Murray gestured at *Le Fantôme*. "That thing."

"I'm not sure I get you," I said. "It plays the flute. It doesn't kill people."

The detective shook his head. "That thing in its hand is a blow gun, not a flute."

I looked at Harry. He nodded.

"The way we figure it," Murray continued, "Mr. Wintour had locked himself into his study to have a look at his latest acquisition. While he was poking around, the gears suddenly started cranking and it raised the blow gun to its lips and shot a poison dart into his neck."

Harry opened his mouth to speak, but then closed it again, apparently lost in thought. Slowly, he circled the desk, examining the automaton from all sides. Then he peered behind the hospital screens to have another look at the unfortunate Mr. Wintour. Emerging again, he dropped to his knees and began a minute examination of the Oriental rug. Occasionally he issued a soft grunt of surprise or satisfaction, but gave no other clue as to what he might be doing.

"Mr. Houdini?" Lieutenant Murray stepped back as Harry, still on his hands and knees, rounded a corner of the dead man's desk. "Mr. Houdini? Is there something in particular you're looking for down there?"

Harry simply grunted and continued his circuit of the desk. I looked at the Chesterfield, where the two men in evening dress were looking on with great amusement.

"Harry," I said, "this might not be the proper time for—"

"Silence, Dash! I am like a bloodhound on the scent!"

"Look, Mr. Houdini," Lieutenant Murray said with some asperity. "We don't need you to tell us whether Wintour is dead or not. We figured you'd know something about how the doll worked, seeing as how you and this Robert-Houdin have the same name."

Harry ignored the remark. "Dr. Peterson?" he called from the floor. "Was Mr. Wintour already dead when he was found?"

"Oh, absolutely," answered the police physician. "Though perhaps you should ask my colleague Dr. Blanton. He examined the body before I did."

"Dr. Blanton?" Harry asked, his head bobbing up from behind the desk. "Who is Dr. Blanton?"

One of the dinner guests rose from a club chair. He was a small, rotund man perhaps sixty years of age, with heavy dewlaps and large, moist eyes. His long, delicate hands seemed to be in constant motion, whether fiddling with the pearl buttons of his waistcoat or adjusting the pince nez he wore at the end of a chain. "I'm Percy Blanton," he said, clipping the spectacles onto his nose. "I've been a friend of Bran's for more years than I care to count. I was just arriving when—how shall I say it?—when the door to the study was opened, so of course I was the first to examine the—let me see—so of course I was the first to examine the subject."

Harry sprang to his feet. "And was Mr. Wintour dead when you examined him?"

"Mr. Houdini—," Lieutenant Murray stepped between my brother and Dr. Blanton.

"No, it's quite all right, Lieutenant," the doctor said. "I don't mind repeating my account."

"That's kind of you, sir, but this man is not an investigator."

It finally dawned on Harry that Lieutenant Murray was exasperated with him. "I do not wish to hamper your investigation or inconvenience Mr. Wintour's guests," he said, adopting a more diplomatic tone, "but what you say concerning *Le Fantôme* seems incredible to me, knowing its workings as I do. I am merely trying to fix the scene in my mind, so as to judge whether the automaton could have acted in the manner you describe."

The lieutenant's hands dropped to his sides. He nodded at Blanton to continue. He didn't look happy about it, though.

"As I told the police," Dr. Blanton said, "Bran—that is, Mr. Wintour—was seated at his desk when I entered the room. His head was forward on the desk and I naturally supposed that he was asleep. It was only when we stepped forward—"

"Pardon me, sir," Harry interrupted. "Who was with you in the room?"

"Why, all of us. Myself, of course. Phillips, the butler. Mr. Hendricks and his wife. And Margaret, naturally."

"Margaret?"

"Mrs. Wintour."

"His wife? Where is she now?"

"I had to take her upstairs and give her a sleeping powder. She was distraught, as you can well imagine."

"I see. And who is Mr. Hendricks?"

"I am," said the gentleman who had been seated on the Chesterfield. He was tall and gaunt-faced, with brown curly hair and a Vandyke beard covering what looked to be a jutting chin. I guessed his age to be fifty or so, though his lined forehead and the dark hollows beneath his eyes made it difficult to judge.

"When Bran invited me here tonight he said he'd made the find of a lifetime," Hendricks said. "If what you say about the automaton is true, I'd say he wasn't exaggerating. I've often heard stories about the Blois collection, but I never dreamed I'd actually see any of it."

"Excuse me, sir," Lieutenant Murray said. "What did you call the collection?"

"The Blois collection," Hendricks said, giving a careful pronunciation. "That's what it's always been called. Blois is the name of the city where Robert-Houdin lived."

"You know something of these devices, then?" The lieutenant seemed to be choosing his words carefully.

"I own a great many automatons, Lieutenant. I dare-say that's why Bran invited me here this evening—to gloat over his prize."

"Have you, ah, any experience of how they work?"

"Indeed I do. I'm in the toy business myself. One doesn't run a manufacturing concern without picking up a thing or two. I doubt if I'm as knowledgeable as Mr. Houdini, but I have a decent understanding of the basic mechanics. Don't look so alarmed, Lieutenant. I'm well aware that this makes me a suspect."

The woman sitting at his side—whose kindly face had encouraged me in my earlier recitation—laid a hand on his arm. "Surely you don't suspect my husband, do you, Lieutenant?"

"Of course he does, Nora," Hendricks said, not unkindly. "I dare say I'm at the very top of the list. There are only a handful of men in New York who could get *Le Fantôme* to work after all these years. Three of us are in this room, and one of us is dead. I can't speak for Mr. Houdini, but I certainly have my share of motives. As soon as you begin to do a little digging, Lieutenant, you'll discover that I'm a business rival of the dead man."

"But the two of you are friends," Mrs. Hendricks protested. "You used to be partners."

"We used to be, darling," her husband said, patting her hand. "I'm afraid that's the point." He turned back toward the desk. "There is something I've been wondering, Lieutenant. Are you certain it was murder? Couldn't it have been an accident, like a gun going off during a cleaning? Who knows how long it's been since anyone has tinkered with those old gears."

"We're looking into that, sir," the detective admitted. "The man who sold the doll to Mr. Wintour is answering questions downtown."

Harry, who had resumed his study of the carpet, looked up in surprise. "You don't mean Josef Graff, do you?"

Lieutenant Murray consulted his notebook. "Yes, Josef Graff. Runs a toy shop, I believe. On the side he arranges purchases for collectors such as Mr. Wintour."

"A fine fellow," offered Hendricks. "I deal with him myself on occasion. You mean to say Josef sold *Le Fantôme* to Bran without offering it to me first?"

"In the circumstances," Lieutenant Murray said, "I should think you'd be grateful."

"You don't suspect old Graff of having a hand in this?" Mr. Hendricks appeared genuinely dismayed.

"I've known the man for years!"

"As have I," Harry said quietly.

"He sold the doll to Wintour," the lieutenant said flatly. "Now Wintour is dead. I think it's reasonable to ask him a few questions."

"Is he being detained?" Hendricks spoke as if dealing with

an impertinent houseboy. "Has Josef Graff been placed under arrest in this matter?"

I glanced at Harry. His face had gone deathly pale.

"So far as we know, he was last to see the murdered man alive," Lieutenant Murray said. "We would be remiss if we did not treat him with some measure of suspicion."

"See here!" Hendricks was on his feet now. "Graff is a feeble old man! You can't just bung him in jail because—"

"With respect, sir," Lieutenant Murray interrupted, "there are elements of this investigation with which you are not familiar. I would ask that you defer to my judgement for the time being." The policeman's tone was even and deferential, but there was no mistaking the core of iron.

Hendricks studied Lieutenant Murray's face for a moment and saw that it was pointless to argue. "I just don't understand the point of detaining Mr. Graff, that's all," he said, sitting down beside his wife. "He's a harmless old man."

My brother had been silent during this exchange. Now he rose from his contemplation of the floor and carefully brushed at the knees of his trousers. "I have completed my examination of the carpet," he announced.

"Have you?" Lieutenant Murray turned to face my brother, his lips pressed together in amusement.

"I am prepared to announce my conclusions," Harry continued.

"Your conclusions?" The lieutenant was smiling broadly now. "Look, Mr. Houdini, as I said before, we just want you to show us how the automaton works."

"I will do so, of course. At the same time, I will also demonstrate that Josef Graff had nothing whatever to do with Mr. Wintour's death."

"I beg your pardon?"

"Josef Graff had nothing whatever to do with Mr. Wintour's death. He may have sold *Le Fantôme* to the dead man, but he is completely innocent of any wrong-doing. I promise you that on my mother's life."

"And how can you be so certain of that?"

"Because *Le Fantôme* did not kill Branford Wintour."

All traces of amusement drained from Lieutenant Murray's face. His eyes became very still, the way a terrier's will when he's about to take a chunk out of your hand. "May I ask how you arrived at that conclusion, Mr. Houdini?"

"Because there is no red dot," said my brother.

Dr. Peterson, the police physician, perked up at this. "No blood, you mean? There was a bit, if you looked closely, but the puncture wasn't deep enough to cause any serious bleeding."

Dr. Blanton, Mr. Wintour's friend, nodded his head in vigorous agreement. "In some cases, the poison need not even enter the bloodstream directly. The smallest scratch is sufficient to—"

"I did not mean blood," Harry said. "I refer to a red dot of a very different kind. A red dot that only Houdini would think to look for. I have made an exhaustive search, gentlemen, and there is no red dot on the body, or on the floor, or on the desk."

Lieutenant Murray locked his hands behind his back. "I think you'll have to explain yourself for us, Mr. Houdini."

"Of course," my brother said, warming to the role. "You and your men cannot be faulted if you are slow to grasp this. It is a matter where only the rarefied knowledge of Houdini can be of service."

"Uh, Harry—?" I began.

"That's all right," Lieutenant Murray said to me. "Please, Mr. Houdini, we'd be ever so grateful if you could put us on the right track here." He held up his hands for silence. "Boys? Could I ask you to stop with all this unnecessary police work for a moment? It seems our visitor here has stumbled upon the solution to our little problem, and I think we should all give him our attention."

There was general laughter from the men in uniform, and even Mr. Hendricks and Dr. Blanton appeared amused. A lesser man might have resented the lieutenant's facetious tone. Harry, with his steel-plated vanity, did not notice. Instead, he puffed out his chest and smoothed his lapels, a gesture he invariably made when he was about to take the stage.

"Thank you, Lieutenant Murray," he said. "I must first correct a misstatement in the lieutenant's kind introduction. I do not claim to have solved the murder." A ripple of mock protest went up among the officers. "No, no," Harry said. "I only wish to demonstrate that *Le Fantôme* is blameless. You see, when you have eliminated the impossible, whatever remains, however improbable, must be the truth."

He surveyed the group of young officers. "First, I will need a volunteer from the audience. You, sir" —he pointed to a strapping patrolman— "may I prevail upon you to join me here at the front of the desk?"

The officer received a desultory round of applause as he stepped forward.

Harry reached into his pocket. "Your name is—? Robbins? Very good. Now, Mr. Robbins, I hold here in my hands a perfectly ordinary pack of playing cards—"

Lieutenant Murray gave a loud cough. "Look here, Houdini—"

I put a hand on his arm to restrain him. "Give him three minutes," I said in a low whisper. "He's on to something."

He gave me a look that suggested I had just staked my life on the fact.

"Officer Robbins," Harry continued, "will you examine the cards and confirm that they are all different? You may shuffle them, if you like." Grinning nervously, the young patrolman gave the cards an awkward shuffle.

"Thank you," said Harry. "Now I will ask you to deal five cards off the top. Do you see the five ivory tiles in front of *Le Fantôme*? I want you to place one card face down on top of each tile."

Robbins bent over the desk, biting his lower lip as he dealt out the five cards.

"Very good," said Harry. "Now, while my back is turned,

select one of the five cards and show it to the aud—to the other gentlemen."

Robbins lifted a card—the five of clubs—off the desk and held it up for inspection.

"Now replace the card," Harry continued, "but remember what it was. You are finished now? Excellent. Now, with the help of *Le Fantôme,* I shall attempt to locate the card you selected."

"See here, Houdini," said Lieutenant Murray, "you can't tamper with that thing—it killed a man tonight."

"I assure you it did not."

"Besides, there's no key to turn it on."

"It does not require a key," Harry said. "Observe." He stretched his finger across the desk and depressed a glass bead on the figure's headdress. We heard a faint click, and slowly the tiny figure stirred. In spite of himself, Lieutenant Murray watched in fascination as the cross-legged figure slowly moved its head from side to side, as if studying the five cards spread out before it. We heard a soft creak as *Le Fantôme's* left arm bent and its hand rose to stroke its temple, as though lost in contemplation. Abruptly, the figure's head snapped upward and its mouth opened in a crude simulation of a smile. I cannot claim that it was a pleasant smile. In fact, it was downright spooky. Then the left arm straightened and pointed to the middle card in the row of five.

From the Chesterfield, Mrs. Hendricks began applauding at the apparent conclusion of the effect. Her husband and Dr. Blanton joined in, as did a handful of the policemen. *Le Fantôme* nodded its head as if to acknowledge the applause.

"You see?" Harry cried. "It is a harmless trick, a simple effect with cards. Officer Robbins, you may now turn over the card that *Le Fantôme* has indicated. It is the card you selected, is it not?"

Robbins looked at the card, hesitated, and looked again. "Uh, no, sir," he said. "I picked the five of clubs. This is the nine of diamonds."

"What? Impossible!" Harry darted forward and snatched the card from the patrolman's hand, glaring at it with undisguised annoyance. "This cannot be!" He winced at the sound of sniggering from the back of the room. "*Le Fantôme* is foolproof! Possibly its workings have become fouled through the years of disrepair, or perhaps I failed to—"

We never learned what Harry might have failed to do. Throughout his tirade, a remarkable change had come over *Le Fantôme*. Unseen by Harry, who had his back to the desk, the automaton stirred to life once again. This time, its right hand—which held the tiny bamboo tube—rose from the folds of its robe. With a swift, sure movement, the figure raised the tube to its lips in the manner of a blow gun. Lieutenant Murray gave a cry of warning and hurled himself across the desk at my brother. The pair of them crashed to the floor just as some ten or twelve of New York's finest dove for cover.

No poison dart came. Instead we heard a gentle puff of air and the sound of a wet splotch. Very deliberately, my brother disentangled himself from Lieutenant Murray, dusted off his trousers, and rose to his feet.

"I appreciate your concern for my safety," he said, "but I assure you it was not necessary. You will see that one of the remaining cards is now marked with a spot of red pigment." He held up the card to show a blob of red coloring. "This is what *Le Fantôme* expels from its pipe—and the only thing it is capable of expelling. So you see, *Le Fantôme* cannot be the culprit. Therefore, someone else must have slipped into this room, killed Mr. Wintour, and slipped out again without disturbing the locks or arousing the suspicions of the household. I suspect, Lieutenant Murray, that this will alter the direction of your inquiries."

The lieutenant said nothing. He stared down at *Le Fantôme's* wooden smile while the tendons in his neck worked back and forth.

"Oh, and one last thing," my brother said. He held up the card with the red splotch. "Officer Robbins, would you care to show our friends the card which *Le Fantôme* has marked?"

Robbins flipped the card face-front to show the five of clubs.

From the desk, we heard a soft wooden creak as *Le Fantôme's* lips pulled back in a chilling smile.

3

THE INSIDE TALKER

"HARRY," I SAID, AFTER WE HAD WALKED A FEW BLOCKS FROM THE Wintour mansion, "you really can't treat the police like that."

"Why can I not?" he asked.

"It's disrespectful. Lieutenant Murray is just doing his work. It's one thing to make a suggestion. It's another to humiliate him."

"I needed to demonstrate that *Le Fantôme* could not have been the instrument of murder."

"It would have been enough to explain it to him. You didn't need to put on the whole song and dance routine."

He seemed to consider it. "It is my nature," he said. "I see these men in uniform and something in me grows angry. Men in uniform have not always been kind to me—to our family." We walked on for a few moments in silence before he continued. "Besides, it is what I do," he said, as if considering the matter for the first time. "I escape from restraints. Chains. Ropes. Handcuffs. One day, this will mean something to people—to the immigrants who escaped to America just as our mother and father did. They will see a man escaping from fetters and they will recall their struggles. They will think of freedom."

I studied his face as we passed under a street lamp. My brother was not a man given to introspection. When it came, however, it was generally worth the wait. "But you are probably right," he allowed. "If I took an improper tone with Lieutenant Murray, I will apologize in the morning."

"Are you certain that you're right about this?" I asked. "Isn't it possible that the automaton could have fired the dart?"

"Yes," he admitted, "but not without a splotch of red pigment. There is no firing mechanism apart from a bladder filled with liquid. This is squeezed between two cogwheels so that a small amount of dye squirts forth. If the poison dart had been loaded into the figure's blow pipe it might possibly have been propelled into the victim's neck, but not without an accompanying splash mark."

We stopped at a corner and waited for a horse and trap to pass by. "I find that possibility very unlikely, though," Harry said. "If I were attempting to stage manage the murder of Mr. Wintour, I would never place my confidence in so unreliable a device. What is the likelihood that a poison dart fired in such a way would find its target? It seems incredible to me that it should have struck Mr. Wintour at all, much less that it hit him in a vulnerable spot. How could the murderer even be certain that the blow pipe would be facing in Mr. Wintour's direction when it fired?" He shook his head. "If I were a murderer, I would not be content to leave so much to chance."

"But if *Le Fantôme* didn't kill him, how did the murderer get out of the study? It was locked from the inside."

"A pretty problem, is it not?"

"Yes, Harry. A pretty problem. Do you have the answer?"

"I confess I do not," he said. "Although no doubt the Great Houdini could think of at least seven ways to enter the study undetected. But I must gather more data. After all, I never guess. It is a shocking habit—destructive to the logical faculty."

" 'Destructive to the logical'—is that another bit of wisdom from the pages of Sherlock Holmes, by any chance?"

He pretended not to hear me.

"Where are we going, by the way?" I asked. "The house is in the other direction."

"We're going to see Josef Graff."

"The magic dealer? He's being held at police headquarters!"

"I'm aware of that, Dash. That's why we're going to see him. I want to assure him that the Great Houdini will secure his release at the earliest opportunity."

"Harry—"

"Did I not prove beyond all doubt that *Le Fantôme* could not have been the cause of Branford Wintour's death? And yet, when I insisted that Mr. Graff be released, Lieutenant Murray refused!"

"He didn't refuse, Harry. He merely said—"

"—that it would be necessary to confirm my 'interesting speculations' before the suspect could be released. Yes, Dash. I heard him. What twaddle! Such is the man whom you would have me treat with greater respect."

I hauled out my Elgin pocket watch and popped open the cover. "It's late, Harry. They won't let us in at this hour. We'll have to wait until morning."

"Well, perhaps not quite that long," Harry said. "First we will call on Mrs. Graff. The poor woman is undoubtedly distraught."

"That's a good idea," I said. "Perhaps you could run the shop for her until Mr. Graff is released."

"Run the shop? Don't be foolish! I intend to see her husband vindicated! The Great Houdini will not rest until Josef Graff is released from his bonds!"

"I think we'd better leave the crime-solving to the police," I said. "We might be more useful keeping his business open."

Harry sighed. "You have no imagination, Dash."

It was a familiar refrain, as my brother had long despaired over my lack of imagination. Not three days earlier, my lack of imagination had been very much on his mind when I tried to talk him out of an especially hare-brained bridge leap. I should explain that Harry had been leaping from bridges since the age of thirteen—usually wearing a pair of handcuffs, or tied in sturdy ropes, or wrapped in a long length of heavy chain. As a magician, his stage manner was indifferent at best. As an escape artist, he was unparalleled. He would stand atop the guardrail of a high bridge, trammelled up in some impressive restraint, and whip his audience into a state of frenzied anticipation as he described his "death leap" into the frigid waters below. When the leap finally came—usually after a tender word of farewell to Bess—the crowd would literally gasp with horror. I don't know how many times I stood by watching as tearful young ladies gripped the railing and scanned the smooth surface of the water below, where seconds earlier Harry had splashed to his "watery destiny." What they did not know, these impressionable young admirers, was that Harry had usually sprung the cuffs or slipped the ropes before he ever hit the water. His showman's instincts told him not to make it look too easy, so he would remain under water while the minutes ticked away, silently treading water below the surface. His lung capacity and endurance were phenomenal, having been honed by long practice sessions in the family bath tub. At his peak, he could remain underwater for five minutes, so that when at last he broke the surface, waving the handcuffs or ropes above his head, the roar from the crowd would be deafening. It seemed to them that they had seen a man cheat death. Actually, they had seen a man who could hold his breath for an uncommonly long time.

Harry was never content to let this stunt alone. He was forever adding more chains and leaping from higher vantages in an attempt to add drama to the escape. Then one day he announced his intention to jump off the new Brooklyn Bridge—wrapped in fifty pounds of iron shackles. It seemed to me, I told him, that he could accomplish much the same effect with a leap from the top of our apartment house. At a certain point, I tried to explain, it really didn't matter whether he was leaping into water or onto solid ground. Harry wouldn't listen to my arguments about the unprecedented height of the bridge, or the added danger of the extra restraints. When it became apparent that I couldn't talk him out of it, I appealed to a higher authority—I mentioned Harry's plan to our mother. She took him aside for a quiet word, and the subject of the Brooklyn Bridge leap was never mentioned again.

Harry continued to list my failings as we rode the Sixth Avenue elevated down to Broadway. He kept talking as we got off and walked five blocks south. He finally ran out of steam when we reached Graff's Toy Emporium.

Graff's was a narrow shop front in a row of dull-red brick buildings, with a wood-framed display window crammed with rag dolls, hobbyhorses, pinwheels, and every other sort of gimcrack and gewgaw. As boys, Harry and I would sweep the floors and wash the windows just for the pleasure of spending time there. Even then, my brother had little patience for tin soldiers, cloth bears, or any of the other more conventional playthings. At the end of an afternoon's work—when the floors and door handles were gleaming—Harry always made straight for the wobbly green case where Mr. Graff kept the Delmarvelo Magic Sets.

The Delmarvelo "Young Conjurer Deluxe" set came in a sturdy pine box with a hinged top. On the lid, a brightly painted label showed a boy-magician enthralling his friends and family. The boy wore a black cape and top hat over his Little Lord Fauntleroy playsuit, and the table in front of him featured a bowl of fire, a houlette of cards, and a winsome bunny who seemed to be winking broadly. The boy's audience was divided equally among well-scrubbed children, whose faces glowed with admiration, and dignified adults in evening dress, who looked on with gentle approval. My eye always came to rest on a particular girl in the front row, whose blond curls were gathered up in a red bow. She had her hands clasped together and pressed against her cheek, with her head tilted just so, gazing at the boy-magician with frank adoration.

Sometimes, if we had done our work especially well, Mr. Graff would let us take the display set into the back room for an hour or so. Harry would click the metal latch and lift the lid with a quiet note of awe, as if uncovering a holy relic. Inside, the tricks were carefully arranged on a bed of straw. I need hardly say that there were no fire bowls or winking bunnies in the Delmarvelo set, but there were several good-quality tricks made of lacquered wood, richly colored in burgundy and black with Chinese detailing. There was a set of rice bowls that neither one of us ever quite mastered, an excellent set of cups and balls, a vanishing wand with break-away tips, a rising card effect, and a double-double coin tray. My favorite was the tiny wooden ball vase, with its delicate fluted stem and bright red polished ball. The effect was simple: the ball was placed into the cup of a small wooden holder and a close-fitting cap was lowered over it. When the cover was lifted—behold!—the ball had vanished. I've done a great many wonderful tricks since then, and Harry and I once caused an elephant to vanish from the stage of the New York Hippodrome, but I can't recall any effect that gave me quite the same feeling of accomplishment.

"Dash," Harry said as we paused outside the shop. "Have you been listening to anything I've said?"

"Sorry," I answered, returning to the present. "Was it important?"

"Never mind. I don't know why I trouble myself."

I peered through the window into the darkened shop. "Harry, are we really doing any good here? I don't want to raise Mrs. Graff's hopes for nothing."

"It will not be for nothing," he said sharply. "You may be assured of that."

Harry rang a bell that sounded in the apartment upstairs. We saw a fluttering of the curtains at the second floor window. A moment later the glow of an oil lamp was visible in the shop. I caught a glimpse of Mrs. Graff as she made her way to the door. She was a broad, sturdy woman with a lot of spare flesh that always seemed to vibrate in accordance with her moods. Her face, normally red and smiling, now appeared pinched and drawn, and her shoulders appeared to sag under the strain of her misfortunes. Nevertheless, she brightened at the sight of the pair of us waiting in the entryway. "Ehrich! Theodore! It is so good of you to come and see me!" She gathered us both in a rib-snapping embrace.

"It is good to see you, Mrs. Graff," Harry gasped as the last particles of air were squeezed from his lungs.

"We're sorry to call so late in the evening," I managed to add.

"My boys! My boys!" She released us and stepped back, beaming over us both. "Let me look at you! See how big you're getting! Theodore, so tall! Ehrich, so broad!"

"I have embarked on a rigorous course of personal conditioning," Harry said proudly. "I am developing my musculature in a systematic and scientific manner."

"How nice," Mrs. Graff said, as if admiring a child's finger painting. "And you, Theodore? Are you still in newspaper school?"

"Journalism," I said. "No, I've been traveling with Harry and Bess for the past few months, getting involved with the act. I may—"

"You should continue your studies, Theodore. Josef always says—Josef—" her face clouded as she recalled her husband's predicament.

Harry took her hand and gently led her to a chair. "Mrs. Graff," I said, "we don't wish to upset you, but can you tell us a little bit about what happened? When the police came?"

Her eyes welled with tears. "I do not know what I can tell you, Theodore. We were eating our supper when the police came to the door. Such a racket! They dragged Josef away in a wagon. I was down at the police station for two hours, but I could learn nothing. Nothing that made sense, at any rate. They say he killed a man! My Josef, a murderer! He won't even lay traps for the rats, this is how big a murderer he is!"

"Did you know Branford Wintour?" Harry asked.

"Our best customer," Mrs. Graff said. "Although he doesn't come to the shop anymore. Josef goes to see him whenever something special comes along. Mr. Wintour has always been a perfect—no! Is that who Josef is supposed to have killed? Ridiculous!"

"Have you seen Mr. Wintour lately?" I asked.

"No. But his man—what is his name?—Phillips, I believe. Phillips has been here three times in the past week." She gripped a corner of her shawl and twisted it around her fingers. "Mr. Wintour, dead? This is terrible news. How did he die?"

"I'm not entirely certain," Harry said. "Did your husband have a special deal brewing with Mr. Wintour? Was he handling something very unusual?"

She nodded. "He was quite secretive about it, Ehrich, but I know there was a very special item involved and that he expected to earn a large commission. He said he was going to buy me a winter coat."

"Do you have any idea what the item might have been?"

"No."

"Did you ever see the man who was selling it?"

"A queer bird. He would only come to the shop at night. I never saw him."

"Never?"

"No. Josef always asked me to wait upstairs when he came."

"I see. Tell me, Mrs. Graff, have you ever heard of *Le Fantôme*?"

"No." She looked at Harry's face and then at mine. "Ehrich, why are you asking me these questions? What is *Le Fantôme*?"

Harry glanced at me, uncertain.

"We don't wish to alarm you unnecessarily, Mrs. Graff," I said.

"You don't wish to alarm me? My husband is in jail! How could I be more alarmed?"

"Very well," Harry said. "Your husband sold Mr. Wintour a very rare automaton called *Le Fantôme*. The police believe that this automaton shot Mr. Wintour with a poisoned dart."

Mrs. Graff narrowed her eyes at us. "Ehrich, you are joking with me. Theodore, this is not a time for your jokes."

Harry said nothing. I looked at my shoes.

Mrs. Graff's hands went to her cheeks. "Can they be serious? This is why the police have arrested Josef? A poison dart?"

"So it would seem," Harry said. "Your husband is a suspect

because he sold the device to Mr. Wintour."

"A poison dart?" she repeated. "A gun, I could understand. A knife, maybe. A poison dart? It does not seem possible!"

Harry began pacing in front of a case of wooden whirly-gigs. "I have demonstrated to the police that the automaton could not have fired the dart, but they have not seen fit to release your husband. Apparently I failed to convince them."

"Harry," I said, "they only wanted to confirm it for themselves. I told you this before."

"No, no," he said. "The police will only find some other means of laying this crime on Mr. Graff's doorstep. We must find the true killer and bring him to justice!"

"Find the true killer? Harry, you're a dime museum magician! What do you know about tracking down killers?" I had been hoping to inject a note of moderation into the proceedings, but Harry had already moved on to his next rhetorical high note.

"The police have not reckoned with the talents of the Great Houdini!" he cried, thrusting his index finger under my nose. "I will comb this city and roust the evildoers wherever they may lurk! I shall be the scourge of the underworld! Those who—"

"Harry," I said quietly. "Why don't we let someone else become the scourge of the underworld? It'll be enough if we can convince the police of Mr. Graff's innocence."

Mrs. Graff gave a nod of assent. "I just want Josef home again."

"As you wish," Harry said. He took Mrs. Graff's hand and pressed it to his lips. "I shall not fail you, dear lady." He flung his astrakhan cloak around his shoulders. "Come along, Dash! We have a rendezvous with justice!"

Mrs. Graff looked at me and gave a bewildered shrug. "You'd better hurry along, then," she said.

We left the shop and Harry said nothing more until we had worked our way along Delancy Street to the thirteenth precinct station house. As we climbed the marble steps I noticed Harry fumbling in his back pocket. "Just a moment, Dash," he said. "Oh, that's all right, then." He pushed open the heavy wooden doors.

A gray-haired sergeant sat behind the dispatcher's desk. "Can I help you gentle—why, Mr. Houdini! Is that you?"

"Good evening, Sergeant O'Donnell," said Harry. "May I introduce the brother of the Great Houdini?"

"Call me Dash," I said. "'The brother of the Great Houdini' sounds so formal."

"Nice to meet you," O'Donnell said. "So, Houdini, are you here to go another round in the lockup?"

"If you wouldn't mind, Sergeant. Practice makes perfect."

O'Donnell saw the expression on my face and laughed. "You mean he didn't tell you? Your brother has been coming down here for the past three weeks to get himself locked up in our hoosegow."

"Late at night," Harry explained, "so as not to attract attention."

"I thought you wanted attention," I said. "Why have I been breaking my back to get you locked up at Sing-Sing if you didn't want attention?"

"Practice, Dash. The holding cells here were built on the same pattern as those at Sing-Sing."

A uniformed officer wandered past and gave Harry a companionable nod. "So you're a regular down here, is that it?" I asked. "Is that why those officers at the Wintour mansion seemed to recognize you?"

"I suppose so," Harry said, "although I dare say some of them recognized me from the stage at Huber's."

"Oh, undoubtedly," I said. "It's a wonder they didn't ask for autographs."

O'Donnell had pulled out a heavy binder and was flipping through the pages. "You're in luck," he said. "We've only got two guests in there at the moment, and I don't suppose either one will give us any trouble. One's a drunk, and the other's supposed to be a murderer, but he don't look like any murderer I ever saw."

"A murderer?" Harry asked with feigned alarm. "Are you sure it's safe?"

"That old bird won't bother you any. Hasn't said a word since they brought him down from interrogation. Just sits real quiet like. Caught him crying when I made my rounds."

"Well, I suppose it will be all right then," Harry said. "You don't mind if my brother comes along? He's going to time me with his fancy watch."

"Why should I mind?" asked O'Donnell, pulling a heavy ring of keys from a desk drawer. "Follow me, gentlemen."

He led us down a set of dank steel-beam steps to a metal-studded door with a heavy iron crossbar. He lifted the bar and fitted a large key into a reinforced panel-lock, turning it three times clockwise. The door rolled open on rusty casters, and O'Donnell held it as we passed through, sliding it shut behind us once we were inside.

The lockup was comprised of only four cells, two on each side, with a wide corridor running down the center. Four bare lightbulbs dangling from ceiling cords provided the only illumination. It took only a glance to see why the warden at Sing-Sing felt so confident about his escape-proof cells. I'd seen my brother pick his way through some of the toughest, most heavily warded padlocks ever designed, but the locks on these cells were beyond his reach—literally. The prison architects had rigged up a sort of extended hasp, so that the lock wasn't actually seated into the cell door at all. Instead, it was bolted onto the wall a good six feet away, securing a metal cross-beam tight against the cell door. From inside the cell, the prisoner would have no way of reaching the lock. Harry's skill and practice were useless here—he simply would not be able to get his hands on the lock.

"Harry—" I began.

He winked. "A pretty problem, is it not?"

As my eyes adjusted to the gloom, I could make out the dim outline of a man in each of the two cages to our right. Both men appeared to be sleeping. I recognized the one closest to us as Josef Graff, whose plump woodcock shape made him easy to spot even in the dark.

Sergeant O'Donnell ignored both prisoners. "You have your choice of two empty cells this evening, Houdini," he said as our footfalls echoed loudly against the rock floor. "Which will it be? Your favorite there at the end?"

"No, this one, I think," Harry replied, indicating the closer of the two on our left. "I think the bolt and hasp are rusty on the other." Harry had fallen a step behind the sergeant as they moved toward the cell. As Mr. Graff began to stir from his bunk, roused by the noise of our arrival, Harry turned and raised a finger to his lips, warning the old man to stay silent. Mr. Graff registered surprise at the sight of us, but lowered his head and pretended to be asleep.

"You know," said O'Donnell, working on the lock across the corridor, "this bolt feels a little stiff, too."

"Does it?" Harry asked. "Oh well, I imagine that the hardware at Sing-Sing is rusty as well. I will prevail, in any case."

The lock finally gave and O'Donnell pulled the door open with a creak. Harry stepped past him into the open cell. "You know, Houdini," the sergeant said, "if you ever do try this at Sing-Sing, they'll insist on a full body search—just like we give the real prisoners."

From across the corridor, Mr. Graff let out a soft groan at the memory.

"I am aware of this, Sergeant, and I am fully prepared to comply. Would you care to—?" He spread his arms wide.

"I think we'll let it pass," O'Donnell said quickly. He swung the door shut and slid the long cross-beam into place. "I'd better get back to the desk," he said, turning to me. "Just bang on the bars when he wants me to let him out."

"When he—what?"

"When he wants me to let him out. He usually gives up after three hours."

I turned to my brother, who was busy rolling up his sleeves. "Harry? You mean to say you haven't figured out a way to escape from this cell yet?"

"It is proving to be more difficult than I thought," he allowed.

"More difficult than you thought. Suppose I had set up the Sing-Sing stunt three weeks ago, like you wanted?"

"The Great Houdini would have risen to the challenge, as he has done so often in the past."

"My, but he's sure of himself, isn't he?" said O'Donnell. "'Course, he usually doesn't sound quite so cocksure by two or three in the morning. Enjoy yourself, Houdini." He turned and let himself out through the main door.

We stood quietly and listened to the sergeant's footsteps fade. "Ehrich?" came a whisper from the other side of the corridor. "Is that really you? Theodore?"

"Of course, Mr. Graff." Harry came to the front of his cell and dangled his arms through the bars.

"You have come to release me?"

"Release you?" I snorted. "Apparently he can't even—"

"It would be imprudent to release you just now, Mr. Graff," Harry said. "That would seem to confirm the accusation that you murdered Branford Wintour. I trust that you did not murder Branford Wintour?"

"Of course not!" The old man swung his feet off the bunk and walked to the door of his cell. He was wearing a wrinkled windowpane check suit with a gold watch fob dangling from his waistcoat. In happier circumstances he might have passed for a diminutive Kris Kringle with his round head, florid cheeks, and snowy hair and beard. Now, even in the shadowy light of the cell block, the stresses of the day were plain to see. His collar had popped open, his tie was askew, and his face was streaked with tears. "Of course I didn't kill Mr. Wintour! He was my best customer, and a fine man besides!"

"I thought not," said Harry. "Might I ask you to tell me everything you know of this unhappy business?"

"What's to tell? There was a knock on the door, next thing I'm in jail. Dragged off in chains, in front of Frieda. In front of the neighbors. Everyone."

THE HARRY HOUDINI MYSTERIES

"I'm sure that was most unpleasant," Harry said. "Perhaps we should examine the events leading up to your arrest? What can you tell us of *Le Fantôme?*"

"Wretched little creature! I wish I had never laid eyes on it!"

"How did it come to be in your possession?"

An expression of wounded pride crossed Mr. Graff's face. "I am the leading purveyor of magical apparatus and curiosities in all of New York," he said with a certain prim dignity. "It is impossible that such an item should appear on the market without coming to my attention."

"Yes, yes, of course," said my brother quickly. "But exactly *how* did it come to your attention?"

"A most curious thing," he began. "I was sitting in—"

A drink-sodden voice from the opposite cell broke in. "My dear sirs," the speaker began, as if dictating a letter, "I have the honor of requesting a reduction in the level of conversation in and about the vicinity of my present location. Thanking you, I remain, yours et cetera…" the voice resolved into contented snoring.

"That is my fellow inmate," Mr. Graff explained. "An amusing fellow. As I was saying, I was going over the books in my shop late last night when a gentleman began banging at the door. I told him to return in the morning, but he was very insistent. He claimed to be an importer of antiques, and wished to know if I would be interested in seeing a few items from the collection of Robert-Houdin. Naturally, I—"

"Did he give you his name?" Harry asked.

"Harrington."

"What did he look like, this Mr. Harrington?"

"He looked quite a bit like you, Ehrich. Very powerful build, dark curly hair. He could easily have done double work for you."

"Make a note, Dash," Harry said. "Muscular, dark hair, medium height—"

Mr. Graff broke in. "A little less than medium height, I would have said."

"Shorter than I, then?"

"Well…"

"And would you say his features were handsome?"

Mr. Graff hesitated and glanced at me. "Ehm…"

I made a note on my pocket pad. "Perhaps not quite as handsome as Harry, Mr. Graff?"

"No, indeed."

"My dear sirs," came the voice from the opposite cell. "It has come to our attention that the volume of conversation remains at a level which prohibits a normal and healthful sleep. If such confabulation persists, we shall have no recourse but to consult management. Yours sincerely…" The voice trailed off again.

"And what else did your striking visitor have to say, Mr. Graff?" I continued.

"He told me that he represented a gentleman who possessed items from the Robert-Houdin collection. Naturally I questioned him closely in the matter. From time to time one comes across a handbill from the Palais Royal, and I've handled quite a few leaflets from his London appearances, but this gentleman was quite precise."

"The Blois collection?" I asked. "The one that's supposed to have been destroyed by fire?"

"Exactly. But he offered no documentation and naturally I regarded the claim with some suspicion. My doubts vanished when he removed *Le Fantôme* from its wooden case. I have seen a great many treasures in my day. It was I, you will recall, who brokered the sale of Signor Blitz's diaries. It was I who verified the provenance of Anderson's 'Inexhaustible Bottle.' But this was something else again. I don't know how long I marvelled over the figure. I was aware that my visitor was growing impatient, but I could not help myself. A Shakespeare folio could not have interested me more. When I had satisfied myself that the figure was genuine, Mr. Harrington asked if I might be able to find a buyer."

"I can think of dozens of magicians who would be interested," Harry said.

"So can I," Mr. Graff agreed, "but only one or two who could afford it. I offered Mr. Harrington a few names, but he suggested that we might do better to deal with wealthy collectors, rather than magicians, as he might have one or two other items for disposal."

"How many other items?"

"Forty-three."

"All from the Blois collection?"

"Every one."

Harry and I looked at each other. "Then it's true," he said.

"Yes," Mr. Graff said quietly. "The collection exists, and Mr. Harrington wanted me to arrange the sale."

"What did you do?"

"Naturally I sent a message to Harry Kellar. After all, the man is the greatest magician in the entire world—"

"With one notable exception," Harry said.

"Well, Ehrich, you must admit that Kellar is certainly the most successful magician working today. Your own talents have yet to find their proper audience."

"This is so."

"Unfortunately, Mr. Kellar found himself unable to entertain the possibility of purchasing the Blois collection. He has not always had the best of luck with his investments, and it seems his resources are not what they might be just now." Mr. Graff walked to his bunk and sat down. "So naturally I decided to approach my two wealthiest customers—"

"Branford Wintour and Michael Hendricks," Harry offered.

"You know Mr. Hendricks as well?"

"We met him this evening."

"A fascinating man. As I said, only he and Mr. Wintour possess the funds required for such a transaction."

I looked up from my notepad. "Surely this would also have occurred to Harrington?"

"Obviously," Mr. Graff said. "But Mr. Wintour and Mr. Hendricks do not open their doors to every passing dealer with a knick-knack to sell. I have dealt with both men many times. They trust my judgement, and prefer to make their acquisitions through me. Mr. Wintour, you may have heard, is especially careful in this regard. He is—was, I should say—considered something of a recluse."

Harry gripped the bars of his cell. "When we spoke to Mr. Hendricks, he made no mention of having been approached by you."

"I did not approach him. Mr. Harrington suggested that I meet with Mr. Wintour first to hear what he was prepared to pay for the lot. Then I was to call on Mr. Hendricks and see if he would be willing to raise the offer."

"A bidding war," Harry said. "Who knows how high the price might have gone?"

"Indeed. And having set my commission at three per cent, I was naturally eager to find out. I arranged a meeting with Mr. Wintour at four o'clock this afternoon."

"The last to see him alive," Harry murmured.

"Certainly not," Mr. Graff said with some heat. "The man who killed him would have been the last to see him alive."

"Of course," Harry said quickly. "It is merely an expression. How did Mr. Wintour respond when you showed him *Le Fantôme*?"

"He received me with the greatest possible courtesy, as always. He arranged for tea and a platter of herring canapés which he knows I especially enjoy. A true gentleman."

"No doubt, but—"

"I believe the herring is cured in aspic, which is what makes it so delicious."

"But the automaton? How did he react to *Le Fantôme*?"

"He was besotted. He thanked me extravagantly for having brought it to him, and expressed the greatest possible eagerness to acquire the rest of the collection."

"Did he make an offer?"

"A most generous one, in my view. I would be very surprised

if even Mr. Hendricks could have matched it. Of course, I did not even have the chance to contact him before"—he gestured at the dank walls of the cell block— "before I found myself here."

"Was it your impression that Mr. Harrington would accept Mr. Wintour's offer?" Harry asked.

"I did not have any means of communicating with him. It seems he had traveled up from Philadelphia, and came directly to my shop from the train station. He had not yet even taken a hotel room. He told me he would return to hear Mr. Wintour's offer on Wednesday evening at the same time."

"Tomorrow," Harry said.

"Indeed." Mr. Graff cast a forlorn eye at his surroundings. "I do not expect to be able to keep our appointment."

"You have told all this to the police?"

"Of course, but I'm not certain they believed me. I was not able to supply much in the way of useful information concerning Mr. Harrington. The police said they would send a man 'round to check the hotel registers, but I doubt if they will locate him."

"Why is that?" I asked.

"In my business, one's clients are sometimes less than candid about their circumstances. Mr. Harrington is not the first client I have ever dealt with who appeared late at night, so as to avoid unwanted attention. Often they are financially embarrassed, and do not wish to attract the attention of their wives and their creditors. I do not think the police will find Mr. Evan Harrington's name on any hotel register."

"Evan Harrington?" I closed my notebook.

"Yes. Do you know him, Theodore?"

"It's the title of a novel by George Meredith."

Mr. Graff sighed heavily. "It was probably the first thing that came into his mind. Too bad he was not a fan of Mr. Twain. Those names I would have recognized." He took out a pocket square and dabbed at his eyes. "And I am likely to remain here until the police locate this man, whomever he might be."

"Dash and I will find him, Mr. Graff," Harry said. "You may rest assured of that."

"Thank you, Ehrich. You are a good boy."

"What time were you supposed to meet with him?"

"Eleven o'clock, but if he's involved in this business, I don't expect he will keep the appointment."

"We'll find him in either case," Harry promised.

"One last thing," I said. "When you left Mr. Wintour, *Le Fantôme* remained in his possession?"

"He insisted on it. He indicated that he was going to have it examined to confirm its authenticity. I arranged to collect it from him in the morning."

"Did Mr. Wintour give you any reason to feel that he might be afraid in any way? Looking back, do you have any reason to imagine he might have feared for his life?"

Mr. Graff stroked his beard before responding. "I do not know if it is significant, but there was a phone call while we were talking. I offered to excuse myself, but Mr. Wintour asked me to wait. I walked away from the desk to give him some privacy. He has a marvelous collection of books, which I took the occasion to admire. I did not hear all of what was being said, but his tone made it clear that it was not entirely pleasant."

"Perhaps someone was threatening him?"

"I did not get that impression. Mr. Wintour was a very powerful man. Such men make enemies. When he finished the telephone call, however, he said a curious thing."

"Oh?"

"He said, 'Graff, my friend, never do business with family.'"

"Good advice," I said, with a sidelong glance at Harry.

"Possibly," Mr. Graff said. "But whom can one trust if not family?"

"Very true," Harry agreed. "And now, if you will excuse us, Mr. Graff, my brother and I should be getting along."

"Thank you for your time, sir," I said. "Harry, do you want

me to bang on the bars for Sergeant O'Donnell?"

"I don't think that will be necessary, Dash."

"No? I don't see that the lock has moved any closer while we've been talking."

"Has it not? I think perhaps it has." He began to unfasten his trousers.

"Harry? I don't mean to be indelicate, but what—?"

"I have a length of coiled watch-spring strapped to my leg. It should extend my reach just enough to reach the lock, and give me enough flexibility to work the pick."

"Suppose O'Donnell had searched you?"

"He would have found it easily," Harry admitted. "That is a problem for tomorrow. First, I must conquer the lock, then I will worry about concealing the spring." Hugging the wall closest to the lock, Harry extended his right arm through the bars as far as he could reach, which left his fingertips a good yard or so from the lock. He pulled his arm back and coiled one end of the watch spring around the end of a stout, double-diamond lock-pick.

"This should do it," he said, pushing the flexible steel through the bars and guiding it toward the lock. "By straightening out this spring, I can use it as a reaching rod. You see? It seems to be working."

Mr. Graff and I watched as Harry eased the end of the heavy lock-pick toward the lock. For a few moments it bobbed up and down like a fishing pole as the metal spring strained beneath the weight. "I must get a feel for the balance," he said. "There was no way of practicing this beforehand."

Gradually, I could see that Harry was getting control of the reaching rod. Cautiously, he began guiding the pick toward the keyhole but it repeatedly bounced off the lock plate. "I'm getting closer each time," he said. "Now, if I can just—if I can just—"

I don't know how long my brother stood there flailing about in the dim light with that strange piece of metal. Occasionally I heard a dull scratch of metal as the pick bounced off the lock. Sometimes there would be a faint flash as light from the overhead bulbs glinted off the metal spring.

Perhaps an hour passed in this fashion. I was sitting on the floor with my back against the door, and had nearly fallen asleep when a cry from my brother brought me to my senses. "Dash!" Harry cried exuberantly. "At last! The pick is in the lock! Now it should be child's play to—"

And that's when the spring broke. Harry watched in mute horror as his lock-pick clattered to the floor.

"Bad luck," said Mr. Graff.

"My dear sirs," said our drunken friend in the opposite cell, "once again I feel compelled to—"

"Silence!" Harry snapped.

Mr. Graff and I looked at one another. Not another sound was heard for a good ten minutes or so.

"Well, Harry," I said at last. "It's getting quite late. Shall I call for Sergeant O'Donnell?"

"Indeed not," my brother said. "If you would be so good as to hand me the lock-pick, I shall begin again."

4

TURNING THE TIP

HARRY MADE THREE MORE ATTEMPTS TO ESCAPE FROM THE LOCKUP that night, and failed each time. He kept his arms folded and his mouth shut when Sergeant O'Donnell finally came to release us, and would not even return my "good night" when I dropped him at home. I hoped a night's sleep would restore him to his usual bull-headed arrogance.

In those days, Harry and Bess were living in my mother's flat on East Sixty-ninth Street, an arrangement that appealed to him for two reasons—it was cheap and it kept him close to Mama. There would have been room for me, too, but I fancied myself as a bit of a man about town, and imagined living at home might cramp my style. I kept a room in Mrs. Arthur's boarding house, only seven blocks away, where I very occasionally enjoyed an evening of whist and cigars with my fellow lodgers. Apart from this, I might just as well have been living in a monastery.

Harry and Bess were seated at the breakfast table when I arrived, while Mother busied herself at the stove. Harry still looked a bit crestfallen.

"My darling Theo!" Mother called as I came through the kitchen door. "Sit down! I will bring you a little something!"

"No, thank you, Mama," I said, removing my trilby. "I have already breakfasted with Mrs. Arthur. Good morning, Bess."

"Hello, Dash," my sister-in-law said. "You boys were out a

bit late last night, weren't you?"

"Speak to your husband about that," I answered. "I would rather have been home sleeping."

"You say you've had breakfast?" Mother asked. "It cannot have been enough. You look thin! Sit!"

"I'm fine, Mother. I'll take a cup of tea, if there is any left."

I sat down at the breakfast table while she began clattering around in the cupboards. I couldn't tell you how many days began that way in those years, with Harry and Bess sitting at their places and my mother darting from table to stove. I once had occasion to visit Professor Einstein at his laboratory in Princeton, and I must report that it seemed quite a modest affair compared with my mother's kitchen. She never used one pot where three would do; she never finished serving one meal before starting preparations on the next. One navigated the room as though crossing a busy thoroughfare, bobbing and weaving amongst the simmering goulashes, cooling breads, whistling kettles, and clattering cake pans. Many times I would call at the house on a summer afternoon to take my mother for a drive, only to find that she could not leave her stewpot and basting spoon. "You go along, Theo," she would invariably say. "The pot needs minding."

As for my brother, he was never happier than when our mother was clucking over him. He sighed with satisfaction whenever she placed a dish of his beloved Hungarian pepper roast in front of him. His face glowed as she poured out his tea, giving him a peck on the forehead as she did so. From my vantage across the table, however, I would often see a flicker of despair pass over my sister-in-law's face whenever Mama tucked Harry's napkin under his chin, or cut up his kippered herring into bite-sized pieces. I resolved that it would be different for me, if I were ever fortunate enough to marry.

I had arrived just as Harry was buttering his first slice of brown toast, an operation of enormous delicacy. Harry required three coatings of paper-thin butter slices to achieve the required perfection, and each of these had to be spread to the very edge of the bread—but not beyond—in precise, surgical strokes. "Have you seen *The Herald*?" Harry asked, pausing in his exertions long enough to pass the newspaper to me. He had folded the front page to an item in the third column.

MAGNATE FOUND DEAD

MILLIONAIRE WINTOUR POISONED AT FIFTH AVENUE HOME

"Horrible! Horrible!" cries Distraught Wife

Wealthy manufacturer Branford Howard Wintour, the reclusive patron of the arts, was found dead at his home late yesterday, the apparent victim of a bizarre poisoning. Police would not confirm whether a strange mischance or a sinister murder plot had claimed the life of the famed businessman.

Mr. Wintour, a collector of rare toys, evidently succumbed to the deadly toxin while examining a recent acquisition. As of last night, the nature and source of the poison were unknown. Although police would not confirm foul play in the matter, a suspect has been taken into custody.

The item continued for several paragraphs, detailing the dead man's long record of philanthropy and public service, but adding little to what Harry and I had learned the previous evening.

"It is an obscenity, is it not?" Harry declared as I lowered the newspaper.

"Tragic, certainly," I answered.

"It is an offense against decency." He took an angry bite of his now-perfected toast.

Ah, I said to myself, Harry's not referring to Wintour's death. He's referring to the fact that the newspaper failed to mention his name.

"Strange mischance," I said, quoting from the account. "They seem to be allowing for the possibility that Wintour's death was accidental."

"Ridiculous! The police merely wish to give themselves an excuse if they fail to unmask the murderer."

"I don't know about that," I said. "If *Le Fantôme* had actually killed Mr. Wintour, I suppose it's possible that his death might have been an accident."

"The device might accidentally have fired a poison dart?"

"Suppose some earlier owner had altered the mechanism to shoot a dart instead of a red blotch. Maybe this person wanted it to be a different sort of trick. Instead of marking a card, maybe he wanted to have it puncture a balloon. And maybe the dart wasn't poisoned at all—or not intentionally, anyway. Maybe it was simply coated with some resin or adhesive that happened to be poisonous. It could have happened that way, couldn't it?"

"Seems a bit far-fetched," Harry said.

"Far-fetched? A famous millionaire has been found in his locked study with a dart in his neck. All bets are off."

"Yes," Harry said. "It is quite a puzzle. That is why it appeals to the Great Houdini. He is a master of puzzles."

"When were you planning to unravel this puzzle?" Bess asked. "Aren't we still working the ten-in-one?"

"Dash will do some scouting around during the day," Harry told her. "He will be my eyes and ears. Then we will report our conclusions to the police."

"Harry, I don't think the police are interested in receiving any further assistance from the Brothers Houdini. Thank you, Mama," I said, as she set a cup of tea before me.

"You are content to leave Josef Graff in jail?"

"Of course not. But I'm confident that the police will get

to the bottom of the crime eventually, and that Mr. Graff will be released."

"Possibly," said Harry. He picked up a second slice of toast and resumed the intricate buttering maneuver. My mother, meanwhile, had placed a soft-boiled egg before me.

"There you are, Theo," she said happily. "Just as you like it."

"Mama, I told you—"

"That looks delicious, Dash," Harry said.

"But—"

"So kind of Mama to prepare it for you."

With a sigh, I picked up the egg spoon she had laid for me. Many times in my career I have allowed myself to be chained and roped and tossed into the frigid waters of the Hudson River. It is an experience I much prefer to soft-boiled eggs.

"Besides," said Harry, noting my squeamishness with quiet amusement, "you saw for yourself that the police were completely misled by *Le Fantôme*. It is a wonder they did not handcuff the little doll and cart it off to jail along with poor Mr. Graff."

"Lieutenant Murray may not have understood how the automaton works, but he had the good sense to call someone who did. He seems very reasonable to me. What's more, he's an official detective and you're not."

Harry regarded me with genuine curiosity. "Dash," he said, "you really *do* think this matter would be better left to the police." He said it as though the possibility had never occurred to him.

I spooned a cool, gluey blob of soft-boiled egg into my mouth. "Why, that's amazing, Harry! However did you deduce that?"

"I will ask your indulgence only for one day. This evening, we shall keep Mr. Graff's appointment with the mysterious Mr. Harrington."

"No, we won't," I said.

"I beg your pardon?"

I swallowed hard as a second greasy mouthful trickled down my throat. "We should leave that to the police. Mr. Graff told them everything he told us. We shouldn't get in their way."

"Dash is right," Bess said. "Besides, Mr. Harrington would hardly carry on with business as usual once he's seen this morning's paper."

"Why not? As I demonstrated last night, *Le Fantôme* did not kill Mr. Wintour."

"No," Bess continued, "but something did, and Mr. Harrington's deal is off in either case."

"Which would make him all the more anxious to come to an agreement with Mr. Hendricks," Harry agreed, "so he will keep his appointment as scheduled. He does not necessarily know that Mr. Graff is in jail. The newspaper did not mention him by name."

"Harry—"

"Bess," Harry said, reaching for her hand, "I must try to find this Harrington person. It is the only way of verifying Mr. Graff's story."

"I still agree with Dash," Bess said. "It would be better to leave it to the police."

Harry released Bess's hand and folded his arms. "Mama, do you see? My brother and my wife are conspiring against me."

"That's nice, dear," said mother, who never listened very closely when she was cooking.

"I will make a bargain with you," he said to both of us. "Dash and I will go to the Toy Emporium this evening at the appointed hour. If we catch sight of Lieutenant Murray or any of his men, we will let the matter rest in their capable hands. If not, we will wait to see if Mr. Harrington presents himself. Is that agreeable, or would you prefer to let Mr. Graff rot in jail?"

"Of course not, but—"

"In the meantime, Dash, you must do a favor for me. You are still friendly with that newspaper gentleman?"

"Biggs? You know perfectly well that I'm still friendly with Biggs." He was referring to a childhood friend of ours who now worked the city desk at the *New York World*. We had renewed our acquaintance during my brief flirtation with a career in journalism, and he occasionally planted a friendly notice about Harry or me in the theatrical columns. Even so, he and Harry had never gotten along.

"I want you to go down to his office and see if you can come up with anything more about the Wintour case. The police may not wish to pool information, but the men of the press are every bit as diligent at gathering facts, and far less difficult about sharing it." He took a slurp of tea. "The press is a most valuable institution, if one knows how to use it."

I couldn't really see any objection, especially since Biggs was usually good for a racing tip or two. "That seems fair enough," I said, reaching for my hat. "I'll meet you at Huber's after work."

"Just a moment, Theo," said my mother. "Have you finished your egg?"

"Yes. Delicious. But I must run now."

"A moment, my son. I have a surprise—a magic trick of my own!" She reached out a frail hand for the china egg cup. "Voila!" she said, whisking it away with a flourish. A second egg had been concealed in the hollow stem of the cup. It wobbled onto its side and rolled lazily towards me.

"God!" I cried.

"Marvelous, yes?" said my mother. "Harry brought me a whole set. Now you can enjoy your first egg without worrying that the second one should get cold!"

"Wonderful, Mama," I said, weakly.

Harry just sat back and grinned.

I caught a streetcar down to the offices of the *World* and found Biggs toiling over an angled compositor's desk. He looked, as always, as though he had just been roused from a deep sleep. His wavy red hair rose and fell at odd angles from his head, and shadows ringed his pale blue eyes. The drowsy appearance also extended to his clothing. He wore a baggy gray tweed suit with an open waistcoat and loosely knotted wool tie. Such attire was considered rather too casual by the older, more conservative rank of newspapermen, but Biggs considered himself part of a new, more progressive breed of journalist. He often told me that a good newsman was required to blend in with "just folks."

"Dash, you old codworm!" he shouted when he saw me lingering in the doorway. "Just the man I've been longing to see! I'd planned to go looking for you at your mother's place this afternoon."

"You wouldn't have found me," I said, tossing my trilby onto a battered stand in the corner. "I'm at Mrs. Arthur's boarding house now."

"I know," he admitted, "but the last time I called on your mother she served me the most extraordinary piece of lemon cake. Sent me into raptures. I was rather hoping—"

"It's blackberry torte today," I said. "Why did you want to see me?"

"Why? You know perfectly well! All of New York is buzzing about the Wintour murder! You and that crazy brother of yours were right there on the spot! The police have the place locked up tight now. We sent our best man with a fat wad of bribe money, but he couldn't get past the roundsman on the door. So come on, Dash. Tell me all."

I pulled up a chair and gave Biggs a brief sketch of the crime scene while he made notes on a block of paper. He interrupted me every so often to ask for a clarification or an extra bit of detail, and I did my best to supply the answers. "All that money," he said when I'd finished, "and he gets done to death by a toy!"

"Perhaps not—"

"Well, whatever. The police will sort it out soon enough. In the meantime, the *World* will keep its readers informed of the 'diligent perspicacity' of our Lieutenant Murray." He scribbled a few more notes and then set down his pen. "So why have you come, Dash?" he asked, lacing his fingers behind his head. "You've made my job quite a bit easier, but I suspect your motives lay elsewhere."

"I was hoping for some background on Mr. Wintour," I said. "I know he made his money in toys, but—"

"Juvenile goods," Biggs said. "He was very touchy about being called 'The Toy King.'"

"Juvenile goods, then. I'd just like to know a bit more about the man."

Biggs regarded me with interest. "Why, Dash? Is there something you haven't told me? I know you're concerned about this fellow Graff, but you really can't expect—"

"It isn't every day that I find myself at a murder scene," I said. "I'm curious about the man's history. Perhaps it's ghoulish of me, but as things stand now I feel as if I've walked in on the third act of a play."

"That's the journalist in you," Biggs said, hopping down off his stool. "It was a mistake for you to follow your brother onto the stage. Follow me. I'll turn you loose in the crypt." He led me through a warren of offices to a dim basement chamber arrayed with row after row of dusty wooden filing cabinets. "Malone would have pulled the active file for the obituary," Biggs said, working his way toward the back of the room, "and of course all the notes from last night will still be upstairs, but there should be plenty of background material left." He pulled open a creaky file drawer and withdrew a fat sheaf of yellowed documents. "Enjoy yourself, Dash," he said, handing me the file. "I'll be back for you in an hour or so."

I found a seat atop a wooden crate and sat down to read. I confess that I found little of interest. There were a handful of admiring profiles describing Mr. Wintour's progress from office boy to magnate, and still more articles that gave details of his various civic interests and contributions. The phrase "pillar of the community" got repeated airings, as did the descriptive "reclusive millionaire." I noted a handful of names that seemed to recur several times—Mr. Hendricks, Dr. Blanton, and various other business associates and fellow benefactors—but apart from that I discovered little worth mentioning to Harry.

I had closed up the sheaf of papers and was preparing to leave when a clipping from Aubrey McMillan's society column caught my eye. It was dated three years previous, in April of 1894, and announced the engagement of Branford Wintour to Miss Katherine Hendricks, the only daughter of his longtime business associate Mr. Michael Hendricks. The wedding was to take place the following June.

I reached into my pocket for the clipping I had torn from that morning's paper. In the fashion of the day, it told me only that the deceased was survived by Mrs. Branford Wintour. It seemed to me, however, that I had heard Mrs. Wintour's given name mentioned the previous evening, and that it was not Katherine. Margaret, was it? Mary?

Biggs returned to find me still puzzling over the clipping. "What do you have there, Dash?" he asked.

I showed him the engagement notice. "Do you know anything about this?"

"Come on, Dash," he answered, "surely you remember—oh! Of course! You'd have been out of the city. Making bunnies vanish in Toledo or some such. Quite the scandal, that was. The society drama of the fall season."

"What happened?"

"It seems our Mr. Wintour had a bit of an eye for the ladies. While he was courting Miss Hendricks—a surpassingly lovely woman, by the by—he was also carrying on a bit of a pash with the Screech."

"The Screech?"

"I take it you've not met Mrs. Wintour?"

"I have not had that pleasure."

"Her voice is said to excite amorous feelings in barn owls. Quite the domestic martinet, as well. Can't keep staff, they say. Her father shoveled coal for a living, so she's thought to be a bit short on the social graces. Quite a looker in her own way, but I wouldn't have taken her over Miss Hendricks. See here—," he stepped over to a distant file drawer and riffled the pages for several minutes, eventually producing an announcement of Miss Hendricks's presentation ball. A pen-sketch of the young woman accompanied the article, showing a lovely, heart-shaped face with lustrous lashes and a fragile mouth.

"Apparently she wanted to go on the stage," Biggs said, "but her mother wouldn't hear of it. She'd have done well with that face."

"Not any stage I've ever played," I said. "She'd stop the show." I looked up from the image. "So how did Wintour come to throw her over for someone called the Screech?"

"Destiny forced his hand. Seems he and the Screech were discovered taking the country air together on the eve of his own engagement reception. He tried to hush it up, but Michael Hendricks got wind of it and called the wedding off. Hendricks also severed his business partnership with Wintour, though it seems that Hendricks got the worst of the arrangement. Meanwhile, Wintour tried to salvage his social standing by marrying the lady whose honor he had stained."

"Sounds like a fairly miserable outcome for everyone."

"Yes, well, perhaps Mr. Wintour found some consolation in his three-million-dollar fortune, his mansion on Fifth Avenue, his private railway car, his—"

"All right. I get the point." My eyes rested again on the sketch of Miss Hendricks. "Tell me, whatever happened to her?"

"Oh, she won't be long on the market. There's some British lord squiring her about town now. After her fortune, they say." He read my eyes. "I think she may be just a hair out of your league, Dash."

My face must have gone crimson. "You may be right," I said, with a cough. "In any case, much obliged." I stood up and reached for my hat.

"Don't be in such a hurry, Dash," Biggs said. "I'm on my way to cover the Wintour service at Holy Trinity. You're welcome to come along if you wish. You can carry my pencil."

"A funeral service? Already?"

"Apparently the Widow Wintour is in something of a hurry."

"But the police can hardly have completed their investigation so quickly. There was talk last night of giving the body a thorough medical examination."

"My thought exactly," Biggs said, cinching up his necktie. "All the more reason to go and have a look at the mourners. In any case, it'll be a chance to see all the wealthy and powerful friends lined up in a row. New York society wouldn't dare to miss this send off. Come along, I might just take you to lunch afterwards."

Biggs chatted amiably about his recent turf losses as we made our way uptown in a horse and trap. Soon we found ourselves at the newly built Church of the Holy Trinity, high on Second Avenue. "New York wasn't meant to hold so many people and buildings," Biggs said, gazing up at the church's soaring Gothic tower. "Soon they'll have to start putting them all underground."

We climbed the wide steps and Biggs made himself known to a church official stationed by the door. We were shown into one of the transepts where other members of the press had assembled. I always tend to feel subdued and reverential in any church or cathedral, even if the religious beliefs of the celebrants don't happen to correspond with my own. Biggs suffered no such inhibitions. He spent several moments glad-handing his colleagues in hushed but exuberant tones, and introduced me to various reporters from the *Times* and the *Herald*. I slipped behind a column to jot down their names, hoping that I might call on them to publicize Harry's next engagement—should he happen to secure one.

Biggs motioned me forward and we leaned against a wooden railing that commanded a view of the front rows of the nave. He kept up a running side-of-mouth commentary as each mourner was led up the center aisle. "The tall, grim-looking fellow is Michael Hendricks, but of course you met him last night. There have been rumors that the two of them were trying to patch up their differences. Hendricks is said to be desperate for capital. And there's his good wife Nora—look at her! Waving and nodding like some sort of duchess! She's much admired for her charity work amongst the lower orders, although said to have a weakness for French wines. Who's that behind her? The little fat fellow with the battered top hat?"

"That's Dr. Blanton," I whispered. "He was also there last night."

"Ah! So that's the good doctor. The Screech's lap-dog. I've heard all about him. Nearly half of his practice is absorbed in drawing up powders and potions to soothe Mrs. Wintour's delicate nerves. No doubt he's been kept on the go since the unhappy event."

Biggs and I both scribbled a few notes on our pads. "See the young swain coming up behind?" he continued, indicating a bluff and hearty-looking fellow carrying a swagger stick. "That's Mrs. Wintour's younger brother Henry, the family wastrel."

"I don't recall seeing him last night," I said.

"I wouldn't have thought so. Wintour couldn't stand the sight of him, but his wife was grooming him to step into the family business. He's just back from a grand tour of Europe, which was supposed to give him some seasoning. Look at that smirk! Can't wait to get his hands on his brother-in-law's fortune. His sort always makes me want to—well, well! You would seem to be in luck, Dash! Unless I miss my guess, the young lady moving up the aisle is none other than Miss Katherine Hendricks, the late Mr. Wintour's old flame." He indicated a slender figure in a black, close-fitting frock, wearing a low hat trimmed with netting.

"Steady, Dash," Biggs said, elbowing me in the ribs.

"She's extraordinary," I said. "I've never seen anything to compare."

"There are many who would agree with you, including that tall fellow just to her left—who, if I'm not mistaken, is her current beau."

I fixed my attention on the gangly figure Biggs had indicated. "Who is he?" I whispered.

"I can't be certain, but I believe it's Lord Randall Wycliffe, seventh earl of Pently-on-Horlake, if I recall correctly, come to find a wealthy American bride to shore up his family's dwindling fortunes."

"That fellow is a British aristocrat?"

"They don't all have brush moustaches and monocles, Dash. Wycliffe is considered quite a catch, though it's said he's not terribly well-endowed between the ears. Still, he's good-looking enough."

I studied the sandy blond hair, strong chin, and cool blue eyes of the young Englishman. "She could do better," I said.

"Could she now?" Biggs chuckled. "Ah—here comes the main attraction. The Widow Wintour, in all her glory." A tall, thick-set woman was making a slow progress up the center aisle, stopping every few steps to clutch an armrest or guide rail, as though the sheer weight of her grief made walking difficult. Her constitution would surely have been the only thing delicate about her, as I've known professional boxers who appeared frail in comparison.

"At the time of her wedding she was considered a real peach," Biggs told me. "That was scarcely three years ago. Apparently the marriage didn't agree with her." We watched as Mrs. Wintour paused to clasp the hands of well-wishers.

"She'll play this scene for all it's worth," Biggs muttered, "although everyone knows she and her husband seldom spoke to one another. She'll be well provided for, though, and she'll never want for company so long as she holds onto the Wintour fortune."

"Really, Biggs," I said, raising an eyebrow at my friend. "The woman is attending her husband's funeral! Have you always been such a cynic?"

He gave me a wide grin. "I used to be plucky and high-spirited, Dash, but I found it grated on people's nerves." He jerked his head toward the seats. "So there you have it, my friend. The ex-partner turned rival; his plump, socially ambitious wife; their stunning daughter; her boorish, titled suitor; the ne'er-do-well younger brother; the grieving widow; and the sycophantic family doctor. Which of them killed the reclusive Branford Wintour, and how will the bold young Dash Hardeen prove it?"

"I don't know that any of them killed Wintour," I said, waving aside his facetious commentary. "Certainly the police don't think so."

"Ah, yes!" Biggs said. "The kindly old toy peddler. Let's not forget him, wasting away in jail, with only the Brothers Houdini to defend his honor. Will they succeed in rescuing him from the clutches of—"

"Biggs," I said, "you really are an ass."

"I've been hoping someone would notice," he said. "Seen enough? I have all I need. We really should make our escape now—before the tributes begin."

We slipped out just as the opening notes of an organ processional sounded, and Biggs led me toward the Second Avenue elevated. Soon enough we were seated opposite one another in a dark-panelled booth at Timborio's, a restaurant and saloon favored by journalists. Biggs studied the menu and made inquiries about the gamecock, and I suppose my expression must have betrayed the state of my finances. "Order whatever you like, Dash," Biggs said. "The *World* will see to it."

"Oh no," I said. "That's quite all right."

"You're a valuable resource, Dash. You and your brother are the only men outside of the immediate family and the police department who've been inside Fortress Wintour since the Dreadful Event. If you think I'm letting you roam free, only to be pounced upon by those leeches at the *Times*, you've another think coming."

"I've already told you everything I can," I said.

"Not everything, I think. Do you mind if I order for both of us?" He set down the menu and organized a rather lavish luncheon spread that featured a fish starter, followed by the gamecock and roasted carrots, with brandied pears to follow. He then summoned the wine steward and ordered up a bottle of Burgundy that he assured me was "quite drinkable," though my knowledge of such things was fairly limited.

"All right, young Theodore," Biggs said when the wine had been decanted, "what makes you and the swaggering Harry think you can solve the Wintour murder?"

"I told you. The police wanted Harry to tell them about the automaton. We're not trying to solve the murder."

"So you said. Forgive me, but everything your brother knows about automatons—or any other subject for that matter—could be printed very comfortably on this wine cork. Your brother could very easily have shared the sum total of his knowledge with the police without pausing to draw breath. He is not, shall we say, a deep thinker. And yet here you are, the faithful brother, racing about trying to scare up information on the Wintour set. This is more than idle curiosity, I think."

"Mr. Graff—" I began.

"Yes, yes," he waved his hand impatiently. "I know all about Mr. Graff and his charming little toy emporium. That certainly explains why the Handcuff Czar should bother himself in the matter, but what about you, young Dash? Aren't you getting a bit old to be trailing along in Harry's wake?"

"He's my brother," I said simply.

"Dash, I'm aware of that. We grew up together, as you'll recall. And don't tell me again how he dragged you from the East River and saved you from drowning. He tells me himself every time I see him."

"He did pull me out of the East River."

"I know that. But he was also the one who pushed you in, remember?"

I lifted my wine glass and stared into the bowl. "I know that you and Harry have never gotten along," I began. "He can be a bully. He can be arrogant—"

"—if you happen to catch him in a good mood."

I set down my glass. "You don't know him as I do."

"Nor would I care to, based on my past experience of him."

A waiter arrived with our fish course. I waited until he had withdrawn into the kitchen. "Do you see those doors?" I asked, gesturing toward the back of the restaurant.

"The doors to the kitchen?" Biggs asked, spearing a piece of fish.

"Behind those doors, there will be two or three young boys in shirtsleeves washing dishes over a steaming basin of hot water. Harry and I did that job off and on for fourteen months, usually for five hours at a time, sometimes two shifts a day. At the end of a shift our hands would be so red and shriveled that my mother would rub them with cooking fat. I was twelve years old at the time."

"Dash—"

"I'm not trying to impress you with my tale of hardship and woe. Plenty of people come from poor families, and lots of them had it tougher than we did. What I'm saying, though, is that Harry always managed to keep his eye on something better. We'd stand there side by side at the wash basin, and he'd fill my head with stories of the fantastic things we were going to do with our lives—travel the world, have adventures, perform for royalty. Even then, I could always spot a huckster, but my brother was no huckster. He honestly believed that these things were certain to happen. All he had to do, he always said, was to be ready when the time came. So he'd finish washing the dishes and then he'd go home and practice."

"That's the part I've never quite understood," Biggs said, dabbing at his mouth with a napkin. "Why did he want to be a magician? Why not an athlete, say, or a captain of industry?"

"Some boys want to grow up to be president. Harry wanted to be Robert-Houdin. I used to take it for granted—having a brother who could produce cakes from an empty hat, or find coins in my nose and ears. It took me some time to realize that not every family had one."

"Dash, I've seen you perform. You're every bit as good a magician as Harry."

"Kind of you to say so, but actually I'm not. No one is. I truly believe he's going to be the most famous man in the world."

Biggs shook his head sadly. "Like Kellar you mean? Or Signor Blitz? Dash, these tricks and stunts will only take him so far. Even the best magicians in the world are still only magicians. Who will remember Kellar ten years from now?"

"I yield to no one in my admiration for Kellar, but Harry is something entirely new."

"The escape artist business, you mean? Dash, not everyone shares Harry's fascination with handcuffs and ropes. I think your brother is betting too heavily on this idea. Will the public pay money to see a man who can—what?—get out of things? It's a strange notion for an entertainment. People tie him up; he escapes. Frankly, I don't see the appeal. There's some novelty, perhaps—like a fire-eater or a circus strong man—but nothing more."

"You think so, do you?"

"I do."

I took another swallow of wine. "There was a lock-smith when we were growing up in Appleton—before my father brought us to New York. The locksmith's name was R. P. Gatts, and Harry used to help him take locks apart and put them back together. One day Mr. Gatts let Harry have a big rusty padlock from somebody's old grain locker. Harry took it home and we found a length of chain somewhere, and that's the first time I can remember him ever trying an escape. I wrapped the chain around his wrists and cinched the padlock so tightly that the chain actually bit into his wrists. Harry insisted on that—the chain had to be as tight as possible."

"And he escaped in a jiffy," Biggs said dismissively. "Leaving you wonderstruck."

"No," I said. "He didn't escape that day. Or the day after. Or the day after that. But every day for three weeks I wrapped the chain around his wrists and snapped that rusty old padlock into place, and then I'd sit back and watch. One day the neighborhood kids came to the yard to get us for Red Robin, but when they saw Harry struggling with that lock they dropped their sticks and their balls and sat down on the grass beside me. And they came back the next day. Harry pulled and tugged at that chain until his wrists went raw. He kept at it every afternoon until it was time to go in for supper. Then I'd unfasten the padlock and he'd shrug his shoulders and say, 'Same time tomorrow.' Some days his arms would be covered with blood and bruises. He never complained. He told our mother he'd fallen out of a tree."

Biggs reached for his cutlery as the gamecock arrived. "Still, he did escape eventually, and you were dazzled, and the neighborhood boys lifted him up and carried him through the neighborhood in triumph. Is that it?"

"No, Biggs, that's the whole point. I honestly don't remember if he ever did escape. All I remember is the struggle. That's where the drama of the thing was. Day after day I sat there on the grass surrounded by our friends and we just watched—mesmerized. These were kids who had no patience for card tricks or coin flourishes. But they spent hours watching Harry—just to see if he could do it." I smiled at the memory. "He was nine years old at the time."

"All right, Dash," Biggs said, "I see your point. But do you really think that a bunch of kids in Appleton is the same thing as a New York audience?"

"So far as Harry is concerned, there's no difference."

Biggs fell silent for several moments, fixing his attention on the food. "You still haven't answered my original question, Dash," he said after a time. "Suppose that everything you say is true. Suppose that Harry is about to conquer the world with his daring feats of escape. Where do you fit in?"

"That should be obvious," I said.

"Enlighten me."

"He couldn't do any of it without me," I said, draining my wine glass. "My brother needs an audience."

5

THE WORM-SHAFT MAN

WHEN I LEFT TIMBORIO'S I STILL HAD A GOOD THREE HOURS before it would be time to meet Harry at the dime museum. I decided that a walk would clear my head. I set off without any fixed sense of a destination and after a time found myself standing outside the Wintour mansion on Fifth Avenue. Taking up a position across the street, I spent nearly an hour watching as expensive carriages rolled up and a series of well-wishers climbed the steps to pay their respects to the widow.

After a while I rolled a cigarette and began wondering what I was doing there. The answer came to me when I saw Mr. Michael Hendricks and his daughter, the lovely Katherine, coming down the steps from the house. I tossed my cigarette aside and hurried across the street. "Mr. Hendricks?" I called.

He stopped and turned toward me. "Yes? Can I help you, young man?"

If anything, Hendricks appeared even more gaunt and haggard than he had the previous evening. Seeing him at close range, however, I was struck by the bright energy in his eyes. They gave the impression of an eager boy trapped in an old man's body.

"I'm terribly sorry to disturb you, sir," I began. "You see, I—"

"You're the young magical fellow from last night," he said. "You and the other boy—your brother, was it?—the pair of you made quite the fools of New York's finest, I must say."

"I'm afraid my brother can be a bit overly zealous," I said. "We didn't mean to leave the police with egg on their faces."

"Nonsense! The law needs a bit of humbling now and again. Keeps them on their toes. What can I do for you, young man? Houdini, was it?"

"Houdini is my brother. My name is Hardeen. Dash Hardeen."

He stuck out a hand which, to my surprise, was red and rough like a curtain-puller's. "Good to know you, Hardeen," he said, pumping my hand with unexpected strength. "I'm Michael Hendricks, and this is my daughter, Katherine."

I raised my hat to Miss Hendricks and she returned a dazzling smile. A more polished young man might have offered a comment on the weather, or ventured some other remark of topical interest. I chose instead to stand motionless with a frozen rictus of a smile stamped on my features, swaying slightly in the autumn breeze. The power of speech had abruptly fled. It would have taken a keen eye to detect an appreciable difference between myself and a lamp post.

"Mr. Hardeen?" said Hendricks. "Was there something you wanted from me?"

"Yes, sir," I said, struggling to regain my composure. "I wondered if I might ask you one or two questions about Mr. Wintour."

"Are you some type of investigator?" he asked.

"No, sir, I'm not. And I don't wish to burden you at such an unhappy time, but a good friend of mine has been detained in this matter, and I've promised his wife that I would do what little I could to assist in clearing his name."

"Yes," Hendricks said. "Poor old Josef. Are the police still holding him?"

"Yes, sir."

He studied my face, apparently trying to gauge my usefulness. "Hardeen, is it? What sort of name is that? Italian?"

"Hardly, sir. It's a stage name. I make my living, such as it is, as a performer. My brother thought it best if I took a different name. He feels there's only room enough for one Houdini in the world."

"I see. Why don't you walk along with us for a moment, Mr. Hardeen?" He held out his arm to his daughter and I fell in step beside them. "Well, Mr. Hardeen," he continued after a moment, "I don't know what I can tell you that you didn't see for yourself last night, but I'm absolutely certain that Josef Graff had nothing whatever to do with this thing. That man once walked half-way across Manhattan to return four cents to me—a real honest Abe, that one. I tried like anything to put him in my carriage, let my driver take him back home, but he wouldn't hear of it. Said it would end up costing me more than the four cents." He laughed. "We could use more like him in this city."

"You and Mr. Wintour both had dealings with Mr. Graff, didn't you, sir?"

"Oh, certainly," he said. "Though I never felt that Branford got any particular pleasure out of his collection. I sometimes suspected he bought up these things simply to keep me from getting my hands on them. He had quite a competitive streak."

"When Mr. Graff came across an unusual item, would he usually let you see it first? Or did he take it to Mr. Wintour?"

"Me, I would have said. I tried to make it worth his while."

"Last night, you appeared surprised that *Le Fantôme* had been shown to Mr. Wintour without your knowledge."

Hendricks stopped walking and reached into a pocket for his coin purse. "Katherine," he said to his daughter, "would you mind seeing if that flower girl has something for my buttonhole?" He slipped a coin into her gloved hand. It was a transparent device to send Miss Hendricks out of earshot for a few moments, and she frowned at him to show what she thought of it. In spite of her obvious displeasure, she turned without further protest and made her way toward the flower stall at the corner.

Hendricks watched her go, then spoke to me in a lowered

tone. "I admit that I was surprised when I heard about the automaton," he said. "A real treasure like that—something with so much history attached to it—I would have expected Mr. Graff to come straight to me. When I heard otherwise I was afraid that—I thought perhaps—," he paused, gazing reflectively at his coin purse. "Well, Mr. Hardeen, I suppose it's no secret that my business has been going through a stormy patch. That's why I happened to be at Branford's place last night. I was hoping we might revive our association in the light of a particularly delicate deal I have in the works. I could have used his—well, no matter. In any event, when I heard that Mr. Graff offered the automaton to Branford first, I was afraid he'd heard rumors of my recent reversals. A man like Josef Graff wouldn't have wanted to embarrass me. If he thought I couldn't afford *Le Fantôme* he would simply have taken it elsewhere. But I can't afford to let that sort of thing pass unchallenged. Those sorts of rumors—those sorts of assumptions about my finances—could prove highly damaging. Appearances count for a great deal in New York and any hint of—"

He cut himself off as Miss Hendricks returned with a white carnation. "Have you and Mr. Hardeen finished talking about money?" she asked, threading the flower through her father's buttonhole. "Or was it some other topic too coarse for my delicate ears?"

"Nothing for you to concern yourself over, my dear," Hendricks answered.

"You're a very exasperating man, Father," Miss Hendricks said. "Don't feel left out, Mr. Hardeen. I've brought a flower for you, too."

"Why—why, thank you," I stammered as she arranged the flower on my lapel.

"There," she said. "You look quite smart now."

"Flowers are very lovely," I said, inanely. Her perfume appeared to be clouding my mind.

"I'll tell you another thing about Josef Graff," Hendricks said as we continued walking. "They'd better let him out of jail soon, because I can't get my train set-up running. He just sold me a big new locomotive with a double set of pilot trucks, and I can't get the blasted thing to work. Need him to come up and show me."

"Compound gears or worm-shaft?" I asked.

He stopped short. "Worm-shaft," he said. "Are you a model train enthusiast, Hardeen? A collector, perhaps?"

"Hardly," I said. "But I used to work for Mr. Graff, and I know my way around the switching yard."

"Just the man I've been needing," he said, patting his daughter's hand. "Come along and have a look at my set-up. We'll give you tea afterwards. Perhaps we can impose upon Katherine to join us, so that you won't find the experience entirely disagreeable."

Mercifully I had fallen a half-step behind them, so that no one saw the bloom of crimson on my cheeks. Miss Hendricks, walking arm-in-arm with her father, appeared to be admiring a row of blossoming trees as if they had amused her in some way.

We walked on for a time while Hendricks chatted enthusiastically about a line of new trains he expected from "those upstarts at Ivers." He solicited my opinion of a new type of collector pivot, and wondered idly whether such a device might have some practical application in the nation's railways. He had just begun to describe the loading ramp of his new lumber car when we reached our destination. "Ah! Here we are," he announced. "Be it ever so humble."

In truth, the structure could only have seemed humble in contrast to the sprawling luxury of the Wintour mansion. Mr. Hendricks's home proved to be a stately four-story wooden manor with a mansard roof and no fewer than seven brick chimneys breaking the roof line. We passed through a black wrought iron gate and followed a tree-lined walk to the front door, which was opened by a uniformed butler as we reached the top of the steps.

"Thank you, Becking," said Hendricks as the butler took his

hat and coat. "Mr. Hardeen and I will be in the study."

I passed my coat and my trilby to the butler and followed Hendricks into a room off the main hall. Closing the door, he loosened his tie and headed for a sideboard covered with bottles and decanters. "Now, Mr. Hardeen," he said, rubbing his hands together, "what can I offer you?"

The study made a dramatic contrast to the room where we had seen Branford Wintour's body the night before. Where Mr. Wintour's study had appeared extravagant but sterile, Mr. Hendricks had created a private sanctuary with little regard to appearances. Books lay open on the arms of battered leather chairs. Papers and correspondence were stacked haphazardly on cluttered occasional tables. Stray articles of clothing were draped over the back of a plush sofa. A battered captain's desk stood in a bay window overlooking the street, its surface barely visible beneath an overlay of documents.

"Forgive the mess," Hendricks said. "The house-maid only gets in here once or twice a month. Even that's too often, if you ask me. Now, what can I get you? I'm having a whiskey and soda."

"That will be fine," I said. Hendricks poured two hearty measures of Walker & Sons whiskey into a pair of glasses, then squirted a stream of aerated water from a tall glass gasogene. "Your good health," he said, handing one of the glasses to me.

I raised my glass to return the salute. "This is a splendid room," I said.

"Thank you, young man. What do you think of this?" He indicated a low platform that curved along the wall of a corner turret. A bewildering double-horseshoe pattern of model train track covered the surface, with more than a dozen switch-points on the straights.

"Incredible," I said. "You've merged three different track patterns."

"Four," he said. "I got tired of watching it go around in a circle. This way I can run several trains at once, just as you would on a real railroad." He took a healthy snort of his whiskey. "Damned silly thing for a grown man to do with his time and money. Katherine says I'm just a boy who refuses to put away his toys."

"My brother and I are professional magicians, Mr. Hendricks. Is that any sort of occupation for a grown man?"

He gave a short, barking type of laugh. "Let me show you the problem with my train." He stepped over to a wooden box and clicked the lever that sent electricity coursing through the tracks. A set of indicator dials began to waggle impressively.

"I don't believe I've ever seen this type of train set before," I said. "Is it new?"

"It's not widely available just yet," he answered. "I have some money in the company."

"'The Minotaur,'" I said, reading the model name off the side of the locomotive. "Isn't this the same type of train Mr. Wintour had in his study? Was this another area where you and Mr. Wintour competed?"

"Trains? Hardly." He stood for a moment, listening to the hum and crackle of the tracks as they warmed up. "As a matter of fact, we tried several times to develop a model train set of our own, but I'm afraid it never came to very much. After we dissolved the partnership, neither one of us pursued the venture." He twisted a dial on the control box. The locomotive emitted a whistle blast and its firebox began to glow. "A shame, really. Branford was the best damned businessman in the entire city. Who knows what we might have done." He pressed a plunger-button and a black locomotive slowly inched forward, gathering speed as the reach rods and draw bars loosened. "My wife hates this train set," he said. "She's convinced I'll burn the whole house down one day."

"It looks as if your grounding wires are more than adequate," I said. "I think Mrs. Hendricks can rest easy. Tell me, were you surprised when Mr. Wintour invited you to dinner last night?"

"Surprised?" He watched as the train gathered speed on a straight section of track, heading into a double-switch plate. "Yes, Hardeen, I suppose I was. But in a town this size, it was getting difficult to carry on avoiding one another. I'd often see him across the room at a restaurant, or reading a newspaper at the club. At first we pretended not to notice, but after a while it began to seem pretty damn silly. I supposed he felt the same way—or so I hoped, at any rate. So I was quite pleased by the invitation."

"Did you have a chance to speak with him?"

"No, sir, I did not. He never came out of the study after Nora and I arrived. We were kept waiting in the morning room." He watched as the locomotive clattered over the switching plate and promptly derailed, plowing straight into the side of a wooden boxcar. "Damn. Just painted that, too."

"I think I see your problem," I said. I stripped off my suit coat and crawled under the platform. "Switch off the power for a minute, would you?"

He tripped the power lever and the hot buzzing ceased. "You know," he said, "I was quite looking forward to seeing Branford again." I heard the sloshing of his whiskey glass. "It's so rare that I meet someone who shares my interests. I was looking forward to telling him about my trains. Nora thought I was building up my hopes for nothing, though. About working together again, I mean."

I rolled over onto my back and tinkered with a loose ground bolt. "Why is that?" I asked.

"Branford's wife. I'm afraid she doesn't care for me."

"Or Miss Hendricks, I would imagine," I said from beneath the platform. I couldn't see his face, but he took a moment to reply.

"Hell," he said. "I suppose that's no secret. Bran was supposed to marry Katherine some years ago. He was smitten with her, and she was fond enough of him, though she thought of him more as an uncle than a husband, I'd venture to say. In any case it seemed a really splendid idea to the pair of us, sitting over port and cigars in the Century one night. We never spoke directly of the business advantages, but it was clear that we'd be uniting the two empires, as it were."

I crawled out from under the train platform to find Hendricks addressing his remarks to his whiskey glass, his face a study in remorse.

"In my own defense, I never forced the matter on Katherine," he continued. "She seemed quite keen on the whole thing. I think Bran may have filled her head with queer ideas—giving her some sort of role in the company or some such. My daughter holds many peculiar views. Reads a great deal of Susan B. Anthony and the other one. What's her name? Elizabeth Cady Stanton. In any case, at least Bran took the time to listen to my daughter when she spoke, which is more than I can say for this pompous young ass who's squiring her about at the moment. Anyway, my daughter's engagement soon came to grief, as you undoubtedly read in the society pages. Why any right-thinking man should leave my daughter at the altar is beyond my ken." He set down his glass. "I'm talking rather a lot, aren't I?"

"Not at all, sir," I said. "I apologize if I've broached an unpleasant subject. I believe I've found the solution to your other little problem, though." I switched the train set back on and sent the locomotive hurtling toward the troublesome portion of the track. It cleared the turn easily and stayed on course for two more high-speed circuits.

"My God, Hardeen!" Hendricks cried. "You're a genius!"

"Hardly, sir. I just loosened two of the bolts holding the track onto the table. There wasn't enough give. The vibration was causing the train to jump the track."

"Damn it, I tried that. I got too much sway from side to side. The train still derailed."

"I compensated for that by replacing these bolt-pins with match sticks. The wood is soft enough to absorb the vibrations but it still controls the wobble."

Hendricks put his face close to the switch-plate and examined my jury-rigging.

"It's not exactly picturesque," I said. "You may want to paint—"

"Brilliant!" he cried. "Just brilliant! Have you any training in this area?"

"Training?"

"Engineering background? That sort of thing?"

"I've toured with a traveling circus for months at a time. Believe me, when you're stuck in Wichita with a broken hinge on your drop-trap, you get pretty good at fixing things with whatever's at hand."

Hendricks watched as the train eased past the turn and headed for the straightaway. "I may have some work for you, Hardeen," he said. "I just might, at that."

We sat together in that room for the better part of two hours, drinking his whiskey and playing with his train. He reminisced a little about his younger days with General Sherman's XV Corps at Vicksburg, and I talked a bit about touring the backwaters with a medicine show. Sometimes we just sat quietly and watched the train. I don't know that I've ever spent a more pleasant time.

It must have been late afternoon by the time I found my hat and got up to leave. Hendricks tried to get me to stay for dinner, but I had to get down to Huber's and meet Harry. As he led me out of the study, Hendricks invited me to stop back again any time. I know he meant this in all sincerity, but we both realized that starving young magicians don't simply drop in on Fifth Avenue millionaires. He took my visiting card and repeated what he'd said about sending some work my way. I shook his hand and thanked him for his company. The butler could hardly wait to close the door behind me.

I had walked only half a block when I heard footsteps rushing up behind me. A woman's voice called my name. I turned to see Katherine Hendricks hurrying toward me.

"Mr. Hardeen!" she called. "I was afraid I'd missed you!"

She was flushed and out of breath as she reached my side. "Father said that you would be staying for tea! I expected I would have had a chance to see you again!"

I removed my hat, wondering why such a charming and lovely young lady should have been so anxious for my company. "I fear that your father and I lost all track of time, Miss Hendricks," I said. "We were entirely absorbed in the workings of his train."

She dabbed at her face with a square of linen. "I really must speak with you," she said. "May I walk with you for a bit?"

"Certainly." I extended my elbow and she rested her gloved hand on my forearm.

She appeared to be struggling to compose her thoughts, and waited until we were out of sight of the house before speaking again. "Well, Mr. Hardeen," she said with a delicate cough, "the trees are very colorful at this time of year."

"Indeed," I answered.

"In the spring there is such a lovely fragrance from those bushes. What do you suppose they are? Lilacs? I'm not very clever at that sort of thing."

"Magnolias, I believe."

"Magnolias! How marvelous!"

"Miss Hendricks? Did you really pursue me into the street to inquire about the fall foliage?"

She bit her lower lip. "Of course not. You must think me very stupid, but I'm not quite certain how to begin. It is not often that I meet someone who—someone with—forgive me, Mr. Hardeen."

I glanced down at her exquisite profile and felt my cheeks grow hot. Could it be? Did I dare hope? During our brief walk home from the church, had I somehow managed to capture her attention? Had she been charmed by my rugged demeanor? Captivated by my knowledge of model train sets? It did not seem likely, and yet here she was, clinging to my arm and struggling to express some inner torment.

"May I speak candidly, Mr. Hardeen?" she said at last.

"Please do," I said.

"I feel that I must—indeed, I *know* that I must—"

"Yes?"

"I must speak to your brother."

I stopped walking. "My brother?"

"It is quite urgent."

"May I ask why?"

"My father told me of your brother's wonderful exploit at Mr. Wintour's home last night. I understand that his demonstration of the little doll—the automaton—was quite masterly. It seems to me that he may be just the man to help me with a certain difficulty I am facing. He seems so terribly clever."

"Perhaps you might wish to take the matter up with my brother directly," I said, glancing at my pocket watch. "If you hurry, you may just be able to see him vanish a bowl of goldfish at Huber's Museum."

Miss Hendricks had not missed the coldness of my tone. "I did not mean to suggest that you are not just as clever," she said quickly. "The two of you work together, do you not?"

"We did. My brother's wife performs his act with him now."

"I did not mean that. I meant that you were both present last night—in the room where Mr. Wintour was discovered."

"We were."

"You saw Mr. Wintour? His body, I mean?"

"Yes."

"Is it likely that you will be returning to Mr. Wintour's home at any time in the future?"

It seemed a very odd question. "I only meant," Miss Hendricks continued, sensing my hesitation, "that perhaps the police might have more questions for you and your brother? About the room in which Mr. Wintour died?"

"I really couldn't say, Miss Hendricks. I suppose it's possible, but I see no reason to presume so."

"Still, it is possible that you might find yourself in Mr. Wintour's study at some point in the future, is it not?"

"May I ask why this matter is of such interest to you?"

"Yes, I suppose I really ought to stop talking in circles." She paused and untied the chin strap of her bonnet, allowing her long auburn hair to flow about her shoulders. "If I seem unduly circumspect, Mr. Hardeen, it is because I fear I may be making too much of nothing."

"Go on."

"You are aware that Mr. Wintour and I were once engaged to be married?"

"Indeed."

"Although our engagement ended badly, I never thought ill of him. I am an ambitious woman, Mr. Hardeen, and Mr. Wintour was one of the few men I've met who did not laugh at my ambitions." She paused, as if daring me to belittle the notion of an ambitious woman. When I did not, she continued. "It was no longer possible that Mr. Wintour and I should ever meet, but we corresponded occasionally."

"I see."

"I assure you that these letters were not indiscreet in any way."

"Then why does the matter trouble you so?"

By way of reply, she stepped to the curb and raised her rolled parasol into the air. A private carriage clattered towards us from down the street. "I asked the coachman to follow behind," she explained. "I thought it might afford a bit of privacy."

The carriage pulled up beside us and I helped her inside. As I pulled the door closed she rapped on the roof with her parasol. The driver flicked the reins and we set off down Fifth Avenue.

"As to these letters," she continued, resuming the conversation where it had left off, "I am being courted by a gentleman from England just now."

"Lord Randall Wycliffe," I said.

She looked at me in surprise. "You seem to know a great deal about me, Mr. Hardeen. Did my father mention Randall to you?"

I shook my head. "My brother isn't the only clever one in the family," I said.

"I see. And do you know Lord Wycliffe?"

"No."

"He comes from a stuffy old family with a big castle somewhere. A mansion, I suppose, not a castle. In any case it's very old and it seems that his ancestors all fought in the War of the Roses or some such thing, and his family cares a great deal about appearances and propriety. When Randall began calling on me, my previous engagement to Mr. Wintour was considered a black mark against me. By his family, I should say. They would have preferred that I had spent my life to this point in a boarding school. Of course, Randall isn't like that at all. He doesn't care a hoot about my past. 'What's done is done,' he says."

"Very wise," I remarked.

"Oh, yes. He has very modern views."

"I'm not sure I see your difficulty, then."

"His family has grave reservations about my suitability, Mr. Hardeen. And I'm afraid that when I became aware of these objections, I behaved foolishly. I wrote to Mr. Wintour to seek his advice. Several times."

"And Lord Wycliffe objected?"

"He does not know."

"But surely if he is everything you say—"

"I said some rather indiscreet things in these letters, Mr. Hardeen."

"Oh?"

"Very indiscreet."

"Ah."

"Yes. So you see, Mr. Hardeen, when I heard that Mr. Wintour was dead—murdered, of all things—it placed me in a very uncomfortable position." She began worrying at the fingers of one of her gloves. "You wouldn't happen to have a cigarette, would you?"

"A cigarette?"

"Don't look so shocked, Mr. Hardeen. You men seem to think that just because—"

"Miss Hendricks," I said, interrupting what promised to be a lengthy peroration, "a woman of my acquaintance not only smokes cigars but also dines on the stubs for the amusement of paying customers. The prospect of a young lady with a cigarette holds no terror for me." I took out my little tin of Shearson's and rolled a cigarette for each of us. She accepted a light and leaned back against the leather seat of the carriage, inhaling with evident satisfaction.

"To return to the matter of the letters—" she began.

"You are afraid that these letters will be discovered among Mr. Wintour's effects."

"Just so."

"And if they were to be discovered?"

"My engagement to Lord Wycliffe would surely be called off."

"That would be regrettable, of course," I said. "But I'm not entirely certain how I can be of assistance in the matter."

"I want you to recover the letters for me, Mr. Hardeen."

I glanced at my reflection in the glass window at the side of the carriage. I did not appear to be a lunatic, but she had apparently mistaken me for one. "Well," I began slowly, "that might present something of a problem. How do you propose I might go about it without rousing the suspicions of the police?"

"I'm sure you and your brother could slip into Mr. Wintour's study somehow. There must be a way. Whoever killed Mr. Wintour found a way. Your brother proved as much last night."

"Yes, but we don't know how it was done."

She laid her hand on mine. "I'm sure you could manage it, Mr. Hardeen. I have such confidence in you."

I looked deep into her extraordinary blue-gray eyes and I saw only connivance. I knew that she was attempting to take advantage of me. I knew that she regarded me as a social inferior, and perhaps a witless dupe. I knew all of this and more, and yet I could not bring myself to turn away. She thought me capable of great cunning and bravery, and I did not wish to disabuse her of the notion. "How is it that the police did not find these letters the other night, Miss Hendricks?" I asked cautiously.

She pulled her hand away. "Mr. Wintour always kept my letters in a special place. Pressed in the pages of a volume of poetry I once gave to him. Elizabeth Barrett Browning. The sonnets. Do you know them, Mr. Hardeen?"

"No," I said, "but I'm well up on limericks involving commercial travelers."

She favored me with a winning smile. "I'm not sure if Mrs. Browning's talents ran in that direction, but I invite you to judge for yourself. Mr. Wintour kept the volume on the lower shelf of the case nearest the fire. The binding is stamped in gold."

"Surely it is safe enough there? Mr. Wintour had thousands of books in his study. I find it unlikely that your letters will be discovered any time soon, if ever."

"I could not stand the uncertainty, Mr. Hardeen. I must know that the letters have been recovered and destroyed. It is the only way of putting my... my indiscretions behind me."

"Miss Hendricks, I really don't know that I can—"

"I'll pay you, of course. Anything you like. Only you must not fail me."

"It is not a question of payment, I assure you. It is a matter of—"

"If you fail me, Mr. Hardeen, my engagement to Lord Wycliffe will surely be broken. I doubt if my reputation would stand this a second time. Father would be crushed. Could you really stand by and allow this to happen?"

I looked again into those expressive eyes. I should have liked to say many things. I might have told her, for instance, that I would have rejoiced to hear that her engagement to Lord Wycliffe had been broken. I might also have revealed that I planned one day to be a wealthy man, and headline an act that would tour all the major capitals of Europe. And I might even have added that I shared her fondness for the poems of Mrs. Browning, especially the one that began "How do I love thee?"

I told her none of these things. Instead, I simply folded my arms and said, "I'll see what I can do."

~6~

THE KING OF KARDS

"THAT WOMAN KILLED BRANFORD WINTOUR," MY BROTHER SAID. "There can be no doubt."

"How do you figure that, Harry?" I asked.

"Because she's trying to get a gullible, love-struck young swain to cover her tracks," he answered. "That would be you, Dash. She's playing you for a fool."

"That thought had occurred to me, Harry," I said. "But it doesn't necessarily follow that she killed Mr. Wintour."

We were crowded behind the scenery flats at Huber's Museum, where Harry and Bess still had two more rotations of the ten-in-one ahead of them. In between shows I filled Harry in on the Wintour funeral and my visit to the Hendricks mansion. My brother listened with keen attention, though the details of my encounter with Miss Katherine left him indignant.

"Certainly she killed him," Harry insisted. "What other explanation can there be?"

"I can think of several," I said, "including the one she gave."

"You believe that?" Harry scoffed. "She wrote this man an indiscreet letter in a moment of weakness and she needs us to recover it? Absurd! She wrote to arrange a secret meeting. Wintour gladly assented, hoping to renew their illicit acquaintance. Once inside the study, unobserved by anyone in the house, she killed him. Simple as that."

"How did she get out again? The room was locked from the inside, as you'll recall."

Harry leaned in toward the mirror of his makeshift dressing table, dabbing at his eyebrows with a heavy pencil. "I haven't worked that out yet," he admitted. "But I will. Women are not to be trusted, not even the best of them."

"What a perfectly horrible thing to say!" cried Bess, who had been listening intently while she repaired a hole in one of her ballet slippers.

Harry turned to her and shrugged his shoulders. "I'm sorry, my dear. It was a remark of Mr. Sherlock Holmes."

"Mr. Holmes never married, I take it?"

"Regrettably, no." He turned away from the mirror as Miss Missy, the Armless Wonder, appeared nudging her little tea trolley before her. Of necessity, Missy supplemented her meager salary from Huber's by selling tea and cakes outside the theater after each show. She never failed to attract a long line of customers, most of them drawn by the sheer novelty of a tea lady who gripped the dainty china handles of the pot and cups with her feet. When her customers had gone, Missy made the rounds of the other performers. With her cheery disposition and pleasing smile, Missy was one of the most winning women I've ever known. She also happened to brew the worst tea in New York, but she needed the extra pennies so badly that no one ever had the heart to refuse a cup.

"I have a little trouble picturing Miss Hendricks as the murderer," I said, watching as Missy poured out three cups of tea. "In the first place—yes, Missy, I'll take milk. Lots of it. In the first place, I'm hard pressed to see a motive for such a thing." I reached over for my cup. "Furthermore, if she did kill him, she would have been perfectly able to remove the incriminating letters herself. Yes, Missy. Delicious, as always."

"Perhaps she was interrupted before she had a chance to recover the letters," Harry said.

"It's possible," I admitted, "but it hardly seems likely."

"I think that we should speak with this Lord Randall Wycliffe," Harry said. "Perhaps Miss Hendricks is trying to shield him. Perhaps he's a jealous type, and Miss Hendricks had written to warn Mr. Wintour. That would incriminate him if the letters were discovered. Lord Wycliffe could well be the true murderer."

"Harry, according to you, half of New York is under suspicion."

"I still think we should speak with him."

"What's the point? After tonight, you and I are no longer in the detective business. Remember our agreement? We'll go to the Toy Emporium this evening to see if Mr. Harrington appears. After that, we're done."

"But until then, you have agreed to help me gather information, have you not?"

"I agreed to see Biggs," I said. "I even checked out the lay of the land with Hendricks and his daughter. But I'm not about to—"

"Only until this evening," he said, cutting me off. "After the last show, we shall call on the young aristocrat." He stood up and started off toward the performance platform. "But first, my public awaits."

"Tell me again how we're going to get into the Cairo Club, Harry?"

"It is a gambling club, and I am the King of Kards. What could be simpler?"

"I see. Wouldn't it be easier to call on Lord Wycliffe at his hotel? I believe he's taken a suite at the Belgrave."

"No, we must not put him on his guard. That is why I asked young Jack Hawkins to shadow his movements. A messenger boy attracts very little attention, but he sees a great deal. Jack tells me that Lord Wycliffe departed for the Cairo less than an hour ago. We have the opportunity to observe him going about his business, unaware that he has come under the watchful eye of the Great Houdini."

"But we're not members of the Cairo. It's rather exclusive."

"Something will present itself. We must be prepared to seize our opportunity when it comes."

"Harry—"

"Trust me, Dash. As you say, it will all be over after this evening."

We were standing in the kitchen of the apartment on Sixty-ninth Street, and we were wearing nothing but our undergarments. After the last show, Harry and I had taken Bess back home and wolfed down a couple of bowls of borscht with brown bread. Then Harry led me into the back room where our old costume trunk was stored. After a fair bit of rummaging, he located the old tailcoats we used to wear as the Brothers Houdini. We would need our evening clothes, he explained, in order to present ourselves as a pair of young gadabouts seeking diversion in one of the swankier gambling establishments. I looked at our wrinkled old costumes, with their worn knees and shiny elbows, and doubted that anyone would mistake us for young gadabouts. My impressions were confirmed by our mother, who refused to let us out of the house in such shabby-looking garments. She insisted on touching up the old costumes with a hot iron, which left us standing in front of the kitchen fire in our linen, waiting for her to finish her ministrations.

"Uh, Harry," I said, "have you ever been to the Cairo?"

"Of course not. It is a club where men go to smoke and gamble. I do neither. Why should I go there?"

"Actually, Harry, it's a place where men do many other things in addition to smoking and gambling, and I just sort of thought it might not be the ideal setting for an encounter with young Lord Wycliffe."

"Ah! I see what you mean!" He tapped his forehead with an index finger. "There is drinking, as well! That might possibly work to our advantage!"

"That's not precisely what I meant, Harry. Some of the men

who go to the Cairo are looking for—" I broke off as Bess wandered into the kitchen. "Er, Bess, I wonder if you wouldn't mind—?"

"Come, now, Dash," she laughed. "I've seen a man in his underthings before."

"Well, yes, but—"

"For goodness sakes, Dash. Harry thinks nothing of stripping down to a loin cloth when he does a bridge leap—"

"It is a swimming costume," Harry interjected, quietly.

"—but you're embarrassed to be seen in your long-drawers. Sometimes I wonder how the two of you came to be in the same family."

"But I was only—"

She put her finger to my lips to silence me. "Harry," she said, "I think what Dash is trying to tell you is that the Cairo caters to a certain class of young men who are not quite as virtuous as you are."

"So I hear!" he said excitedly. "They drink and smoke and gamble!" He gave a knowing wink.

"Well, Harry," Bess said carefully, "it is possible that there may also—," she caught herself as Mother appeared with our trousers.

"Mama," said Harry, "we are going to an illicit nightclub! Can you imagine?"

"That's nice, Ehrich," Mother said.

Bess leaned over and whispered in my ear. "Keep an eye on him, will you, Dash?"

"I always do," I answered.

"Besides," Harry continued, "we are not due at Mr. Graff's shop for another three hours. If I don't keep you on your feet, you'll fall asleep in front of the fire."

"Which sounds like a very attractive notion to me," I answered. "What possible reason could this Mr. Harrington have had for insisting on such a late meeting?"

"Mr. Graff assured us that this was not so unusual. Possibly

Mr. Harrington is on the run from the law. The automaton may have been stolen from its rightful owner."

"Perhaps," said Bess, "but if *Le Fantôme* was stolen, Lieutenant Murray would have known of it."

"Not necessarily. It would almost certainly have come from a collection in Europe. That would surely fall outside of Lieutenant Murray's jurisdiction."

"At least Lieutenant Murray has a jurisdiction, Harry," I said. "We're just busy-bodies."

"No imagination, Dash. It is your greatest failing." He turned away and pulled on his trousers.

Moments later, the Brothers Houdini descended to street level. Resplendent in our rabbit-scented tailcoats and top hats, we headed toward the night club district on foot to conserve what little cash we had between us. As Harry had promised, an opportunity to get inside the Cairo presented itself almost immediately. We arrived just as two carriages drew up at the entrance, disgorging a large group of high-spirited young men. Seizing our chance, we darted between the two carriages and mixed in with the herd, so that we were swept along into the main parlor of the club without anyone taking note of our shabby clothes or empty wallets.

Inside, Harry and I took up a position beside an enormous potted palm. Before us stretched a vast billiards room with a row of four green baize gaming tables beyond. Young women circulated with trays of clear effervescent liquid which I knew to be champagne, although I had never seen this exotic wine before. The ladies who carried these trays, I could not help but notice, were dressed in an arresting form of dishabille. After a moment, one of these fascinating creatures made her way towards us.

"May I offer you gentlemen a beverage?" she asked.

"Thank you, no," said Harry, frantically averting his eyes. "Alcohol is detrimental to the careful balance of the bodily humors."

"He means he doesn't drink," I said, trying to be helpful.

"What about a cigar, then?" she asked.

"Tobacco is also forbidden if one wishes to preserve the vital forces," Harry told the potted palm.

"You?" she said to me. "Worried about your vital forces?"

I tugged at the lining of my pockets to signal that I had no money.

"Call me if you change your minds," she said, turning away.

"My God, Dash!" Harry cried. "These women are barely dressed!"

"I hadn't noticed," I said.

"What sort of place is this?" he asked, genuinely confused.

"It's the sort of place where men go when they desire the society of ladies. I tried to tell you this earlier."

"The society of ladies? Would it not be better to remain at home? When I desire the society of—oh." His mouth contracted into a tight, open circle as the realization hit. "Oh," he said again.

"Harry, take a breath. Your face is bright red."

"We should leave this place."

"Fine by me."

"After all, it is hardly the sort of place where one is likely to find an English lord!"

"He's right over there."

"What?"

I pointed to the nearest of the green baize gaming tables, where Lord Randall Wycliffe, seventh earl of Pently-on-Horlake, was enjoying a hand of cards. He had a cigar clipped between the fingers of his left hand, and a glass of whiskey within easy reach. He did not seem at all troubled by any absence of aristocratic decorum.

"His lordship is younger than I imagined," Harry said.

"I know what you mean," I agreed. "He should have white hair and mutton chop whiskers. Maybe a cavalry sword."

We edged closer. The game was poker—five-card Betty—and his lordship appeared to be winning, judging by the tall stacks of blue and red wooden chips in front of him. Two older players sat scowling across the table at him, and a large knot of onlookers had gathered to see the handsome young foreigner relieve them of their money.

Harry and I stood and watched for a time. I'm no stranger to the game of poker, and it was clear that all three men were experienced players. The older men played a solid but conservative game—nursing a pair or three-of-a-kind, drawing two or three cards and hoping for the best. Lord Wycliffe, who played a riskier and more aggressive game, appeared to be toying with them. At the finish of each hand, when the bets were made, he would gaze across the table and sigh heavily, as if filled with regret over the failings of two particularly dim-witted pupils. Then he would lay down his hand to show a straight or a full house. "One has to take chances in this game," he said more than once. "Wouldn't you agree?"

"Dash," Harry whispered, "he's cheating."

"You spotted that, did you?"

"Is it not obvious? Does no one else see what's going on?"

"Harry, nobody here knows what to look for."

"It seems perfectly obvious to me. I can hardly believe that anyone with a pair of eyes and a brain could allow himself to be taken by so craven a manipulation. One day I really must write up a book on this subject. Or a trifling monograph, at the very least."

"'How to Cheat at Cards'?"

"Something of that nature. If I may warn the unwary and deter the youth of this land from the fascinations of the green cloth, I shall feel that my efforts have not been in vain." He turned his attention back to Lord Wycliffe. "He's not even very good at it!" he said indignantly. "With a few simple lessons I could have improved his technique many times over."

"It seems good enough. He's making a pile."

"*The Right Way to Do Wrong.*"

"What?

"The title of my book. *The Right Way to Do Wrong*."

"Catchy."

We looked on as Lord Wycliffe won another hand and swept in his chips. A murmur of appreciation rose from the onlookers. A sallow blonde in a green satin concoction had now attached herself to his lordship, squeezing his arm and sending up a delighted laugh with each win.

"What shall we do?" Harry whispered. "We can't very well make an open accusation! He might take offense!"

"So?"

"Well, he might demand satisfaction!"

"A duel, you mean?" I turned and looked at the young Englishman, who was appraising the girl in green as though she might be a race horse. "He doesn't strike me as the type to go in for pistols at dawn. Harry, I have an idea."

"Yes?"

"You wanted to stay alert for whatever opportunity presented itself. We've been handed one on a platter. When I give you the signal, I want you to strip off your tailcoat and start doing those ridiculous 'muscular expansionism' exercises of yours. All right?"

"My exercises? But—"

"Just this once, Harry, follow my lead and do exactly as I say. When I give you the nod, go into the routine."

He continued to grumble through five more rounds of play, but I managed to ignore him. Lord Wycliffe, I noticed, was beginning to get cocky. Up to this point he had allowed himself to lose a hand occasionally, just to keep his marks hooked, but with his new blond friend at his side, he began to take every hand. At the finish of each game he would smirk and say, "Sorry, chaps," which was a phrase I had never before encountered outside of a penny dreadful.

After about half an hour, Lord Wycliffe's opponents threw down their cards and declared themselves finished for the evening. "Anyone else?" asked the young Englishman, glancing at the crowd of onlookers. "The evening is young yet, surely."

Seeing that there would be no takers, he stood up and began to gather his chips.

I seized the moment. Pushing forward as the rest of the crowd dispersed, I appeared suddenly at his elbow. "Well played, your lordship," I said, as though he and I had met before. "May we assist you in cashing in your winnings?"

"Kind of you," he said.

"Not at all." I swept the chips into my top hat. "If you'll just follow me?"

"You see, I'm rather busy just now," he said, slipping an arm around the waist of the girl in green. "May I collect them at a more convenient time?"

"I see no difficulty," I answered. "If you'll just step over to the cashier's window, I'll give you a receipt."

"But—"

"It won't take but a moment."

He whispered into the ear of his young companion and slipped something into her hand. "Very well," he said to me. "Let's be quick about it."

With Harry trailing behind, I led Lord Wycliffe out of the main parlor and through a smaller room where a team of bartenders was busily mixing cocktails. "Where are we going?" Lord Wycliffe asked. "I've never been back this way before."

Neither had I, but there was no reason for him to know this. "We'll need to open the safe," I said. "We don't ordinarily keep such large reserves of cash out on the main floor."

"But I told you I only wanted a receipt."

"I'll need to verify that we have the cash on hand. Bear with us, sir." I found a heavy Dutch door and pulled it open. Behind it lay a flight of bare wooden steps leading down into a cellar. "Follow me, sir," I said, heading down the stairs. Harry brought up the rear.

At the bottom of the stairs we found ourselves standing on the dirt floor of a large wine cellar. "This can't be right," Lord Wycliffe said. "What are we doing here?"

I nodded at Harry. He shrugged, peeled off his tailcoat, and laid it neatly across a wooden wine bin.

"Just a few questions, if you'd be so kind, your lordship. We must take precautions when a player enjoys such a remarkable run of luck."

"But what are we doing in the wine cellar?"

"A simple precaution. To avoid any possible embarrassment." Harry took two quick intakes of breath, rather in the manner of a snorting bull. Then he pressed his fists together at his chest and flexed his muscles, so that his arms and torso bulged alarmingly.

"I don't know just what you mean," said Lord Wycliffe, glancing anxiously at my brother's peculiar display. "Say, what's he on about?"

Harry gave two more bull-snorts and cocked his fists at shoulder level. His arm muscles pulsed and throbbed beneath the fabric of his shirt.

"We don't often see a player of your caliber here in New York," I said, ignoring my brother's posturing. "It's fortunate that you don't pass this way often."

"Yes, well." Lord Wycliffe's eyes shifted nervously from Harry to me. "I had a bit of luck, is all."

"Luck? You do yourself an injustice, sir."

"Look, I really don't know what you're suggesting. Are you going to give me a receipt, or—?"

"Hot down here, don't you think?"

"I'm sorry?"

"Hot. Stuffy. Unseasonable."

"Yes, but I'm not sure I—"

"Better take off your coat, sir."

His eyes locked on mine. Harry, meanwhile, had dropped into an awkward squat and had his arms flexed over his head. "I think perhaps I'd best get back upstairs," said his lordship.

"If we could just ask you to take off your coat, sir," I repeated.

"I don't—I don't—," he glanced at Harry, who had begun to

make a strange bovine sound, as if he might throw a calf. Lord Wycliffe looked back at me. "This is intolerable."

"The coat."

His shoulders sagged. "Oh, all right." He began to peel off his jacket. "I don't know how you spotted it."

The hold-out was a masterly construction of wood and leather webbing, with straps and buckles at the elbow and wrist. A flexible trident-style clip ran along the inner forearm and a circle of leather was cinched tightly around the chest. When the cards were held normally, with the elbow bent, the trident clip remained flush with the cuff of the jacket. Whenever the player gave a long deep breath—sighing over an opponent's misfortune, for instance—the clip extended six inches forward, delivering one or two fresh playing cards into the player's cupped palm. At the same time, any inconveniently low cards could be whisked away. A card worker like my brother, who could cause an entire pack to appear and disappear at his fingertips, could perform simple switches of that sort with his bare hands. For anyone who didn't happen to be a "King of Kards," however, a wooden hold-out was the next best thing.

"That's a beauty," I told Lord Wycliffe. "Who did it? Anderson's?"

"A firm in London," he answered, dejectedly.

"How much do you owe, your lordship?"

"You mean here? Or in toto?"

"Just here."

"Quite a lot. Upwards of three hundred dollars."

Harry's eyes widened, but he continued with his regimen, which had now broadened to include some very energetic leg-stretching.

"Your winnings tonight would have just about cancelled that out."

"Nearly. What will happen to me now?"

"That depends on you. The management doesn't have to know about this unfortunate development."

His eyes brightened. "You're not with the Cairo? But I thought—"

I shook my head.

"I—I can pay you," he said quickly. "Let me cash in the winnings and I'll do right by you. You have my word."

I shook my head again. "We're going to ask you some questions. You will answer them truthfully."

He drew back, and his eyes seemed to grow hooded. "Questions? What do you mean?"

"I understand that you are engaged to Miss Katherine Hendricks," I said.

"What's that to do with anything?" he snapped.

"Her father is very wealthy."

"I am aware of that," he said stiffly.

"How do you suppose he would react if he knew that his future son-in-law was gambling away Miss Hendricks's dowry in a flop house?"

"Are you threatening me? Is this to be blackmail?"

"We'll discuss that in a moment. As I said, we wish to ask you a few questions."

"And if I refuse?"

"We'll pay a call on Mr. Hendricks."

"Damn it!" he cried. "Damn it all to hell!"

"Your lordship," said Harry, without pausing in his exertions, "I will thank you to watch your language."

Lord Wycliffe's eyes moved from Harry to me and back again. "Common thugs, that's what you are," he said. "Look at you. With your hair tonic and your bad shoes. I don't know what sort of dodge you're trying to put over on me, but I'm putting a stop to it right now. Pay a call on Michael Hendricks? The pair of you? You'd never get past the door."

I stepped up close and held his gaze for a moment. "Mr. Hendricks was right," I said. "You *are* a pompous ass."

He backed up half a step. "You've never met Michael Hendricks in your life," he said.

"When was it that your name was raised?" I asked myself. "When he showed me his new locomotive, the Minotaur? Or was it when Becking appeared with the humidor? Funny, I really can't recall. Of course, we'd both had quite a bit of Walker's by that stage."

Lord Wycliffe pressed his lips together. "You're a detective of some sort, is that it? The old man hired you to check up on me."

I would have preferred to let the assertion go unanswered, but Harry couldn't help himself. "Yes, Lord Wycliffe," he said proudly. "We are amateur sleuths."

"Be that as it may," I said quickly, "would you be so good as to tell us when you last saw Branford Wintour?"

"Wintour! Is that what this is about?"

"When did you last see him?"

"Why, I've never met the man! Wintour was something of a hermit, I understand. Rarely came out of that whacking great pile of his."

"You're aware of the past relationship between Mr. Wintour and Miss Hendricks?"

His eyes flared for an instant. "Water over the dam," he said coldly.

"Has your fiancée had any contact with Mr. Wintour since their engagement was broken?"

"None whatever."

Harry opened his mouth to speak, but I held up a warning finger.

"Can you account for your whereabouts last night?" I continued.

"My whereabouts? See here, I'm not obliged to answer any more of these questions." He took out a heavy gold watch and made an elaborate show of consulting the time. "I have half a mind to—"

"Harry."

My brother straightened up and took a step towards his lordship. That was all it took. The young man skittered backward three steps and raised his arms as if fending off a blow. "All right!" he cried.

"Where were you last night?" I repeated.

He gave a resigned shrug. "I was here, actually. And I lost rather a lot, in case you might like to know."

"Can you produce witnesses to that effect?"

"I should prefer not to," he said. "I was—you see, I wasn't gambling the entire time, if you take my meaning."

"But I take it you weren't alone, either?"

"No."

"For the entire evening?"

"That is correct."

"And where were you before you arrived here?"

"I was having tea with Miss Hendricks and her mother."

"I see." I took a moment to study his face and found myself wanting to mash it like a turnip.

Lord Wycliffe brushed his lapels and tugged at his cuffs. "If there's nothing else, gentlemen?"

I decided to play my ace. "So tell me, Lord Wycliffe, however did you acquire *Le Fantôme*?"

I have to give the man credit. He barely flinched. He blinked twice, but that was about it. His upper lip remained as stiff as one could wish.

"I think perhaps we should repair to a quieter room," he said as a wine steward appeared on the wooden steps. "If you'll follow me?"

"Dash," Harry whispered, as we followed him up the steps. "How did you know? This is extraordinary!"

"His watch, Harry. It's from Blois."

"Robert-Houdin's home town. I see. But that did not necessarily mean that Lord Wycliffe was the owner of *Le Fantôme*."

"No, but I figured it was worth a shot."

"Is he the killer? Should we apprehend him?"

"His story seems pretty solid, Harry. But let's see what we can get out of him."

THE DIME MUSEUM MURDERS

"Extraordinary." Harry shook his head as we weaved through the crowded gaming parlor. "I saw, but I did not observe."

"What?"

"Nothing. It is nothing."

Lord Wycliffe led us up the main staircase to the second floor of the house. We passed down a central corridor and hooked left into a narrow sitting area. He seemed to know his way around, I noticed. He knocked on a closed door and, receiving no answer, turned the handle. "This way, gentlemen," he said. "We'll have a bit of privacy."

It was a small room, papered in wide stripes of a violet hue. A bed with a tall wooden headboard was the central feature of the room, with two chairs and a small dressing table arranged alongside. A beaded floor lamp provided the only illumination.

Harry and I each took a chair, leaving Lord Wycliffe to perch awkwardly on the edge of the bed. He folded his hands across one knee and spent a moment with his eyes closed, chin sunk onto his chest, before speaking again.

"I did not kill Branford Wintour," he said at last.

"And yet," I said, "you've been at great pains to conceal the fact that you are the man trying to sell *Le Fantôme*, the device that the police believe to be the murder weapon."

"The automaton didn't kill Wintour! The very idea is absurd!"

"Patently absurd!" Harry blurted out. "Why, the very notion is—"

"What we believe is not at issue," I said.

"I wasn't even there last night!" Lord Wycliffe insisted.

"No, but when you saw the newspapers this morning, you should have come forward."

His shoulders sagged. He pulled a gold case from his breast pocket and offered us a Turkish cigarette. They looked very inviting, but up to that point I had managed to conceal my smoking habits from my brother, so I waved them away.

"Can you blame me for keeping silent?" he asked, lighting a cigarette for himself. "I'm in an impossible situation. It was necessary to keep the transaction silent from the beginning. I couldn't let Michael Hendricks know about my—my financial difficulties. And I promised Katherine I wouldn't gamble anymore. I simply—well, I thought it best if I could just sell off a few trinkets, settle my debts, and start fresh. Now, with Wintour's death, I'm in a hell of a position. Before I was merely a scoundrel. Now I'm thrown into a murder. It's impossible." He gave a heavy sigh, sending a rich and inviting cloud of cigarette smoke in my direction.

"I'm afraid we don't understand your impossible situation," I said. "How did you come to be in possession of *Le Fantôme?*"

"My family, of course," he said airily. "You know the sort of thing. My mother was French, and we had a good deal in the way of French watches, mantel clocks—that sort of thing. Terribly good workmanship. I rather took it all for granted when I was growing up."

"All from Blois?"

"I think so, yes."

I could see Harry struggling to hide his excitement. "And automatons? Were there a great many automatons in the house when you were growing up?"

"One or two. Perhaps more. Terribly clever things. Father would sometimes wind them up and make them go for the guests. Marvelous things."

Harry's face fell. "Only one or two?"

"Perhaps a few more. A dozen or so? I never took much notice before."

"How many do you have with you in New York?" Harry asked.

"Just the one. I wanted to see what sort of price it would fetch before I had others sent over. The funny thing is, you see, that I never would have realized how valuable they were if not for Michael Hendricks. He has any number of the things scattered around that giant playroom of his, and I shudder to think what ridiculous prices he payed for them. But of course

I couldn't very well stroll in and say, 'Would you like to buy my automaton so I can clear my debts?' The whole thing had to be very hush-hush."

I looked on longingly as he lit another cigarette. "So you engaged Mr. Harrington as your intermediary?"

Lord Wycliffe's head snapped up in surprise. "How do you know about him?"

"Just tell us who he is and how you found him."

He shook his head slowly. "That's the queer thing about it. He found me. About three weeks ago, here at the club. I'd never seen him before or since. I'd been losing quite heavily that night, and we got to talking at the bar. He mentioned that every so often he was able to help a sportsman such as myself out of his difficulties."

"Sportsman?"

"That was his term. He was quite delicate about the enterprise. He asked me if I had any bothersome old family jewelry or antiques that I might like to convert into working capital. Again, that was exactly how he phrased it. So I had *Le Fantôme* crated up and shipped over, and he agreed to see what he could do about selling it off."

"Did he mention that he would attempt to sell it to Branford Wintour?"

Lord Wycliffe shook his head. "He only said that he would make the necessary arrangements."

"For a fee?"

"For a twenty-five per cent commission of the sale."

"Twenty-five? That seems rather steep."

"I thought so, too. But one pays a premium to ensure discretion."

"I suppose so. Where can we find Mr. Harrington?"

"But, Dash," Harry said, "we're going to see—" I shot a withering look in his direction.

Lord Wycliffe appeared not to notice. "You're not going to—you can't just—" He shifted awkwardly on the edge of the bed.

"I really would prefer to keep my name out of this matter."

"We have no interest in your private affairs. For the moment, we only want to speak with Mr. Harrington."

"You're not in the employ of Michael Hendricks?"

"No."

"Then what is your interest in this matter?"

Harry straightened up in his chair. "To see that justice is—"

"That'll do, Harry," I cut in. "Like yourself, Lord Wycliffe, we would prefer to keep our interests private. Now, if you'll tell us where we might find Mr. Harrington?"

He sighed heavily. "There's a saloon on Mott Street. Wilson's. He would send me a note and we'd meet there. That's all I can tell you."

"You're certain?"

"I only met the man three times. Once here at the Cairo, and twice at Wilson's."

"And what does he look like?"

Lord Wycliffe took a moment before responding. Then a wry smile spread across his features. "To tell you the truth," he said, jerking his thumb in Harry's direction, "he looks a bit like your friend there—nasty, brutish, and short."

"That man killed Branford Wintour," Harry said, as we hurried toward Delancy Street.

"How do you figure?" I asked.

"It's perfectly obvious. Lord Wycliffe was jealous of Miss Hendricks's continued association with Mr. Wintour. He saw the older man as an obstacle to his future happiness."

"I didn't get the impression that he was even aware of Miss Hendricks's continued association with Mr. Wintour."

"That was the impression he wanted to give, so that we wouldn't suspect him. He's a very clever man."

"He doesn't strike me as all that clever, Harry. Besides, I suspect that Branford Wintour would have been more useful to Lord Wycliffe alive than dead. He needed the money from the sale of *Le Fantôme*."

"Perhaps," Harry allowed, "but I'm going to keep my eye on him."

"Harry, how many times do I have to say it? After tonight, you and I are no longer in the detective business. We'll tell Lieutenant Murray what we learned and he can check Lord Wycliffe's story for himself."

"If that's how you feel, why were you so insistent on getting a description of Mr. Harrington? Why did you want to know how to contact him? After all, we have an appointment with him in twenty minutes at Mr. Graff's shop!"

"I know that, Harry, but I'm not banking on Mr. Harrington to keep the appointment. Lieutenant Murray may find the information helpful."

"Can you really wash your hands of this affair so easily?" Harry asked. "I saw you questioning Lord Wycliffe just now. I could hardly have done better myself. You were quite—"

"Imaginative?"

"I was going to say skillful. You played the scene quite brilliantly."

"That's just it, Harry. I wasn't playing a scene. This isn't some costume melodrama. It's all been just another performance for you, hasn't it? Another role for the Great Houdini."

"I'm not play acting," he said, as we rounded the corner onto Delancy Street. "Our friend is in prison. Or have you forgotten?"

"I could hardly forget, Harry. Not with all these helpful reminders you keep delivering every three minutes."

"You should need no reminding. Mr. Graff has been our friend and protector for many years."

"I know, Harry, but—"

"Like family. That's how he has treated us."

"I know, Harry, but—"

"You and I might still be washing dishes or cutting ties if not for Mr. Graff."

"I know, Harry, but—"

"Anyway, if I have been guilty of embracing my role as amateur sleuth a little too vigorously, at least we may be able to ring down the final curtain tonight. Let's see if Mr. Harrington appears."

The door to Mr. Graff's shop was locked and the windows were shuttered. Harry tugged on the door, then pressed his nose to the glass to peer into the darkened front room. "There's no one in there," he said. "I could pick the lock easily enough, but I don't want to alarm Mrs. Graff."

Harry pressed the bell and glanced up at the apartment above. "No answer," he said. "Perhaps she has gone to stay with her sister in Brooklyn. What time is it?"

I looked at my Elgin. "Harrington should be here in fifteen minutes, if he's coming."

"We may as well get out of the street, then." Harry flipped open a fat leather wallet and withdrew a sturdy two-pin curl-pick. I heard a sharp snick as the lock gave way. "I must speak to Mr. Graff about this. Bess could have picked this lock with her ivory comb." He pushed the door open.

It took a moment for our eyes to adjust to the gloom. We were accustomed to seeing Mr. Graff's shop filled with children. In the dark, it took on a strange and sinister aspect. Shadows played over the marionettes; tin soldiers and straw dolls appeared to be leering at us in the guttering light from the street. "I'll put on some lights," Harry said, feeling his way toward the back room. "Then I will tell you my plan."

"Your plan?"

"Yes. My plan to wring a confession from Mr. Harrington."

"Harry, whoever this Mr. Harrington is, we don't know that he killed Branford Wintour."

"He's in it up to his neck," Harry said. "All we have to do is—" He gave a strangled cry.

At first I thought he had been attacked by some unseen assailant in the back room. I ran forward and saw that it was something much worse. "My God, Dash! My God! Who—who would do such a thing?"

Frieda Graff lay on her back in a dark pool of blood. Her eyes were open and fixed on some distant point, and her arms were flung over her head as if to ward off a blow. An angry purple swelling covered the right side of her face, just below the jaw hinge. A bone-handled carving knife lay on the floor beside her.

I sprang forward, stamping my foot on the wooden floor to drive off a trio of rats. Kneeling beside her, I felt for signs of life.

"Dash, is she—?"

"Yes."

"God," he said softly. "God, no."

I reached up to close her eyes, as I had seen my father do.

"Dash, that word. American slang?"

I looked up and saw him pointing at the blank wall behind us. There was a word scrawled in blood. "Yes, Harry," I said. "American slang."

"What does it mean?"

"It refers to her religion, Harry."

I watched his face. His mouth tightened into a hard line and his cheeks darkened. Something clear and eager seemed to fade from his eyes and I never saw it again.

"The police," he said quietly. "Come, Dash, we must call the police. Perhaps they—" He stopped as if seized by the throat. "Dash! Hurry!" He grabbed my arm and literally hurled me toward the door.

"Harry—what—?"

"Run!" He was out the door before I could utter another syllable.

We were still in our evening clothes, and my opera shoes weren't exactly suited for high speed, but I managed to keep within a few paces of Harry as he sprinted across Lispenard Street, hooked left onto Broadway, and set off along Canal. By now my lungs were seared with pain, but I kept going. I'd figured out where we were headed.

Harry turned onto Mulberry Street and bounded up the steps to the precinct house. Sergeant O'Donnell looked up in surprise as Harry threw open the heavy doors.

"Mr. Houdini—?"

"The cellblock! Hurry!"

"But—!"

Harry charged past him and crashed through the doors to the stairwell. Gripping the bannister like a pommel horse, he vaulted over the railing and onto the lower stairs, covering the two flights in a single fluid motion.

"Houdini!" O'Donnell called from the top of the stairs. "You can't—!"

Lock-picks spilled from Harry's leather wallet as he scrabbled for the proper tool, all the while shouting Mr. Graff's name through the metal grille of the access door. He had the lock tripped by the time I reached him, and I helped to pull back the heavy door.

"Mr. Graff!" he shouted, pushing past me into the cellblock. "Mr. Graff! Are you—?" Then O'Donnell found the light.

The old man hung at the end of a leather belt at the center of his cell, swaying slightly, a piece of paper pinned to his chest. A stool lay on its side below him.

Harry dropped to his knees, his mouth working convulsively, though he made no sound. He pressed his fists to his temples as if to force the terrible scene from his mind. O'Donnell gripped the bars of the cell, his eyes moving from the dead man to my brother to the lock-picks scattered on the floor.

I fell back against a bare brick wall, unable to catch my breath. My head swirled with questions, but one thing had become perfectly clear.

My brother and I were no longer playing a game.

~~~ 7 ~~~

THE HUMAN TELESCOPE

"ALL RIGHT, HOUDINI," LIEUTENANT MURRAY SAID. "LET'S HAVE IT from the beginning."

Harry laced his fingers around the coffee cup he had been clutching for three hours. "I can add nothing to what I have already told you."

The lieutenant turned to me. "How about you, Hardeen? Anything to add?"

"I'm happy to go over the details again, if I can be helpful."

He looked at us both, his expression wavering between dark suspicion and genuine curiosity. We had been sitting at a table in the police interview room for the better part of the night, relating the events of the evening for perhaps seven different officials. The lieutenant had listened attentively to each reiteration, apparently uncertain as to our motives and trustworthiness. Two floors below us, a team of police investigators combed through the cell where Josef Graff had died.

"Tell me again how you knew that the old man was in danger," Murray said.

"It was obvious," Harry replied. "Mrs. Graff had been killed. Clearly the murderer felt it necessary to silence her. He would not kill the wife and leave the husband to talk."

The lieutenant nodded. "So you've said. But with respect, Houdini, Mrs. Graff's murder looks a whole hell of a lot like the work of a gang. Hit over the head, cut up the side. Gang boys. Irish. Italian. We see this sort of thing often enough, though it doesn't always make the papers. All those immigrant neighborhoods packed together. There's always a bad element, always young people looking to make trouble."

Harry stared listlessly at a map of the city pinned to the wall across from him.

"And Mr. Graff," Murray continued, "that looks to have been a suicide. There was even a note pinned to his chest. 'Forgive,' it said. It would have been natural enough for the old man to take his own life. He felt disgraced—you said it yourself, Houdini—and his wife's death would have pushed him over the edge. My superiors are tempted to close the book on the whole thing. Chalk up Graff's suicide as an admission of guilt in the Wintour killing."

"You don't believe that, Lieutenant," Harry said with quiet certainty.

The lieutenant let out a heavy sigh. "No, I don't." He stood up, linking his hands behind his back as he walked to a grimy window. "I might have believed it, if you two hadn't stirred up the waxworks. But now? The timing is wrong."

"Timing is very important in my business," Harry said.

"No one was due to check the cells until tomorrow morning. By then, there might have been time for Graff to have heard about his wife. Possibly. If her body had been discovered last night, one of his neighbors might have brought him word; shouted it up to him through the alley window. We would have had no way of knowing one way or the other. It probably would have been ruled a suicide."

"I'm not sure I see the problem," I said. "The killer must have been seen entering the building. Mr. Graff was dead when we got there, so he must have been killed sometime before midnight. The killer would have had to pass Sergeant O'Donnell in order to get down to the cells."

Lieutenant Murray laced his fingers behind his neck.

"You'd think so, wouldn't you?"

"What do you mean?"

"A few minutes before eleven, a pretty young girl comes running through the doors of the station house. She says her poor aged mother has turned her ankle just outside and please, Mr. Policeman, could you help us get home? Well, this young lady is such an attractive creature, and Sergeant O'Donnell is such a courtly gentleman, that he leaves his post and helps the girl with her elderly mother. Must have been gone for half an hour or so."

"Leaving the desk unattended," I said.

"Precisely."

"He never thought to check the cells when he returned?"

"I gather it's not the first time the sergeant has deserted his post. He had no reason to think anything was out of order."

"In theory, then, Mr. Graff wouldn't have been discovered for another six or seven hours." I tilted back in my chair. "We only found Mrs. Graff's body because we were supposed to be meeting this Harrington character. She might have been there for days before anyone found her."

"She'd have been found last night," Murray said. "We got a call, someone reporting a disturbance. The roundsman was on his way to have a look when he spotted the two of you tearing out the front door, looking guilty as hell." He turned away from the window. "If you hadn't run straight to a police station, I'd have you under lock and key for killing the old lady."

"Why that's the most—!"

"Harry, we were seen fleeing from the store. It would have been a natural conclusion."

Harry folded his arms and glowered.

I turned back to the lieutenant. "Is it possible that whoever killed Mrs. Graff was attempting to pin her murder on us?"

"Three bodies in two days," Murray said, ignoring my question. "All connected to this little toy."

"A very expensive toy," Harry said.

"Three people. A lot of killing over one little toy."

"As I have said," Harry continued, "it may be only one of—"

"I know, I know. A valuable cache of magical treasures. I still don't buy it. Whoever killed Wintour is covering his tracks. He didn't want the Graffs to be able to identify him. Still—" he leaned across the table, his palms flat on the scarred surface. "You're sure the wife never saw this guy?"

"Yes," said Harry. "She said he only came to the shop late at night. What else did she say? Oh, yes. She said that he was 'a queer bird.'"

Murray let out another sigh. "That's wonderful. I'll just comb the city until I find a queer bird." He jerked his head suddenly toward the door. "All right, gentlemen, I'm through with you for the night. Stay out of my way and don't bring me any more bodies."

Harry opened his mouth to reply but I grabbed him by the shoulder and pulled him out into the night.

We walked in silence to Mother's apartment building. When we got there, I could see the outline of Bess standing in the window, waiting for Harry. He glanced up at the window. "Tomorrow we begin again to look for Mr. Harrington," he said. "Call for me in the morning."

I nodded. "What about the dime museum?"

"I'll send a wire in the morning," he answered. "I have a new job now." He turned and walked into the building. I waited, looking up at the shadow in the window. After a moment, I saw Harry fold his arms around her. I turned and jammed my fists into my pockets, keeping my head down as I walked the six blocks to the boarding house.

The following morning at half past nine, Phillips the butler answered our knock at the door of the Wintour mansion. "Mrs. Wintour is expecting you," he told us, as if surprised by this information.

The butler conducted us through the vast entry hall and down a wide corridor lined with Impressionist paintings and

Chinese urns. There was also a suit of armor clutching a pikestaff, and one of those big glass domes with a stuffed pheasant in it. I half-expected to see the eyes in one of the paintings follow our progress down the hall.

At the far end of the corridor Phillips opened a set of double doors into the family greenhouse, a two-story glass cathedral filled to capacity with exotic plants and trees. Mrs. Wintour, wearing traditional black and a veil of thin netting, sat at a small glass table some twenty yards away. Dr. Blanton, looking somber in a gray frock-coat, hovered at her elbow.

The butler announced us and withdrew as Mrs. Wintour extended her hand in our direction. Harry crossed the distance to the table in a graceful sliding run and raised the hand to his lips, clicking his heels as he did so. I contented myself by removing my hat.

"It is kind of you to see us, Mrs. Wintour," said my brother. "I know how difficult it must be for you to receive callers at such a time."

"Indeed, Mr. Houdini. But your note was so kind, and the flowers were so lovely. If I can help in any way, I feel I must."

Biggs had been right about the abrasiveness of Mrs. Wintour's voice. A drowning cat would have been positively tuneful in comparison. Even Harry, with his face composed in a mask of sympathetic charm, could not entirely conceal a wince. "Your courage is an inspiration," he said. He held out a covered bowl he had been cradling beneath his arm. "My mother wished you to have this," he said.

Mrs. Wintour tugged at a corner of her veil. "What is it, may I ask?"

"Chicken soup."

The widow hesitated, apparently trying to decide whether to find the gesture charming or gauche. After a moment, a crooked smile broke across her features. "Please set it down here, Mr. Houdini," she said, gesturing at the glass table. "It is really too kind of your mother. You must tell her how exceedingly grateful I am."

Harry smiled and nodded.

"Forgive me," Mrs. Wintour continued, "I have been rude. May I introduce Dr. Blanton, my personal physician?" She indicated the grim figure at her side. "My nerves are in a bit of a state at the moment, and he has been seeing to them."

"Of course. We met Dr. Blanton the other night." Harry and I nodded at the doctor, who gave no more response than the suit of armor in the hall.

"May I offer you tea?" Mrs. Wintour asked. She had raised her veil and placed a lorgnette to her eyes, giving my brother a frank appraisal. She seemed to be warming to him by the moment.

"We will not impose on you any longer than necessary," Harry said. "We merely wished to gain your consent to examine your husband's study."

"Bran's study? Whatever for?"

"To uncover a means of slipping in and out without disturbing the locks."

"The locks? Percy?" She glanced uncertainly at Dr. Blanton.

The doctor cleared his throat. "It would appear these men wish to ascertain if anyone might have entered Branford's study and—I mean—on the night in question."

Mrs. Wintour turned to us. "The police have already been here this morning," she said. "The matter is entirely too distressing. I thought everything was settled. But now—but now—" Her voice was rising steadily to an even more challenging timbre.

"Mrs. Wintour," Harry said, "we have no wish to upset you further. We merely wish to examine the scene."

"I take it that the little shopkeeper was a friend of yours?"

"He was," Harry said.

"You have my sympathies. However, I really don't see why you should hope to learn anything by examining my husband's study. The police have been very thorough."

I broke in, sensing that Harry was about to share his views on the police investigation. "My brother is a professional escapologist," I ventured. "Problems of this sort fascinate him."

"A what?" The lorgnette returned to Mrs. Wintour's eyes.

"An escape artist. He makes his living by escaping from things—handcuffs, ropes, straitjackets, packing crates—"

"Does he, indeed?"

"Yes. He enjoyed a remarkable success on tour last season."

"I will soon be the eclipsing sensation of America," Harry averred. "Nothing on earth can hold Houdini a prisoner. I—"

"So naturally," I interrupted, "in his distress over the tragic circumstances of your husband's demise, it occurred to Harry that he may be able to shed some light on how an unwanted visitor might have gained admittance."

Mrs. Wintour wrapped a brocade shawl around her shoulders and spent several moments studying the young man who liked to be tied up. Then, languidly waving the lorgnette at Dr. Blanton, she said, "Percy, show them to the study." The doctor began to frame a protest, but Mrs. Wintour held up her hand. "I see no harm," she said, curtly.

With a shrug, the doctor motioned for us to follow him.

"And Mr. Houdini—!" the widow called after us.

"Yes?"

"Do remember to thank your mother for the soup!"

Dr. Blanton conducted us back down the corridor in the manner of a man putting the cat out.

"Doctor?" Harry called after him. "I wonder if you know our brother? Dr. Leopold Weiss?"

"I think not," he said, without turning.

"He is a doctor like yourself."

"Is he. How interesting."

"Another question, if I may?"

Dr. Blanton pulled up and glanced at his watch with showy impatience.

"I did not like to say in front of the lady," Harry said, "but I am convinced that Josef Graff had nothing to do with the murder of Mr. Wintour."

"So I gathered, Mr. Houdini. But I am afraid I do not share this view."

"As you like. I wondered, though, if you might supply a list of the names of anyone who might wish to see harm come to Mr. Wintour?"

Something on the order of a smile crossed the doctor's face—possibly for the first time since the Jackson administration. "A list of Bran's enemies, you mean? You want me to draw up a list of Branford Wintour's enemies?"

"If it would not be too much trouble."

The doctor steepled his fingers. "Mr. Houdini, you could knock down every white pine from here to California and you still couldn't mill enough paper to draw up such a list. Branford Wintour used to boast that he made a business enemy along with every dollar he earned."

"But surely not all of them would have wished to see him dead?"

"Not a businessman, are you, Mr. Houdini?" The doctor turned and continued down the hall. "I will tell you this, though. Bran was working on something unusual these past few months. Something of enormous importance. Wouldn't tell me a thing about it. 'Going to write my name in the history books,' he said. Very mysterious. No doubt he was stepping on some toes with that one."

We reached the entrance to the study. Dr. Blanton pulled out a ring of keys and unlocked the doors.

"You have your own key?" Harry asked.

The doctor paused, holding the key in the lock. "These are Bran's keys. I'm seeing to a few of his affairs until the estate is settled." He passed over the heavy ring. "Leave them with Phillips on your way out. Good day to you, gentlemen." He turned and made his way back down the corridor.

Harry pulled me inside the study and locked the door behind us. Putting a finger to his lips, he pulled me to the center of the room. "That man," he said in a low voice, "is the murderer. He killed Branford Wintour and the Graffs besides. I have him now!"

"Got any proof, Harry?"

"Is it not obvious?" he asked in a hushed, but urgent tone of voice. "As a doctor he could easily have obtained the poison used to kill Mr. Wintour! He had the motive and the opportunity!"

"Motive?"

"Did you see him leering at Mrs. Wintour? A vulture, that's what he is. Can't wait to move in and claim the dead man's territory. Strutting around with Mr. Wintour's keys in his pocket. He's a wrong one, I tell you."

"Harry, if you go to Lieutenant Murray with this ridiculous blather he'll have your head stuffed and mounted like that moose over there."

"I'll get proof. Don't worry about that. Now—" he resumed at normal volume, "—let us see what we can discover about this lock." He walked back to the door and crouched to examine the lockplate. "Dash," he said, pulling a high-powered magnifying lens from his pocket. "Bring me a taper from the fireplace, will you?"

"Can I also get you a deerstalker hat and some shag tobacco?"

"I have a good reason for employing the magnifying glass, Dash. I'm checking for scratches on the bolt mechanism."

I lit a wax taper at the fireplace and carried it over to the door. Harry held it close to the lockplate and peered into the internal mechanism of the keyhole. "Difficult to see anything," he said. He pulled out his lock-pick wallet and selected a tool that did double duty as a screwdriver. With practiced ease he loosened the four corner screws on the brass covering plate and lifted it off, exposing the inner workings of the lock. I peered over his shoulder. It was a heavy gunmetal lever-tumbler lock. Harry fished out the key ring that Dr. Blanton had given us and fitted the heavy bow key over the cam. The twelve-tooth bit on the end of the key fitted smoothly against the tumblers. Harry cranked the key three times. The bolt moved smoothly back and forth each time.

"This is most interesting," he said.

"I don't see anything unusual."

"Exactly. The lock is in perfect working order. No wear or scratches outside of normal key operation. If this lock had been picked, we would see scratches in the soft brass here on the fittings and lockplates. They are perfectly clean."

"Meaning it hasn't been picked."

"It has not."

"What about that locksmith, Mr. Featherstone? He must have picked the lock the other night."

"No, Mr. Featherstone used his master skeleton. He's the one who installed the lock in the first place." He refastened the lockplate.

"Where does that leave us?"

"It means we are looking for some other means of entering the room." He walked to the fireplace and stuck his head up the massive chimney. "Too narrow," he said. He walked to the edge of the elaborate Oriental rug and dropped to his knees. "Help me with this, will you?"

"Praying for inspiration?"

"I want to roll this carpet back and see if there's a trap door beneath."

I joined him on the floor and we took up some twelve feet of rug. "Just as a point of interest, Harry," I said, waving away a cloud of dust, "why would anyone have a trap door in his study, apart from making life easier for a potential murderer?"

"Mr. Wintour had this house built himself," Harry said, "to his own specifications. He strikes me as a man who might have wished to slip out of the house occasionally, without his wife's knowledge."

I had to agree that this was not entirely out of the question. Harry and I crawled over the oak flooring on our hands and knees, pulling and prying wherever there seemed to be a loose joint or an ill-fitting board. When this yielded no results, we began moving pieces of furniture and some of the statuary for spots we had missed. Harry crawled beneath the oblong platform that held the model train set, while I wriggled under the marble-inlay desk where Wintour had died. We finished by tapping at the marble tiles surrounding the fireplace.

"No trap door," I said at length.

"It would seem not."

"What's next?"

"The walls, of course. If there's no trap door, surely there must be a sliding panel!" He began rapping at the back of the fireplace. "Check behind the tapestry," he called over his shoulder. "There has to be a reason why that entire wall is covered."

I walked to the corner of the room and carefully burrowed behind the hanging tapestry. It felt heavy and stifling, and I moved carefully for fear of pulling the entire thing down on top of me. I spent perhaps fifteen minutes making a slow progress from one end to the other, checking the bare wall for any suspicious-looking cracks or seams. It appeared to be entirely solid.

When I finally emerged, I found Harry sprawled on one of the arm chairs. "Give up?" I asked.

He was staring at the tall bookshelves which I had so admired on our first visit to the Wintour mansion. They gave the dead man's study a leathery opulence that I associated with the ruling families of Europe. Every time I looked at them, I imagined myself reclining in one of the stuffed chairs in my dressing gown, a snifter of fine cognac in one hand, perusing one of my custom-bound first editions.

"Dash? Are you paying attention?"

I looked away from the books. "Sure."

"You notice the doors on the bookcases?"

"Of course." Each case was fitted with a latch-frame door. Instead of glass panels in the frames, there was an open lattice-work of hammered brass.

"It strikes me that the doors may have been designed to conceal an entryway of some sort," Harry explained, "but I have examined each one and can find nothing. The cases themselves are firmly anchored to the floor and ceiling, and there is no sign of a sliding mechanism of any description." He looked over at me. "Dash? You seem most distracted."

"I'm just admiring the books, Harry. I suppose I'm wondering how long it would take to read them all."

Harry lifted his head, as if seeing the books for the first time, rather than the shelves. "I have read some of them," he said, gesturing at one of the cases. "*Treasure Island*, by Robert Louis Stevenson. A fine book." He peered intently. "*The Master of Ballantrae*, also by Mr. Stevenson. I have not read that one. Perhaps I shall."

I squinted at the shelves. "Can you really read those titles from here?"

"Of course! Can't you? Our friend at the ten-in-one is not the only one with telescope eyes." He pointed to a row of books near the ceiling. "There is a complete set of Shakespeare. The green volume on the shelf below is Thackeray's *Henry Esmond*. Next to it is *Ivanhoe*, by Sir Walter Scott."

"Hold it," I said. "Harry, I know perfectly well how the 'human telescope' act is done. You memorized those titles while I was flailing away under the wall hanging. Now you're trying to impress me by calling them off as if you're reading them with your telescope eyes. I'm not some boardwalk mark, Harry."

He folded his arms, grinning widely. "You do not believe me?"

"No, Harry. No one has eyes that sharp. Not even you."

"Try me."

I walked to the case and pointed to a leather spine. "What's this?"

"*Tristram Shandy*," he answered.

"Lucky guess. This?"

"*The Vicar of Wakefield*."

"This one?"

"*The Peregrine Pickle*. Perhaps you need spectacles. Dash, you really should be—all right. That one is *Clarissa Harlowe*, by

Samuel Richardson. There is *Martin Chuzzlewit*. That one is *Guy Mannering*. That one is…" His voice trailed off. "Extraordinary," he said.

"I should say so. You have the eyes of a hawk."

"No, not that." He stood up and joined me at the center bookshelf. "*Guy Mannering*," he said, pulling the volume off the shelf. "By Sir Walter Scott."

"Yes, looks as if there's a complete set of Scott here."

"But that belongs over here." He walked to a row of shelves at the other side of the case and threw open the latticework doors. "I saw a copy of *Ivanhoe* on this shelf. I wonder if—yes! Two sets of Scott! Two copies of *Ivanhoe*! Two copies of *Guy Mannering*!"

"Harry, books are just another form of property to a man like Wintour. He probably bought the second set as an investment. Or as part of a collection. How many copies of *Discoverie of Witchcraft* do you have?"

"No, Dash. Look—this second set is very high off the ground, so as to discourage the casual browser. Only Houdini, with his sharp eyes and uncanny powers of observation, would even have noticed it." He darted to the corner of the room and seized a rolling library ladder. "Do you not see, Dash? This second set of Scott novels is a mere facade. We are certain to discover that the spine of each volume has been sliced from its binding and fastened together to form a false layer. We often see illusions of this sort in our profession. It appears to be a row of books, but in reality it is a hiding place!"

Harry climbed to the top of the ladder and reached for the suspect volumes. "Behold! Now we shall see what is hidden behind these shelves!"

Harry gave a sharp tug, expecting to uncover a spring-panel, trip-switch, or some other means of concealment. Instead, an entire set of the collected works of Sir Walter Scott cascaded onto the floor. I believe *The Bride of Lammermoor* hit him on the head. At the top of the ladder, Harry stared at the now-empty shelf in disbelief. "Is it possible?" he asked. "Can it really be perfectly innocent? I simply cannot credit it. Why should the man have two sets of Scott if one of them is not concealing a passageway or a secret compartment?"

"I don't know, Harry," I said. "Perhaps he was uncommonly fond of historical romances."

Harry sat down on the top step of the ladder. "Dash," he said, "there is no secret panel, trap door, or hidden entrance of any kind in this room."

"I was beginning to form that impression."

"Then how did the murderer get in and out?"

"I think we can assume that Wintour knew his killer, and that he opened the door willingly."

"I'll grant you that," Harry said, "though it seems odd that no one else in the household was aware of any visitors. But how did the killer leave the door locked behind him? Someone bolted that door from the inside, and it certainly wasn't Mr. Wintour."

"No," I agreed. "Nor does it seem likely that someone could have arranged a secret meeting with him and then slipped away unnoticed."

"Unless Mr. Wintour himself desired to keep the meeting a secret," said Harry, "which brings us back to the fair Miss Hendricks."

"Yes," I said. "It does, doesn't it?" I walked to the fireplace and scanned the books on the lower shelves. "Let's see... Byron... Wordsworth... Shelley... here we go! Elizabeth Barrett Browning." I pulled a small volume from the shelf.

"Anything there?" asked Harry, climbing down from the ladder.

I flipped opened the front cover to see that the pages had been hollowed out to form a place of concealment. "I guess Mr. Wintour wasn't much of a poetry fan," I said.

"Are those the letters?" asked Harry, peering over my shoulder.

I lifted out a packet of some twenty or thirty envelopes tied with a silk ribbon. The paper was a pale violet hue and heavily scented with perfume. I untied the ribbon and scanned the envelopes. None of them was marked in any fashion. "They must have been delivered by hand," I said, "which means that some third person was privy to their correspondence."

Harry stroked his chin. "Couldn't one of the servants have been running the letters back and forth?"

"Wintour and Hendricks were supposed to be feuding, remember? It would have attracted too much attention if there had been a butler or chambermaid scurrying back and forth. It was probably some mutual acquaintance."

"Hmm. A mutual acquaintance who knew of Mr. Wintour's continued interest in Miss Hendricks. This person could have used this information to arrange a clandestine meeting here in the study."

"My thought exactly."

"Dash, we should read those letters."

"Read them? That's not exactly gentlemanly of you, Harry."

"They may well name the person who acted as courier. It could be a vital clue."

"I admit that, but I don't feel right—"

There was an urgent knock at the doors of the study. "Gentlemen?" called a voice from outside the room. "Are you still in there?"

I shoved the letters in my pocket and slipped the hollow book back onto the shelf. Harry crossed to the doors and unlocked them.

A stocky young man in a checked walking suit stood outside. I recognized him as Henry Crain, the dead man's brother-in-law, whom I had seen at the funeral the day before. He looked to be a year or two short of his thirtieth year—not that much older than Harry and myself—but he carried himself with a certain pompous self-regard that made him seem a great deal older.

"Gentlemen," he said, sweeping into the room, "may I ask why I was not consulted before you made yourself free with my late brother-in-law's rooms?"

"I beg your pardon," said Harry. "We gained permission from Mrs. Wintour. We would not have dreamed of intruding otherwise. I am Harry Houdini and this is my brother Dash Hardeen."

"I'm Henry Crain," he said curtly, ignoring Harry's out-stretched hand. "My sister is in no condition to receive callers. Your presence here is an unwelcome intrusion, and I'm afraid I must ask you to leave immediately." The butler appeared in the doorway with our hats and coats. Harry's face began to turn an angry red.

"I regret any distress we've caused," I said, steering Harry toward the door. "Please accept our apologies, along with our condolences."

"But—" said my brother. "We haven't—"

"Come along, Harry. I'm sure Mr. Crain is a very busy man."

"One moment," the young man called after us. Harry and I paused in the doorway. "What were you hoping to find in there?"

"Your sister didn't tell you?" Harry asked.

"She mentioned some absurd notion involving a secret corridor," Crain said scornfully. "You can't expect me to believe that was your real purpose in coming here?"

Harry opened his mouth to object and I gave him a sharp poke in the ribs with my index finger. "You're quite right," I said, lowering my voice to a confidential whisper. "We're here on behalf of Mr. Harrington."

Harry's eyes widened with alarm. I gave him another poke in the ribs.

"Harrington?" said Crain. "The name means nothing to me."

"May I speak in confidence?" I asked.

Crain narrowed his eyes for a moment. "Would you give us a moment, Phillips?" The butler nodded and withdrew. "I'm a busy man, Mr.—what was it?"

"Hardeen."

"Yes. I'm a busy man, so I think you'd best come to the point."

"Your late brother-in-law had a fine collection of mechanical toys and automatons," I said.

"I'm aware of that, sir. One of the damned things killed him."

"Mr. Harrington takes a very keen interest in automatons," I said. "A very keen interest."

"Go on."

"Perhaps Mr. Wintour's collection has a sentimental value for you and your sister. If so, we won't impose ourselves upon you any longer. If not...?"

I let the half-formed question hang in the air. Crain hesitated for a moment, then motioned us back into the study and closed the door behind us. "See here," he said, "are you saying that this Mr. Harrington will pay good money for these trinkets?"

"It's his business."

He glanced over at the array of wind-up figures on the library table. "You have some cheek, sir. You came in here with a cock-and-bull story about examining the study, but really you just wanted to size up my brother-in-law's valuables."

I turned to make for the door. "I can see that you won't be interested in dealing with Mr. Harrington," I said. "I apologize again if we've given offense. Come along, Harry."

"Wait!" the young man cried. "Wait just a moment." He looked around as though there might be someone else in the room. "I won't entirely rule out the possibility of a transaction," he said in a lowered tone, "but it would have to be done in strictest confidence."

"Of course," I said.

"How do I contact this Mr. Harrington?"

Harry bit his lip nervously.

"Well," I said, "Mr. Harrington is an extremely private person, like yourself. He prefers to work through intermediaries. May we tell him that you would be willing to entertain an offer?"

Crain considered for a moment. "All right," he said, "but you'll have to be discreet. Do you understand?"

"I believe so, sir," I said. "You'll be hearing from us shortly."

"Very well." He led us out of the study and showed us to the front door. "And one last thing, gentlemen."

"Yes?"

"There's no need to mention any of this to Mrs. Wintour. Good day, gentlemen." With that, he closed the door behind us.

Harry waited until we had rounded a corner before speaking. "That man—" he began.

"I know, Harry, I know. You think that Henry Crain killed Branford Wintour."

"Well, don't you?"

"If so, then he did it without any assistance from our friend Harrington. How do you explain that? Are you going to tell me that the entire business of Mr. Graff and the automaton was just a coincidence?"

"Of course not! He's bluffing! He knows perfectly well who Mr. Harrington is, for the simple reason that he himself is Mr. Harrington! He arranged the sale of *Le Fantôme* as a clever pretext in order to—"

"Harry, the only thing we know about Mr. Harrington is that he looks something like you. Henry Crain does not look like you. Benny the Human Skye Terrier looks more like you than he does."

Harry frowned. "It was dark when Mr. Graff met with Harrington," he said.

"Harry."

"All right. But he could easily have hired this Mr. Harrington to do his dirty work for him. You have to admit that he has a powerful motive. He seems to be making himself very free with the dead man's treasures."

"I'll grant you that," I said.

"Seems to me there's only one way to be certain," Harry continued.

"How's that?"

"It should be obvious, Dash," Harry said. "We'll have to find Mr. Harrington and ask him for ourselves."

8

THE LIVING SPONGE

"YOU'LL DO NO SUCH THING," SAID BESS, TUGGING AT THE COLLAR of her cloth winter coat. "Have you forgotten that this Mr. Harrington may well have killed Mr. and Mrs. Graff? You can't just go chasing after him like some sort of cowboy! Leave Mr. Harrington to the police!"

"I'm not afraid of Harrington, Bess," Harry said in a level tone. "I'm not afraid of anything."

"I know that, Harry," Bess answered. "I'm afraid for both of us."

We had just been to see the rabbi about funeral arrangements for the Graffs, which had left Harry in a despondent humor. "Don't you see, Bess? It's my fault that the Graffs are dead. I should have saved them."

"Saved them?" I asked, settling my trilby on my head. "I think you're being a little hard on yourself, Harry."

"Am I? Exactly what have I accomplished in these past few days? I failed to foresee the danger to Mr. and Mrs. Graff; I failed to arrive at any solution to the puzzle of Mr. Wintour's study; I failed to escape from the holding cell at police headquarters. Nothing but failure! I was a fool to walk away from Huber's Museum. Even that modest rung of show business may yet prove too great for my talents. Dime Museum Harry. Perhaps that's all I'll ever be."

"Harry, you're just—"

"I believe I shall return to the tie-cutting factory on Broadway, if they will have me. Perhaps there is a position that would not tax the skills of the Great Houdini." He thrust his hands out and made a clipping motion, as if working a pair of shears. "Snip, snip," he said. "In the future I might do better to rely on my hands, rather than my brain."

Bess clutched his arm and laced her fingers through his. "Harry, you are behaving like a little boy. This must stop." My brother looked wounded at this, but said nothing. I fell in step behind them, marveling once again over my sister-in-law's ability to quiet Harry's tempers. Up to this stage of his life, my brother had done very well behaving like a little boy, with Mama there to stroke his brow and make his cares disappear. Bess, whose fire and spirit had so attracted him during their courtship, would not stand for childishness. "I am not your mother," I often heard her say, "I am your wife."

We walked on for a time in silence, with Bess pausing every so often to look in a shop window.

"Harrington is the key," Harry said, as we climbed aboard a horse-drawn omnibus. "Once he learned that Lord Wycliffe possessed a valuable automaton, he used Mr. Graff to establish its authenticity. Through Mr. Graff, Harrington gained an entree into the reclusive Mr. Wintour's private study—which, I must assume, had been his object from the beginning."

"It's not a bad theory," I said, struggling to keep my footing as the omnibus lurched forward. "But where's the motive? Why should Harrington kill Wintour?"

"There are endless possibilities," Harry sighed. "Money. Revenge. A woman. When we find Harrington we will have our answer."

"Lieutenant Murray will find him soon enough," I said, as we found seats at the back. "He'll act on the information we got from Lord Wycliffe."

"You give him too much credit," Harry said. "That man is a *shmendrick*."

"A what?" Bess asked.

"A good-for-nothing," I explained. My brother tended to fall back on Yiddish whenever he felt especially frustrated.

"Lieutenant Murray will never solve this case," Harry declared. "Not because he isn't clever enough, he simply doesn't care enough. Soon enough he'll have to turn his attention to all the other crimes and killings and thefts that plague this city."

"Branford Wintour's murder won't be forgotten. His money will see to that. His wealthy friends won't let the police rest until they close the case."

"His wealthy friends will prefer a verdict of death by misadventure to an unsolved murder. There will be meetings behind closed doors and the entire matter will be swept under the carpet. You wait and see. As for the Graffs, they'll be forgotten soon enough—especially now that the Toy Emporium is to be sold."

"Sold?" I asked.

"That's why the rabbi took me aside as we were leaving. Apparently there has been an offer to buy the building, and the rabbi hoped I might help to clear out the shop, so that the stock can be sold to benefit the congregation."

"Father's old congregation," I said.

"Yes," Harry said. "That's why the rabbi asked."

"How sad," said Bess. "Of course you'll help."

"Later," Harry said. "It will have to wait until after we've found Harrington."

"The shop is being sold?" I asked again.

"Yes, Dash," Harry said. "Why does that surprise you so?"

I clawed at my jacket pocket for my note pad. A memory was struggling to emerge from the depths of my mind, but—like Harry battling his way out of a strait-jacket—it seemed to be having a hard time of it. "Who's buying the place?" I asked.

Harry shrugged. "A downtown firm. It seems they plan to tear down the building to make room for something new.

There's been a great deal of building going on in the old neighborhood lately."

"Do you recall the name of the firm?"

"Dash, you're looking very strange all of a sudden. Of course I remember the name. Daedalus Incorporated. One could hardly forget such a name."

"Daedalus," I said, flipping through several pages of notes. "I wonder if—ah ha! How very odd!"

"What is it, Dash?" Bess asked.

"You'll never guess who just bought the Toy Emporium."

"I told you. Daedalus Incorporated."

"And do you know who owns Daedalus Incorporated?"

"Who?"

I snapped my notebook shut. "Branford Wintour," I said.

Lieutenant Murray was not on the premises when Harry and I arrived at Mulberry Street to share this fresh revelation with him. We were advised that his shift would end within the hour, and that there was some slight possibility of finding him in Donnegan's Tavern, around the corner on Bayard.

Donnegan's proved to be a dark and fragrant establishment, with sawdust on the floor and paintings from County on the walls. We took a booth near the door, and sat watching an energetic pair of arm wrestlers at the bar. Soon enough Lieutenant Murray appeared, looking even more rumpled than he had that morning, if possible.

To my surprise, he greeted us quite cordially. "Mr. Houdini!" he cried. "Mr. Hardeen! A pleasure to see you again! Come to set the department to rights? Got some fresh information on the Lincoln assassination, have you?"

To his credit, Harry took this in good part. "I have already apologized for my—my exuberance the other evening," he said. "I did not mean to suggest that your investigation had not been thorough. As a further expression of my remorse, we should like to buy you a drink."

"Would you now? That's very grand of you, Mr. Houdini. Mine's a Jameson's and water."

I went to the bar and ordered whiskies for the Lieutenant and myself, and a glass of minerals for Harry.

"Your health, gentlemen," said the lieutenant, when I had carried the drinks back to the table. "I'm pleased to see you. Saves me the trouble of bringing you down to headquarters. I had a few more questions about—"

"That can wait," Harry said. "Did you know that Mr. Graff's shop has just been purchased by Branford Wintour?"

Murray cocked his eyebrows at me, amused. "I had heard something of the sort, Mr. Houdini," he said drily.

"You don't find it at all curious that a dead man should be acquiring business property?"

The lieutenant took a quaff of his whiskey. "Not especially," he said. "Branford Wintour had dealings all over the city. Toys— pardon me, juvenile goods—were just a small part of his trade. I happen to know he had money in several department stores, a baking concern and at least three clothing manufacturers. An empire like that doesn't just shut down over night. Wintour's businesses will keep going for years, even if he isn't around to pull the strings."

"But the Toy Emporium! It's too much of a coincidence!"

"Is it? I've been checking around. Branford Wintour had a finger in nearly every property deal south of Canal Street for the past three years. Apparently he was fond of the neighborhood."

Harry folded his arms. "But who authorized the purchase?"

"The directors of Daedalus Incorporated."

"Do we have their names?" I asked.

The lieutenant shook his head. "I'm working on it, though. I don't like coincidences any more than you do. But you're not going to find any sinister conspiracy here, gentlemen. In all likelihood, the members of the board were simply adhering to a policy established by Wintour before his death." He knocked back the rest of his whiskey. "Of course, there is another possibility."

"What's that?" Harry asked.

"That Branford Wintour has returned from the dead in order to gain control of every toy shop in the city. For all we know, Wintour's tortured spirit is doing a brisk business in cloth bears even as we speak."

Harry lowered his chin, offended by the lieutenant's flippant tone. "I suppose you're prepared to disregard our information about Mr. Harrington just as readily?"

"Ah. That's what I wanted to speak with you gentlemen about. I had an interesting conversation with Lord Randall Wycliffe this morning."

"And?"

"I'm afraid he's denying all knowledge of any Mr. Harrington."

"What!" Harry leapt from his seat. "The man is a bald-faced liar!"

"He's a bald-faced liar who's taking advice from his attorneys," Lieutenant Murray answered. "Sit down, Houdini. I know you're telling the truth. I'm only saying that we're not going to be getting much cooperation from his lordship. It's clear he doesn't want to be involved, and he's willing to stake his word against yours to stay clear of the thing."

"I've never told a falsehood in my life!" Harry insisted. "The very idea is insulting!"

"Is it?" Lieutenant Murray asked. "Were the two of you being strictly candid when you represented yourselves as employees of the Cairo Club last night?"

"We never actually *said* that we—"

"Be that as it may, Lord Wycliffe won't be volunteering any more information, and there's very little I can do about it."

"Where does that leave us, Lieutenant?" I asked.

"Same place we were last night. Three bodies. No way of knowing if their deaths are even connected to one another."

"Harrington," Harry said grimly. "He killed them all."

"So you say, Mr. Houdini, but we have precious little evidence of that. All we know is that he approached Lord Wycliffe about brokering a deal for *Le Fantôme*. That's not a crime, so far as we know. I'm telling you, boys, my superiors would be very happy to see this problem vanish." He fingered his empty glass. I stood up and went to the bar for another round.

"Lord Wycliffe mentioned Wilson's saloon on Mott Street," I said when I returned. "He told us that he met Harrington there."

"So you said this morning. I'm afraid Wilson's isn't the type of establishment where they put out the red carpet for the police."

"How do you mean?" Harry asked.

"You've heard of Jake Stein?"

"The notorious criminal?" Harry's eyes brightened. "The nefarious gangland chieftain?"

"Yes, Houdini," said the lieutenant, rolling his eyes slightly. "That's the one."

"Jake Stein is a habitue of Wilson's saloon?"

"Hardly. No one's seen Jake Stein in years. But he runs every bar and disorderly house down there. A clean officer can't get anything out of those people, and the dirty ones aren't about to bite the hand that feeds them."

"How intriguing," said Harry. "A genuine den of iniquity. Tell me, Lieutenant, if I wanted to have someone killed, is Wilson's saloon the sort of place I might turn?"

"Pardon me?" The lieutenant's mouth twitched with amusement. "You and the wife not getting along, Houdini?"

"My wife is the very center of my existence, sir. Let's say I wished to remove a troublesome business rival. My brother, for instance."

"I don't think you want to have me killed, Harry," I said. "Mother would be very cross."

"I mean a truly first-rate job," Harry continued, ignoring me. "Something that might confuse the police and obscure the motive."

"You're talking about the Graffs," said Lieutenant Murray flatly.

"I am."

He sighed heavily. "You think the Graffs were killed by a hired gun?"

"It seems apparent to me that they were."

"I'm sorry, Houdini, I know these people were important to you, but in all candor—"

"Oh, I don't argue that it was artfully done," my brother said. "That was the reason for my question. Where would I go if I wanted to find someone who could perform such a task?"

"Someone who could kill both of them and make it look like a gang killing and a suicide?"

"Exactly."

"Why, that would take a real magician, wouldn't it, Houdini?"

My brother considered for a moment. "Yes," he said, "I suppose it would."

The two of them debated the matter for some time, with Lieutenant Murray probing us rather more skillfully than we questioned him. I jotted down a good many notes over the course of the discussion, but I noticed that the lieutenant filled many more pages of his pad than I did. He also managed to put away an uncommon amount of whiskey at my expense.

After an hour or so, Lieutenant Murray closed his notebook and rose to take his leave.

"One last thing," Harry said. "If my brother and I should happen across Mr. Harrington, would you be interested in speaking with him?"

The lieutenant's face turned hard. "Don't be a jackass, Houdini. Stay out of my road."

"We meet a good many people in our travels. It's not impossible that we should make his acquaintance."

Lieutenant Murray leaned across the table and thrust his index finger under Harry's nose. "Houdini," he said, "you are quite possibly the biggest son of a bitch I've ever—"

"Lieutenant," said Harry primly, "I will thank you to leave my sainted mother out of this."

The anger drained from the lieutenant's face. "All right," he said with his short, barking laugh, "but you are the most pig-headed, irritating bas—er—individual I've ever come across."

"You are welcome to your opinion," Harry said.

"I'm grateful for that, Mr. Houdini." The lieutenant settled his hat on his head. "Thanks for the drinks, gentlemen. Now go back to pulling bunnies from top hats. Leave the police work to me." He turned and headed for the door.

Harry watched him go, rolling a coin across his knuckles. "What a most unreasonably stubborn man," he said. "One must be more open to opposing views in this world."

"You don't say."

"Oh, indeed! As our late father often said, 'Toleration is good for all or it is good for none.'"

"I don't recall him ever saying that."

"No? Someone else, perhaps."

"Harry, Lieutenant Murray has just shot down virtually every theory and idea you've had about this business. And he's ordered us to mind our own affairs. You seem to be taking this in remarkably good spirits."

"The lieutenant is not the only source of information in this town," Harry said, smiling happily.

"No," I said, tilting my glass back to finish up the last swallow of whiskey, "there's also the library."

"I was thinking more along the lines of Mr. Jake Stein."

A hot jet of whiskey went down the wrong pipe. "Harry," I coughed. "No."

"Why not?" he asked, patting me on the back. "If one cannot get satisfaction from the law, he must turn to the outlaw."

"Harry, this is Jake Stein you're talking about. You don't just pop in for tea with Jake Stein."

"Fine," said Harry brightly. "No tea, then. Just polite conversation." He continued rolling the coin across his knuckles.

Jake Stein is forgotten today, but in our boyhood he was a figure of awe in the neighborhood, a son of immigrants who rose to control much of the criminal activity of the Lower East

Side. As children we spoke of him in hushed tones, as though the mere mention of his name would call down fearsome acts of vengeance upon ourselves and our families. "Careful what you say," the older boys would tell us. "Jake's men can hear you."

I studied my brother's open, smiling face. "So, Harry, you want to march into Jake Stein's office, wherever it might be, and ask him if he killed the Graffs?"

"Well, no," he answered, "that might be imprudent. I want to ask him if he knows of anyone else who might have killed the Graffs."

"You know, Harry, I've seen you do a lot of crazy things. I've seen you sink to the bottom of the East River with one hundred pounds worth of manacles hanging off you. I've seen you—"

"I just want to ask him a question. The man knows everything that goes on around him. He sits motionless, like a spider in the center of its web, but that web has a thousand radiations, and he knows well every quiver of each of them."

"I believe you're thinking of Professor Moriarty. Tell me, why should Jake Stein even agree to see us?"

"Why not? I just want to know if he recognizes the work of a certain killer. He may have an appreciation of such things." He took the coin he had been rolling, held it at his fingertips and then—with a sharp, twitch of a motion—caused it to vanish. "You see that? A perfect back palm. When I see that, I think instantly of the work of T. Nelson Downs, the 'King of Koins.' I have an appreciation of such things. Perhaps it is the same with Mr. Stein."

"You think Stein is a connoisseur of murder?"

He seemed to consider it seriously. "Perhaps, yes. In any event, we must find out or our investigation is at a standstill." He stood up and reached for his coat.

We continued this strange conversation all the way to Mott Street, with Harry refusing to listen to any of my sensible arguments in favor of health and longevity.

"If I've said it once I've said it a thousand times," Harry said, as we stood outside Wilson's saloon, "you have—"

"—no imagination. I know, Harry, I know."

He turned and pushed through the clouded glass doors. I hesitated for a moment, gave a shrug, and followed him in.

At first glance, Wilson's appeared to be a rather nicer establishment than the one we had just left. The floor was clean and the brasswork gleaming, and a row of polished mirrors and gas jets on the far wall gave the room a bright, rosy glow. Only the clientele gave any indication of a less salubrious atmosphere. The scattering of sullen men at the bar, and clustered around the low round tables, gave an unmistakable air of menace.

Incongruously, Harry whistled a happy tune and marched to the bar, where the bartender was mopping the counter with a rag. "I say, good fellow," Harry said brightly, "would you happen to know where we might call upon Mr. Jake Stein?"

The barman stopped polishing the counter. Conversations died. Heads turned toward my brother. If there had been swinging saloon doors, we'd have heard them creak.

"I—I'm afraid I can't help you there, sir," said the barman.

"Not to worry!" said the magnanimous Harry. "But if you should happen to see him—or any of his acquaintances—I would be obliged if you would pass along a message. Tell him that the Great Houdini is looking for him. Good day!"

Harry headed for the door. I followed four steps behind, hoping no one had noticed that we came in together.

"I think that went very well," he said on the sidewalk outside. He pointed to another saloon. "Let's try in here!"

"Harry—" I grabbed his arm but he shrugged it off.

"Honestly, Dash. Sometimes I don't know who fusses over me more—you or Mama."

And so we repeated the scene in every saloon and flop house for three streets running. In each instance Harry would saunter up to the bar, slap his hand on the counter and announce his interest in Jake Stein—"the notorious criminal," as he took to describing him.

The reactions ranged from shock to bemusement to outright laughter, but Harry soldiered on with dogged persistence. "Tell him the Great Houdini is looking for him!" he called at each stop.

We were just exiting a gambling house on Humphrey Street when I noticed that we were no longer alone in our wanderings. There were two of them, stocky rough-hewn characters wearing gray cloth coats and peaked caps. They dogged us through five more stops, keeping a fair distance, but paying close attention. At last, as we worked our way over to Bowery Street, the taller of the pair stepped up and tapped Harry on the shoulder. "Understand you're looking for Mr. Stein?" His cap made it difficult to make out his features, except for his nose. It was clear he had put in some time in a boxing ring.

"Why, yes," said my brother. "Would you happen—?"

Our friend put a finger to his lips. "This way," he said, motioning down an alley.

"Uh, Harry—" I began.

"Come along, Dash!" Harry called over his shoulder, gaily. "Mustn't keep Mr. Stein waiting! Honestly—" he turned to deliver some comment on the intransigence of younger brothers, but the remark was cut short by the thud of a fist to the solar plexus. Harry went down hard, gasping violently for breath. Rough hands twisted my arms behind my back and shoved me against a brick wall. "Not—not fair," Harry gasped, raising himself up on one elbow. "I wasn't—I wasn't set."

Our two attackers glanced at each other, amused by the pluck of the little man with the tidy bow tie. "Did you hear that?" said the one who had floored Harry. "He wasn't set." He grinned and said it again. That turned out to be a mistake.

My brother and I had been fairly green when we arrived in New York some ten years earlier. We did not stay green for long. We learned to make our way with our fists, and there were few neighborhood hooligans and bullies who had not mixed it up with the Brothers Houdini now and again. We were tough boys who grew into tough young men. My brother could bend iron bars in his bare hands. Me, I was just plain scrappy.

"He wasn't set," said the one pinning my arms, still enjoying a nice chuckle over it.

"I wasn't either," I said, and I drove the heel of my shoe into his instep. His grip loosened and I bought some fighting room with an elbow to the windpipe. Harry, meanwhile, plowed his head into the stomach of the shorter man. A metal pipe clattered onto the paving stones.

"Now, my man," Harry said, "we shall see how you do in a fair contest!"

"Harry," I said, fending off a rabbit punch, "just shut up and fight."

"Very well," he said, somewhat exasperated. He cocked his arm and hurled his thunderbolt—a right hand straight to the other man's jaw hinge. It made a sound like a cracking walnut off the hard bone. The man's head snapped back but his feet never moved. He was out before he hit the ground.

This put a healthy scare into the taller one. I saw his hand move under his coat and I figured I didn't want to know what was under there. I sent a kick to the knee and hopped back while his legs melted under him. He dropped to a kneeling position as I grabbed the back of his head and brought it smashing down on my knee, which happened to be shooting upward at the time. His head made a funny sound, too, but his was a whole lot wetter. I let go and he flopped backward in a heap.

Harry examined his knuckles for bruising, in much the way he might have chosen an apple from the corner vendor's cart. "I wasn't set," he said.

"So I gathered. Come on."

We turned and walked toward the mouth of the alley, and that's when we ran into the man with the Smith and Wesson. He was small, red-haired, and he had three friends with him.

One of them was cracking his knuckles, another had a length of chain wrapped around his first, and the third had a knife that he kept flicking open and closed.

"Which one of you is the Great Houdini?" asked the man with the gun.

"I am," my brother said.

"Mr. Stein will see you now."

9

THE GLASS-EATER

THE RED-HAIRED MAN KEPT THE GUN TRAINED ON US WHILE HIS associates dragged our two unconscious sparring partners out of the alley. The pair were loaded roughly into a waiting carriage. When they returned, one of the men held a hank of coarse bailing rope. "Hands behind your backs," said the red-haired man. His voice was strangely high and musical.

"You're tying up the Great Houdini?" Harry asked incredulously. "This is—"

"Shut up, Harry," I said, as a blindfold was slipped over my eyes and tied roughly at the back.

"Nobody needs to get hurt," said the high voice. "We're just taking a little ride."

It's fortunate that gangster movies were still some years away, or I imagine that phrase would have filled me with dread. I wouldn't say I was thrilled about "taking a little ride" in any case, but I didn't know enough to conjure visions of cement overshoes. Harry, for his part, was busy muttering about the indignity of having his hands tied in a "saucy little half-hitch." Happily, our captors seemed to be ignoring him.

We were bundled into a covered carriage and I heard a rap on the roof to signal the driver, who whipped the horses to a brisk trot. In spite of my blindfold, which smelled faintly of salted fish, I was able to hold onto a loose thread of where we were going. I knew the area well, and could track our progress by a variety of sounds bobbing up through the constant clatter of the wooden wheels on granite slabs—the shrill cry of a fruit vendor, the gaseous roar of the elevated train, the tinny wheeze of an organ grinder. Aromas, too, seemed much stronger to me as I sat blindfolded in the back of the carriage. The warm balm of roasting nuts mingled horribly with the sickly stench of an open sewer; the all-pervading funk of horse effluvia blended with the gritty bite of burning coal. Gradually these gave way to the sounds of birds and water, and I realized we were nearing the East River. The granite beneath our wheels now yielded to wooden planking. "We're getting out," the high voice said as the carriage drew to a halt. "Don't even think about giving us the slip." Mercifully, my brother said nothing.

Rough hands pushed me out of the carriage and I stumbled badly as I misjudged the step. Someone took hold of me at the elbow and led me forward, with the ludicrous warning "Watch your step." A change in wind signalled our progress along a dock.

"Step up," I was told. I realized with a shock, as I climbed a shallow set of stairs, that I was being helped aboard a boat of some kind. Several pairs of hands half-lifted, half-pushed me a short distance through the air, and my feet came down with a thump onto a wooden deck. I felt the gentle roll of the water beneath me. I scarcely had time to register these new sensations when I heard the thud of my brother's feet hitting the deck, and a shouted instruction to "bring 'em below."

Someone pushed my head from behind. I bent forward, passing through what was evidently a low doorway. I heard latches working and doors creaking as we passed along a short corridor, then down a steep set of step rungs.

Finally we appeared to reach our destination. I heard a low murmur of voices, and a clinging whiff of stale cigars reached my nostrils. A voice said, "Take off the blindfolds."

We were in a large but sparsely appointed ship's cabin. The furnishings were those of a warehouse rather than a sailing vessel—seven wooden filing cabinets, a dozen packing crates, four ladder-stools, and a flat, highly-polished deal table. Maps of the city covered the wall opposite us, with a spray of yellow-headed pins jabbed in at various points. Four or five young men were arrayed along the map wall, some of them standing, the others perched on stools. A much older man sat in a cane-backed swivel chair behind the deal table. He was squat and pudgy, with cool gray eyes that regarded us from behind a pair of round spectacles. A coil of white hair swept forward from the back of his head, struggling to conceal a wrinkled and spotted pate. A heavy shading of bluish stubble covered his jawline. He waited a moment as we took in our surroundings, then removed a wet panatela from his teeth. "Sorry about the rough treatment," he said. "I'm Jake Stein."

I suppose we merely stared. He certainly did not fit my boyhood impression of a legendary criminal, a man rumored to have beaten a pair of traitorous underlings to death with his bare hands. He looked instead like one of the men I saw playing chess each day in the lobby of my mother's apartment building. Perhaps his only no-table feature was the coarse, labored quality of his voice, which sounded as if it had been dipped in hot oil.

"Which one of you is the Great Houdini?" he asked, gesturing with the cigar.

"I am," my brother said. "It is kind of you to receive us." His tone sounded bright and firm—his stage voice.

"What are you, some sort of circus act? The Great Houdini?"

"I am the world-renowned handcuff king and prison breaker, the justly celebrated self-liberator."

"Come again?"

"I escape from handcuffs and ropes."

"Seems to me we've got you tied up pretty good right now," Stein said, leaning back and swinging his feet onto the table.

"These bonds?" Harry gave an indignant snort. "Child's play. If your associate had not pointed a gun at me, I would have disposed of these ropes in an instant."

"That so?" Stein squinted hard at Harry's face, trying to make up his mind about something. "I'd like to see that. Why don't you just—"

Stein never finished the sentence. Harry's shoulders twitched, and a grimace washed over his features. "Child's play," he said, tossing the untied ropes onto the table.

My stomach clenched as I watched the play of anger and fascination on Stein's features. Clearly he did not care for brash young men. After a tense pause, the old man apparently decided to find my brother amusing. He grinned and clapped his hands. Harry took a bow as Stein's henchmen followed suit. I took advantage of the appreciative climate to escape from my own bonds, though no one seemed to notice.

"Not bad!" Jake Stein said in his painful-sounding growl. "You say you can escape from anything?"

"Nothing on earth can hold me a prisoner," my brother assured him. "The Great Houdini can escape from anything."

"I'll have to introduce you to my wife sometime," said Stein, a remark that drew energetic hilarity from the men along the back wall. Harry grinned weakly. I would guess that he heard this joke perhaps seven thousand times over the course of his lifetime.

"So" —Stein took a drag on his cigar— "you must be the guy who keeps trying to bust out of Mulberry Street, huh?"

"You know of this?"

"Jake Stein knows things, kid. Remember that. Let me know if you ever figure a way out. Could be useful."

This prompted another outburst of mirth from the boys at the back.

Stein pointed his cigar at us. "I guess you boys are pretty good with your fists," he said. "I might just have some work for you some time." The growl trailed off and he gazed at the ceiling, pondering the manner in which the Brothers Houdini might make themselves useful to his operations. For me, this prospect seemed about as attractive as Harry's plan to jump off the Brooklyn Bridge.

Fortunately, Harry did not entirely apprehend the nature of Stein's interest. "Well," he said, "until recently my wife and I were playing at Huber's Museum. Prior to that we enjoyed a lengthy engagement with the Welsh Brothers Circus. In addition to our public performances, we are available for birthday parties, family gatherings, and social functions of all descriptions. I also offer a comprehensive series of lessons in magic and sleight of hand."

Stein's eyes narrowed for a moment, but the grin stayed fixed in place. He threw a don't-this-beat-all look at the back-wall boys. Without realizing it, Harry had dodged a bullet.

"Okay, Houdini," Stein said, "you've been looking for me all over town. What was it you wanted?"

"Two friends of mine have been brutally murdered," Harry began. "They were an elderly couple who—"

"The Graffs. Ran the Toy Emporium."

"Precisely. I am seeking information about this terrible tragedy."

Stein folded his arms across his chest. "May I ask why you think I would know anything about it, Houdini?"

Harry swept his right hand over his head, a stage flourish. "Because, sir, Jake Stein knows things."

It was the right answer. Stein grinned as he swung his feet off the table and knocked his cigar over an ashtray. "I'm not sure what sort of help you're looking for, kid. The old lady got cut up by a gang. The old man strung himself up in a jail cell. What else do you want to know?"

"I am not entirely happy with that explanation," Harry said. "Not happy at all."

Stein cleared his throat—a horrible, gravelled sound. "You want me to find the kids that carved the old lady, is that it? Look, kid, I'm not in the business of—"

"I do not think that Mrs. Graff's death was the work of a gang."

"No?" Stein leaned forward, genuinely curious. "Why not?"

Harry answered at great length, summarizing the events

of the past three days, beginning with our summons to the Wintour mansion. Stein listened closely, interrupting twice to ask for clarification, nodding appreciatively at our exploit in the Cairo Club, and wondering aloud over the puzzle of Branford Wintour's study.

"Harrington, is it?" Stein asked when Harry had finished. "The name was Evan Harrington?"

"Yes."

"Harrington did the job on Wintour, then laced the old couple to keep them mum—that's what you think?"

"Laced?"

Stein sighed. "Killed. You think Harrington killed them to cover his tracks?"

"That is my theory."

Stein gave a hot, gasping noise that I took to be a chuckle. "Evan Harrington. A wooden nickel of a name if ever I heard one."

"I am aware of that, of course," Harry said. "It may surprise you to learn that my name is not actually Harry Houdini."

"Is that so, Ehrich?"

My brother stiffened.

"Ehrich Weiss," Stein continued, "and his brother Theodore. Sons of the Rabbi Mayer Samuel Weiss. A good man, your father."

Harry gave a faint cry of surprise. "You knew him?"

"Not to speak to. I heard him two or three times, though. Morning services. I liked the look of him. Very devout. Not like these young ones today. I was sorry to hear he'd passed."

Harry paused, momentarily bewildered. "It is kind of you," he said.

"How is your mother?"

"She is well, thank you."

"Good." Stein bit the end off a fresh cigar. "I'm still not quite certain how I can help you," he said, as one of the wall-boys stepped forward to light his cigar. "What is it that you want from me?"

"Let us assume that the Graffs were killed by a single individual, as I have outlined. I wondered if these acts might suggest a pattern to you, if you perhaps recognized a certain—well—"

"Do I recognize the work," Stein said helpfully. "Isn't that what you're asking?"

"Yes. Yes, sir. This person would have to be clever enough to slip in and out of Mr. Wintour's locked study without leaving any trace, but also brutal enough to attack Mrs. Graff with such unwonted savagery."

"You say these toys are valuable?"

"They are not toys."

"Well, whatever they are. Worth a few bucks?"

"Indeed. But I do not think that is why Mr. Wintour was killed."

"I'd have to agree," Stein said. "Nobody I know would go to all that trouble for a bunch of—what was it you called them?"

"Automatons."

"Yes." He sent a cloud of smoke toward the low ceiling. "Here's my problem, Houdini. I can think of any number of punch-and-peel men who could have slipped into Wintour's study without too much trouble. And I know maybe a dozen knife artists who might have done the old lady and made it look like gang boys—if they had a reason to do it. The old man in the cell, I don't know from that. Maybe he killed himself, maybe he didn't. But you see my problem? You're asking me if I recognize the work. If I were looking, I'd be looking for two guys. Not one."

Harry weighed this answer carefully. "In my profession," he said slowly, "one must be able to do many things. When I work in a dime museum, I am sometimes called upon to be a strong man, or a juggler, or a clown. Once I even ran a ghost show. A talented performer wears many hats."

The old man rubbed the stubble on his chin. The door opened behind us and a slight man wearing a black suit and a homburg slipped into the room. Stein did not acknowledge him. "In my business," Stein told us, "matters are different. You got a leaky pipe, you call a plumber. You got a broken door, you call a carpenter. Do you understand me?"

Harry nodded. "Two different men."

"Put it this way," he said. "Whoever killed Wintour had nothing to do with killing the old lady." He looked up at the man in the Homburg, then back at Harry. "You really think she got killed by a working man? You're sure it wasn't just gang boys?"

"I'm sure of it," Harry said.

Stein leaned back in his chair and swung his feet back onto the table. His eyes came to rest on me. "You don't say much, do you, Theodore?"

"Not a whole lot, no," I said.

"But you saw what went on in the toy shop?"

"Uh, yes, I did." I shuffled my feet, self-conscious at having been put on the spot.

"And who do you think killed her?" Stein grinned behind his cigar, enjoying my discomfiture.

I stopped shuffling and looked him straight in the eye, damned if I was going to let him stare me down. "I don't know who killed her," I said. "I don't know if it was a gang of street thugs, or someone trying to make it look like street thugs, and frankly I don't care. All I know is that she was a sweet old lady and she deserved better than to get slit up the belly like a brook trout. My brother and I are chasing all around town looking for someone who might know something. Maybe we'll find something, maybe we won't. Maybe we'll do some good, maybe not. It's better than sitting home with a book."

Harry was looking at me with an expression of interest and surprise, as though I'd just pulled a dripping octopus from a top hat, instead of the customary rabbit. Stein puffed his cigar and glanced again at Homburg man, who shook his head.

"So all you boys want to do is find who did this to the sweet old lady, is that it?"

THE DIME MUSEUM MURDERS

"And her husband," said Harry.

"Mr. Stein," said Homburg man. "This is not—"

Stein held up a hand to silence him. "This thing," Stein said, "I don't like to see this sort of thing on my patch. It... doesn't look well. But I don't want to stir the pot too much. Someone might take offense. But I like you boys. I'm going to—"

Homburg man renewed his objections. Stein silenced him again with a look that could have melted iron.

"I don't know who killed your friends," Stein continued. "I'm not even sure I need to know. But I know who I'd ask about it, if I were you."

"That would be very helpful," Harry said.

Stein wrote a name and address down on a slip of paper. "This gentleman is a pretty cool bean. You want something from him, you got to have money or you got to have muscle. You two don't seem to me like the money type."

"No," Harry admitted.

Stein pushed it across the table at us. "There is one thing," he said.

"Yes?" Harry asked, reaching for the paper.

"Anyone finds out where you got this name, then you boys have got a problem with me."

"That won't happen," Harry said. "We are unusually good at keeping secrets."

"Huh," Stein snorted, still amused by my brother. "I just might have some work for you boys," he said. "I just might at that."

I looked at the cold, grinning face behind the soggy cigar. I hoped he was talking about magic lessons.

10

RETURN OF THE GRAVEYARD GHOULS

AS I RECALL, THE DREAM I WAS HAVING FOUND ME STROLLING ARM-in-arm along Sixth Avenue in the company of Miss Katherine Hendricks, who seemed to find me handsome and fascinating to a degree that surprised us both. We had just paused to admire the window displays at Simpson-Crawford when she turned to me with a coquettish giggle, squeezed my hand, and said, "Dash! Wake up!"

I pulled a pillow over my head. "Go away, Harry."

A hand—definitely not Miss Hendricks's—shook me by the shoulder. "Come on, Dash! The game's afoot!"

I threw the pillow aside and blocked my eyes against the light of Harry's bull's-eye lantern. "Haven't you been to bed yet, Harry? What time is it?"

"A little past midnight."

I fumbled for my Elgin on the table beside my bed. "It's three o'clock!"

"Is it? Well, that's all the better. Come on, get dressed! Mr. Cranston has finally returned!"

It seemed pointless to argue, since he would have stood there shaking my shoulder until morning anyway. I swung my feet onto the floor and padded over to the wash basin, poured some cold water out of the jug, and splashed my face. Slowly, the events of the previous day came back into focus.

THE DIME MUSEUM MURDERS

We had spent the evening lounging outside a brownstone on Twenty-third Street, trying to look inconspicuous. The brownstone belonged to a Mr. Joshua Cranston, whose name and address had been on the slip of paper that Jake Stein had given us. For a time we idled on a wrought iron bench directly across the street, but after an hour or so we feared we would be taken for vagrants. We began strolling around the block, in the manner of two young swells seeking "healthful exercise" along a route that happened to bring them down the same street every three minutes. Soon enough we began to attract unwanted attention from the neighborhood doormen. We returned to the bench across the street, artfully concealing ourselves behind a late edition of the *Herald*.

Almost from the moment we left Jake Stein's presence—his goons, apparently satisfied by our vow of secrecy, had not insisted on blindfolds—I had debated with my brother over the wisdom of pursuing Joshua Cranston. I did not relish the idea of being beholden to a gangland figure, and I sensed that Stein was using us as pawns in some private agenda. Harry brushed aside my objections. "In this world," he told me, "the big thief condemns the little thief."

As night fell, and no lights came on inside the brownstone, we began to suspect that no one was at home in the Cranston residence. We kept watch for two more hours, by which stage my complaints of hunger had reached a pitch that even Harry could not ignore. We agreed to withdraw for the night and resume our vigil in the morning.

It was now apparent that Harry had not gone home after all. "I decided to climb one of the trees across the street," he explained, "so that I would be able to watch the house without drawing attention to myself. It was actually quite comfortable, rather like that leafy old spruce we used to climb in Appleton. In fact, after an hour or so I fell asleep, only to be awakened just moments ago by the arrival of a four-wheeler. Cranston got out and went into the brownstone. Drunk as a lord, I might add."

"You're sure it was Cranston?"

"The coachman addressed him by name."

"Wouldn't we do better to wait until morning?" I asked, reaching for the trousers of my brown wool suit. "He'll be asleep by the time we get back over there."

"Forget the fancy clothes," Harry said. "Wear those old rags from the black art routine."

He was referring to an act we used to do called "Graveyard Ghouls," in which a pair of grinning skeletons were seen to float and dance in a mysterious fashion. Much depended on the machinations of an unseen assistant—myself—who was clothed entirely in black. "What are you planning, Harry?" I asked.

"I simply do not wish to attract attention," he said. "It would not do to appear as a strutting Beau Brummel."

I shrugged and clicked the latches on my old costume trunk in the corner. "Wouldn't we do better to wait until morning?" I repeated as I rooted around in the trunk.

"He is seldom abroad in daylight."

"How do you know that?"

"I know a great deal about Mr. Cranston now. He lives alone, he operates almost exclusively at night, he is extremely partial to wine and spirits, and he is suspected in the disappearance of Muggins."

"Muggins?"

"A poodle belonging to Mrs. Roth."

"And Mrs. Roth would be…?"

"She and her husband occupy the neighboring house."

"How did you come to know all this, Harry?" I asked, pulling a heavy black tunic over my head.

"You'll recall that you abandoned me for a time at the very height of our surveillance?"

"Harry, I had to find a water closet."

"I used the occasion of your absence to make myself charming to Mrs. Roth's nursemaid, who was taking little Jeremy for a stroll."

"When were you going to tell me this?"

"When it suited me."

"Harry," I said, buttoning up my black wool trousers, "normal people sometimes have to answer the call of nature. Normal people sometimes get hungry. Normal people sometimes sleep. I realize that such ideas are foreign to you, but—"

"One of us had to remain alert. And see what has come of it? We are now ready to beard the lion in his den. Good Lord, Dash, stop preening! Every moment is crucial!"

I was now dressed and had been running a comb through my hair. "We're going to knock on the door at three in the morning?"

"Not precisely," Harry said. "Come along, I have a carriage waiting."

We left the boarding house on tiptoe so as not to wake the other tenants, and as we reached the street I saw that Harry had hired an open, two-wheeled coal wagon, though the driver was nowhere to be seen.

"He seemed happy enough to let me use the rig," Harry explained. "Like you, he places his stomach above the demands of work."

We climbed onto the hardwood seat and I took the reins, as Harry was an uncommonly poor driver. I flicked the reins and the horse set off at an easy trot toward Twenty-third Street. It was a beautiful, crisp night, the entire city wrapped in a blanket of sleep. Only the rhythmic clatter of our hooves and wooden wheels broke the stillness. I looked over at Harry, who had pulled the collar of his shaggy astrakhan overcoat up around his ears. His eyes were gleaming. "The curtain is rising, Dash," he said. "The answers are almost within our grasp!"

Within moments we drew up outside Cranston's brownstone. "Now what?" I asked Harry.

"We go to the cellar delivery door," Harry said, swinging a heavy cloth sack onto his shoulder. "If anyone should happen to look out the window, they will assume we are bringing a weight of coal."

"At this hour?"

"Mr. Cranston keeps an eccentric schedule," he assured me. "His tradesmen have had to accommodate him. It is the despair of the neighborhood."

I shrugged and walked the horse and wagon down a narrow service alley at the side of the house, stopping in front of a pair of wooden delivery doors. "Just a moment," Harry said, reaching for his lock-picks. "I'll have these doors open faster than—Dash! How did you manage that?"

"They weren't locked," I said, indicating the open doors. "Nobody locks their doors in this neighborhood."

"Oh," Harry looked a bit disappointed as he tucked his lock-pick wallet back into his pocket. "Well, then. Let us proceed."

"Wait, Harry." I put out a hand to stop him. "We're about to break into a man's home. If we're caught, we'll be arrested. Somehow I don't think Mr. Jake Stein will vouch for us at police headquarters. I need to know what we're doing here."

"It should be apparent," Harry answered in a low voice. "Mr. Stein told us that we would need either money or muscle to get what we wanted from Joshua Cranston. We have no money; therefore, we shall use muscle—as only the Brothers Houdini can."

"And how might that be, may I ask? By creeping around in black clothes?" I peered into the darkened coal cellar. "Suppose Cranston keeps a gun?"

"Then we must rely on the element of surprise," Harry said. He pushed past me and climbed down a half-flight of stone steps leading into the house.

I had little choice but to follow as Harry walked toward the center of the coal cellar. He fished around in the cloth sack he was carrying and pulled out his bull's-eye lantern. Lighting the flame, he adjusted the focusing lens into a narrow beam. "Come along," he whispered. "These stairs will lead us up through the kitchen. The master bedroom is on the second floor at the back."

"How do you know that?" I asked.

"Mrs. Roth's nursemaid told me. She had it from Cranston's valet. Stay behind me."

We crept up the stairs to the kitchen and passed through to a richly decorated parlor. Harry swept the beam of his lantern toward a winding staircase at the front of the house. "Just a moment, Dash," he said, reaching into the cloth sack. "Better put this on." He handed me a strip of black fabric.

It was one of those little domino masks such as Robin Hood or some operatic villain might have worn. "Harry," I whispered, "you're being preposterous! This is the sort of mask you might wear in stage melodrama!"

"We must safeguard our identity," Harry insisted. "Put it on."

"Raffles."

"What?"

"Raffles," I repeated. "You want to wear this mask because Raffles, the gentleman burglar, wears one." My voice had risen dangerously, but I found I was having trouble controlling it.

"Ridiculous," Harry whispered, petulantly.

"That's how you see yourself, isn't it? The Great Harry Houdini, amateur cracksman, slipping away from the ambassador's reception to relieve the duchess of her diamond tiara. Poor old Inspector Murray, the doddering chief of the Sureté, has never managed to apprehend our dashing rogue, who always leaves a pair of silver handcuffs as his calling card. Oh, how many times have the hapless officials of—"

"Stop it, Dash!" my brother snapped. "It's not like that at all. I just thought we would need a proper costume if we are to frighten Mr. Cranston. He will naturally assume that we are dangerous burglars and tell us what we wish to know."

"Harry, no real burglar ever wore one of these things."

He fingered the delicate little mask wistfully. "Let us put them on anyway," he said.

"Suit yourself," I said, shoving mine into my pocket. "But why stop there? Think how frightened Cranston will be if he sees you twirling the ends of a wax moustache."

Harry gave the mask another mournful look. "You have no imagination, Dash," he said, slipping it back into the cloth sack.

Flinging the sack over his shoulder, Harry began a cautious ascent of the main staircase, clinging to the bannister and trying to lighten his tread on the potentially creaky floor boards. I followed suit, though it seemed to me that we had already made enough noise to rouse the dead.

At the top of the stairs we could hear the steady, two-note drone of a sleeping man snoring lustily. Harry flicked the shade on the bull's-eye lantern, masking the beam. Creeping to the door of the master bedroom, Harry nudged it open with his foot.

Cranston lay on his back at the center of a sprawling four-poster bed. He wore silk pajamas and a cotton night cap, and his hands were clasped contentedly over the modest bulge of his stomach.

"He doesn't look much like a killer, does he?" Harry whispered.

"He doesn't look as if he'd harm a fly," I answered. "Or Muggins the poodle, for that matter."

Harry passed me the lantern. "There's only one way to find out. When I give the signal, shine the beam in his eyes. I'm going to give him the fright of his life." He crept to the sleeping man's side and raised his arms in the manner of an animal about to pounce. "Now, Dash!"

I snapped the lantern's shade open and beamed the light onto Cranston's face. At the same time, Harry filled his lungs with air and let out the fearsome growl he had perfected as Yar, the primitive strong man of the dime museum circuit. "Joshua Cranston!" he shouted. "Your moment of judgement is at hand! Rise and face your darkest nightmare!"

Cranston didn't stir. The snoring continued without interruption. Harry furrowed his brow. "He appears to be an uncommonly sound sleeper," Harry said at a more normal volume. He seized the sleeping man by the shoulder and shook him roughly. Cranston began to mumble and swipe at his eyes, as if to bat away the beam of the lantern. "Joshua Cranston!" Harry shouted at an even louder pitch. "Your moment of judgement is at hand! Rise and face your darkest nightmare!"

The sleeping man muttered something that concerned a woman named Dolores, then rolled over and resumed snoring.

I swept the lantern beam to a low table beside the bed. "Harry," I said.

"Wait just a minute, Dash." He gripped the edge of the mattress and gave it a mighty heave upward. Cranston rolled off the opposite edge and onto the floor in a tangle of bedclothes. "Joshua Cranston!" he thundered. "Your day of judgement has arrived! Turn and face your accusers!"

Cranston flailed about groggily for a moment, found his pillow, and went back to sleep. "Harry," I said, "it's going to take more than judgement day to wake this man up." I held out a blue-glass vial.

"What is it?" Harry asked, pulling the cork stopper. "It smells vile!"

"Grunson's Nerve Tonic," I said. "An efficacious and healthful remedy for the treatment of persistent neuralgia and wakefulness."

Harry shoved the stopper back into the vial as if squashing a bug. "So. He is drugged."

"Heavily."

"How long before we can wake him?"

"No way of knowing."

"An hour?"

"At least."

Harry nudged the sleeping man with his foot. "Dash, I have a rather interesting idea."

Two hours later, Joshua Cranston began to stir.

As he slowly regained consciousness, he became aware that much had changed while he was under the influence of his sleeping draught. For one thing, he was no longer in his bedroom. For another, his legs were securely tied. Also, he was dangling head-down from a crane atop the Bayard Building, twelve stories high, looking straight down onto Bleecker Street.

When his screams subsided, he became aware of my brother Harry, dangling head-down beside him at the end of a sturdy rope.

"Good morning, Mr. Cranston," Harry said. "Tell me, whatever became of Muggins the poodle?"

11

THE UPSIDE-DOWN MAN

MR. CRANSTON CONTINUED SCREAMING FOR SOME TIME. HIS VOICE seemed to ebb and flow in the strong winds whipping around the top of the building, and there was a certain fascination in listening to the sound fall away, like a stone disappearing into a well. Tall buildings were not so common then as now, and from our lofty vantage atop the Bayard Building, which had only just been completed that year, we seemed to be looking down on a sleeping village at the foot of some majestic mountain. It made for quite a peaceful scene—apart from the very noisy distress of our companion—with everything shaded a faint lavender in the cool wash of dawn.

Harry, hanging upside-down beside Cranston, waited patiently for him to cease his vocalizations. "I assure you, Mr. Cranston, no one can hear you," Harry said, although we both doubted that this was true. "Do you see how far down the street is? No one is about at this hour." He folded his arms, swaying slightly in the morning breeze.

We had selected the Bayard Building to take advantage of a gear-action construction crane mounted on the ornate cornice, which, during daylight hours, was being used to haul a set of granite angels into position. It had been a considerable chore dragging Cranston's sleeping body across town and up to the top of the building, but the expression on our victim's face more than justified the effort.

"Now then, Mr. Cranston," said Harry blandly, as though opening a board meeting of some kind, "I think we have some business to discuss."

The little man screwed up his eyes and rubbed them, as if to make this terrible apparition disappear. When he opened them again, my brother winked and gave a cheery wave.

"What—what" —Cranston struggled for breath— "what is—why do—what is the meaning of this?" His face glowed red with the blood pooling in his cheeks. He stared at my brother with wild eyes. "I—I have money! Lots of money!"

"Would you be referring to this money?" Harry asked, waving two fat packets of notes.

"Impossible! How did—?"

"One should not place too much confidence in a Bering wall safe, Mr. Cranston. Even if it does have the new dual-chamber pin-plate."

"Keep the money! Just get me down from here! I beg of you!"

"We wouldn't think of keeping your money, Mr. Cranston," Harry said. "However, we may not exactly give it back, either." He peeled off a few bills from one of the bundles and scattered them to the morning wind.

Cranston gave a shriek as the notes swirled and danced about his head. "God! No!" His hands darted out to snatch at the money, but the sudden movement set him swinging back and forth like a pendulum. Apparently the motion did not agree with him. He made a harsh choking noise and clutched at his throat. The contents of his stomach spiralled twelve stories to the street below.

Harry took out his handkerchief, fluffed it open in the breeze, and held it out to Cranston, who reached for it with a tight, fragile movement, as though clinging to the railing on an icy set of steps. "What do you want from me?" he gasped, dabbing nervously at his lips. "Why are you doing this to me?"

"Tell us about Evan Harrington," Harry said.

"Harrington?" A sudden flash of cunning appeared in Cranston's eyes. "I—I do not know who that is."

Harry reached across and gave him a small push on the shoulder that set him swinging back and forth again. "Tell us about Evan Harrington," Harry repeated.

"No!" Cranston cried. "I don't know who you're talking about! I don't know any Evan Harrington! Please stop it!"

Harry reached out and gave another push. "Evan Harrington," he said.

"I can't stand this!" Cranston shrieked, coughing wetly.

"Evan Harrington."

"I don't—"

"Looks a bit like me…" Harry said, giving Cranston another shove.

"Please—!"

"Tried to broker the sale of a valuable automaton…" Another shove.

"I don't—"

"Framed Josef Graff for murder…"

"No—no—"

"Responsible for three deaths in the past three days…" Harry reached out and clutched Cranston by the shoulder, abruptly halting the swinging motion. "I think you can tell me a great deal about Evan Harrington, Mr. Cranston. Begin now, please."

"I don't know a thing about any Evan Harrington! I don't know anything about any murders! You must have me mistaken for—"

"Look up towards your feet," Harry said. "Do you see that handsome fellow straddling the crane? What do you suppose he's doing? Why, it appears as if he's setting fire to the ropes that are anchoring us to the crane!"

"No!" Cranston shouted. "You'll die! You'll die with me!"

"Yes, that is a bother," Harry admitted. "Look! The rope is burning quite merrily, having been soaked in kerosene. I would estimate, Mr. Cranston, that you and I have less than one minute before the fire eats through the rope. Then we will fall to the pavement below. It will be a horrible fate—but then, there have been so many deaths lately."

"I haven't killed anyone!"

"All the more regrettable, then."

"For God's sake! I haven't killed anyone!"

Harry grabbed Cranston's nightshirt and pulled his face close to his. "Name the killer," he said.

"I'm not responsible! A man approached me. He—I'll tell you everything, just put out that fire and haul me up!"

"Tell me now," Harry said calmly.

"You're insane!"

Harry merely smiled. "Who approached you?"

"I—I never met the man. He made contact through an intermediary. Most of them do. But I put him in touch with a man who could do the job. All confidential—safeguarded to ensure mutual discretion. I swear, I don't know who hired me!"

"And you passed the assignment on to someone?"

"I'm not a killer! I'm just the man in the middle!"

"The name, please."

"Fred Gittles. My best man."

"Goes by the name of Harrington, does he?"

"Sometimes. Or Richard Feverel. He goes by lots of names. Please—"

"Where do I find Fred Gittles?"

"Thirty-ninth and Broadway. Number three-six-two. For God's sake—"

And then the rope snapped.

I watched Cranston as he fell. His face crumpled and his arms flailed and a sharp little scream died on his lips as though he'd been kicked in the throat. He and my brother seemed to hang in the empty space for a moment, like fish jumping in a summer stream, and then they began to sink in a twisting, corkscrew motion toward the street below.

They must have fallen ten, perhaps twelve feet before I heard the taut zing of the safety wire. They took a hard bounce and bobbed up and down for a few moments before coming to a lazy, gentle swing at the end of the wire.

"Are you all right?" I shouted, cupping my hands to make myself heard over the rising wind.

Harry, still upside-down, gave a cheery salute. "Cranston is unconscious," he called. "I think that went rather well, don't you?"

We had a far easier time getting Cranston off the building. I had brought along a bottle of nerve tonic, and we administered a generous dose before stuffing him back into Harry's sack. We carried him down to the street and loaded him onto the back of the coal cart, then headed back toward his brownstone.

We debated briefly whether or not to turn him over to Lieutenant Murray, but in the end we decided that such a course might create unwanted problems with Jake Stein. Cranston had told us what we wanted to know; we were happy enough to put him back where we found him.

Dawn had broken by the time we dragged the sack through the delivery entrance and carried Cranston up to his own bed. We put what remained of his money back in the wall safe and removed all remaining traces of our visit. I stood back and watched as Harry settled the cotton sleeping cap back onto Cranston's head. "Perhaps when he awakes he will think it was all a narcotic dream," Harry said.

"Until he sees those rope burns on his ankles," I replied. "Come on, Harry, let's go."

Moments later, as we drove away in the coal cart, Harry looked back at the brownstone and gave a sigh of satisfaction. "The burning rope was a brilliant suggestion, Dash," he said. "I thought the poor man was having an apoplectic fit."

"I'm surprised he didn't," I replied. "You were quite impressive up there, Harry."

"I was, was I not?" he agreed. "A shame that no one witnessed the display but ourselves. I wonder…" His eyes drifted upward at the passing skyline.

We drove on in silence for quite some time. Whenever I looked over at Harry, he appeared to be lost in thought. After ten minutes or so, I cleared my throat.

"Harry—" I began.

"No, Dash—don't bother. All that you have to say has already crossed my mind."

"Then you know that we're not going to capture Mr. Gittles ourselves."

His head sank down to his chest. "I know."

"And you know that we're going to police headquarters to turn the information over to Lieutenant Murray."

"Yes," he said dejectedly. "I know."

I looked over at him again. "I expected more of an argument," I said.

"I'm tired of arguing with you, Dash."

"I mean, be reasonable, Harry. The police take a dim view of citizens who make arrests. What did you think we were going to do? Hog-tie Gittles and dump him on the steps at Mulberry Street? Maybe with a little note pinned to his chest— 'Compliments of H. Houdini'?"

"No," Harry said. "I would have brought him inside."

"It's not how these things are done in New York."

"Perhaps they should be," Harry replied with some heat. "You know perfectly well what will happen when we tell our story to Lieutenant Murray. He'll fold his arms and shrug his shoulders and tell us to mind our own business. I can hear him now. 'The police can manage this investigation quite well without your assistance, Mr. Houdini.' Honestly, Dash, I don't know why you place such confidence in that man."

He pulled his collar up around his chin and would not speak to me for the rest of the ride to Mulberry Street.

To his credit, Lieutenant Murray did not tell us to mind our own business. He didn't even fold his arms or shrug his shoulders. He listened to our story with frank admiration, and knew better than to press too hard when we glossed over certain details—such as our visit to Jake Stein and our abduction of Joshua Cranston.

When we finished, he leaned back in his chair and gave an appreciative whistle. "Joshua Cranston," he said, with a note of reverence in his voice. "The two of you got Joshua Cranston to sing like a nightingale."

"Well," said Harry, trying to appear modest, "I suppose we did."

The lieutenant turned to the desk sergeant who had taken down our statement in longhand. "When was the last time we hauled Old Brassnuts in here, Sergeant?"

"I couldn't say," the sergeant replied. "Can't be more than three weeks, though."

"He tell us anything useful?"

"No, sir."

Lieutenant Murray nodded. "I didn't think so. But somehow when these two boys tapped him on the shoulder, he spat out a name. A real, live name." He shook his head at the wonder of it. "How did you do it?"

"Well," said Harry, perching awkwardly between discretion and boastfulness, "we—we—"

"We got him to see things from a fresh perspective," I said.

"All right," said the lieutenant. "Play it your way. If this pans out, the New York Police Department will be very much in your debt. There may even be a citizen's commendation in it for you." He noted Harry's glum expression and turned to me. "Why's he so gloomy?"

"He wanted to bring you Gittles himself."

"Did he? How'd you talk him out of it?"

"I—"

"I don't suppose you could take us along when you arrest Mr. Gittles?" Harry broke in. "I should like to see this murderer face to face."

"There'll be plenty of opportunity for that at the trial, Houdini. I'm afraid we can't allow civilians to hitch along on an arrest run."

"But—"

"Houdini, you did the right thing coming down here. If you and your brother had tried to snatch this Gittles character by your lonesome, he'd have got himself some fancy-pants attorney and claimed unlawful detention." He stood up and reached for a leather gun holster that had been hanging over the coat rack. "I'd like to have you with us when we nab him, but our hands are tied."

Harry gave a bitter laugh. "If only our hands *were* tied," he said, "that would be the least of my troubles."

Harry continued to sulk as we left the precinct house and returned the coal wagon to its rightful owner. "It's just not fair, Dash," he said as we made our way north to Sixty-ninth Street. "I wanted to hear the man confess. We earned that right."

He kept on in this vein for some time, and I managed to ignore most of it until we found ourselves standing outside the apartment building. "Get some sleep, Harry," I said. "Then you and I had better find ourselves some honest work."

"What, you're not coming in? Mama will have breakfast ready!"

"I'm bushed, Harry. I just want to crawl into bed for a few hours."

He shook his head, despairing over the lay-about habits of his younger brother. "Very well, Dash. Go on home to bed." He sighed and turned toward the building. "Dash," he called after me, "try not to sleep your life away."

I walked the six blocks to my boarding house and wearily climbed the stairs to my room. I felt exhausted, but I knew I wouldn't be able to sleep. I stripped off my dark clothing, took a quick bath, and shaved. Then I changed my linen and pulled on a clean suit. I was back on the street again inside of an hour.

I caught the elevated train and headed downtown. On the way, I chewed over what Joshua Cranston had told us that morning. As far as I knew, every word of it was true. It didn't matter a bit to me. The police were welcome to Fred Gittles.

I wanted to know who hired him. If Cranston didn't know who was pulling the strings, neither would Gittles. That was the name I wanted. That was the only name that really mattered. I didn't know who it was, but I had a hunch.

You may wonder why I didn't share any of this with my brother. The truth is, I wasn't quite as much of a lay-about as he imagined. Much as I loved him, there were times when I would rather have taken that leap off the Brooklyn Bridge than listened to another moment of his self-absorbed prattle. There were times when I preferred to be something other than the brother of the Great Houdini.

It must have been about nine o'clock by the time I reached the Toy Emporium. The door was shuttered and the windows were soaped to discourage gawkers. The police had fastened a warded Hocking padlock onto the hasp. Luckily, my brother isn't the only one in the family who's handy with a crescent-pick. I gave a cheery whistle and handled my pick as if it were a standard key, hoping that any passers-by would think I belonged there.

I had the lock open in seconds. I stepped inside and pulled the door fast behind me. I hadn't been in the store since the discovery of Mrs. Graff's body, and though I knew her remains had long since been carted away, I could not suppress a shudder as I peered into the back room. No evidence remained of the horrors of the previous evening, apart from a greasy stain on the duck's-egg carpet.

I pushed back through the curtain into the main section of the store. A Minotaur Express Steam-Action Electric Train was set up on a display platform at the center of the room. A heavy black circuit panel sat on the floor below, with thick, cloth-covered wires snaking upward toward the track connector points. I reached down and tripped the swing-lever. The crackle and hum of electricity coursed through the circuits.

A wooden panel with seven control knobs sat at one end of the track. I reached across and turned the knob closest to me.

The black cast-iron locomotive gave a shrill whistle. I turned another knob and the draw bars strained as the train lurched forward. I watched for several minutes as the train made a stately progress around the platform, passing beneath a small trestle bridge and through a miniature town, complete with a station, post office, and water tower. A pricing slip dangled from the control box. I reached over and pulled it up. Seven dollars and fifteen cents. I tried to imagine the life of a boy whose parents could afford such a toy.

I switched off the buzzing electricity and unhooked the black locomotive. I lifted it off the track and copied down the model number. Replacing the car on the track, I went back into Mr. Graff's office.

Josef Graff had been one of the smartest merchants in New York, as he himself had told us only two nights earlier. I knew that he would not have stocked such an expensive item if he did not expect to sell two or three of them, and I also knew that he would have kept a careful record of each transaction. I pulled open the file drawer of his battered old desk and found a green stock folder marked with the name "Minotaur." I pulled it out and spread it on the desk.

I read through the file carefully—sales receipts, stock orders, manufacturer's specifications, the works. Then I read it again to be certain I hadn't missed anything. The specifics were a whole lot more detailed than I expected. When I finished, I gathered up the documents and put them back in the drawer. Minutes later, I was back on the street, the door carefully locked behind me.

It took about twenty minutes to get to Sixty-ninth Street. I breezed through the kitchen, said a quick good morning to my mother and Bess, and headed straight for the back bedroom. "Come on, Harry," I said, shaking him by the shoulder. "Wake up. Let's not sleep our lives away."

"What—? Dash? What are you doing here?"

"Get your pants on, Harry," I said. "I know who killed Branford Wintour."

12

THE MINOTAUR

"AT LEAST TELL ME WHERE WE'RE GOING, DASH," HARRY SAID, AS our cab clattered across Broadway.

"Harry," I returned, "you can't expect me to divulge the particulars. It's traditional that the detective remain tight-lipped until he reaches the scene of the crime."

"But—but the Toy Emporium is in the opposite direction."

"The first crime scene, Harry. I said I knew who killed Branford Wintour."

"Is it not the same man?"

"No, actually. I don't think so, anyway. We'll know soon enough."

"The Wintour mansion," he said, as we rolled to a stop outside. "So, the mystery ends where it began! Tell me, Dash, is Mrs. Wintour the murderer?"

"Harry, let's not—"

"The butler?"

"I—"

"The brother-in-law?"

I smiled and put a finger to my lips. "Not another word, Harry." I climbed down, paid the driver, and made my way up the marble steps. Harry followed a few steps behind.

Phillips, the butler, greeted us with the frigid civility one normally reserves for bill collectors. "I do not believe that Mrs.

Wintour is expecting you, gentlemen," he said, "unless you've come to deliver more of your mother's soup?"

"We're here to see Mr. Crain," I said. "Would you please tell him that we've brought an answer from our mutual friend, Mr. Harrington?"

"So, it *is* the brother-in-law," Harry whispered, as the old butler withdrew down the main corridor. "I knew it all along!"

"It's not the brother-in-law," I said. "I just needed an excuse to get back into Wintour's study. Once we're in, find a reason to send him out of the room."

"But—"

"Just think of something, Harry. You're supposed to be the master of misdirection, aren't you? We need to be alone in the study."

"Very well." Harry furrowed his brow as Phillips returned with Henry Crain at his elbow.

"Gentlemen," said Crain apprehensively. "I hadn't expected to see you again so soon."

"I apologize for the intrusion," I said. "Normally we wouldn't think of appearing unannounced. Do you recall the matter we discussed the other day?"

"I do," said Crain, with a furtive glance toward the butler.

"We have some rather urgent news in that regard. Perhaps we might discuss it in the study?"

"I—yes, I don't see any reason why not. Phillips, I shall be in the study. See that we're not disturbed."

"Very good, sir," the butler said, though his expression indicated a certain irritation over Crain's high-handed behavior.

"Follow me, gentlemen," the young man said, leading us toward the study, "we can have a bit of privacy in here."

"That's very kind of you, sir," I said. "Again, I apologize for the imposition."

I noticed that Crain had now taken possession of his late brother-in-law's key ring, having apparently wrested control away from Dr. Blanton. He unlocked the door and showed us into the room, waving us to a seat in front of the dead man's desk. "Now, then," he said. "I take it your friend Mr. Harrington is interested in purchasing these" —he swept his hand toward the toy collection— "these trinkets?"

"He is, indeed, sir," I said. "Would you be willing to entertain an offer?"

"If the matter can be kept confidential. What sort of offer is Mr. Harrington prepared to make?"

"A very generous one."

"Yes, but exactly how generous?"

"Twenty thousand dollars." *What the hell*, I thought to myself.

Crain's eyes bulged slightly. "Twenty thousand dollars," he repeated. "Yes, I believe we might be able to come to an agreement over that figure. How soon might we be able to make the transaction?"

"Mr. Harrington is eager to proceed immediately, if that would be acceptable."

"Yes. Yes, it would."

During this exchange, Harry rose from his seat and wandered over toward the library table where much of the dead man's toy collection was arrayed. "This is a very interesting item," Harry said, fingering a heavy gold medallion. "What is it, exactly?"

"I'm afraid I couldn't say," Crain answered. "I've never seen it before."

"The image is most unusual. A stallion of some kind? Well, no matter." Harry set it down and picked up a cast-iron penny bank in the shape of a barking dog. "Marvelous," he said, tugging the dog's tail to work its hinged jaws. "Absolutely marvelous."

"To return to the matter at hand," Crain said, "as I have mentioned, I do not wish to upset my sister by involving her in this business. We shall have to proceed carefully."

"Mr. Harrington is the very soul of discretion," I said, wondering how much longer I would have to keep up my end of the conversation. I shot a look at Harry.

"A very impressive collection, Mr. Crain," my brother

said, stepping away from the library table. "You're to be congratulated, sir."

"Why, I—thank you."

"Dash," said Harry, turning to me, "may I have my pills now?"

"Your pills?"

"Don't tell me you've forgotten them?"

"I—"

"Never mind. I'm sure it's nothing. Now then, Mr. Crain, I should like to offer our assistance in the matter of—of—" Harry staggered forward suddenly, his hands flying to his throat.

"Mr. Houdini? Are you all right?"

"I—I'm sure it's nothing—I" —he pulled at his collar— "you must forgive me—I should not have—"

"Mr. Houdini?"

At this, Harry's eyes flickered and rolled back in his head. His shoulders twitched once, then again, as though he were dangling at the end of a fishing line. A faint, croaking sound escaped from his lips as his body went limp. He pitched forward onto the carpet, landing with a heavy thud.

"Harry!" I cried, springing from my chair.

"Is he all right?" Crain crouched down beside me. "What happened?"

I rolled Harry onto his back. His eyes were open and his features were composed in an expression of serene resignation. "M-mustn't blame yourself, Dash," he struggled to say. "Tell Bess—tell her I love her." A cool glaze came over his eyes and his right arm flopped onto the floor in front of Crain.

"My God! Mr. Hardeen, he's not breathing!" Crain snatched up Harry's arm. "There's no pulse!"

"Get a doctor!" I shouted. "Find Dr. Blanton! Hurry!"

Crain leapt to his feet. "I'll be back as quickly as I can!" he cried. He flung the door open and rushed into the foyer, calling loudly for Dr. Blanton.

I stood up and closed the door behind him. Then I lifted a sturdy ladderback chair and wedged it under the door handle.

I walked back and bent over the fallen form of my brother. His eyes were much brighter now, and the tranquil expression had broadened into a gleeful smile.

"Was that really necessary?" I asked.

He stood up and brushed off his clothing. "You wanted him out of the room. He's out of the room."

"Couldn't you have sent him to fetch a newspaper?"

"Where's the drama in fetching a newspaper?"

I had no answer for that. "Come on, Harry, we'd better get to work. He'll be back here with Dr. Blanton any second."

"Don't worry, I can always go back into the act."

"That shouldn't be necessary." I had crossed the room to make a slow circuit of the model train platform. "How did you stop your pulse, by the way?"

"Ah! An old trick of the Indian fakirs." He reached inside his suit coat and withdrew the gold medallion he had been admiring earlier. "This is just the right size and shape. I had it pressed between my ribcage and the inside of my arm. It temporarily cut off the flow of blood to my arm."

"Not bad," I said.

"I wonder if it would fool a trained physician?"

"Let's not find out. Come over here, would you?" I had dropped onto my hands and knees to study the heavy oblong platform upon which the train set rested. "Here's something we missed when we were sniffing around yesterday."

"Those bolts, you mean? I made a note of them. They're simply there to anchor the pedestal to the floor."

"Not exactly, Harry. There's a big difference. I wouldn't have noticed if I hadn't compared this train to the set-up in Mr. Graff's shop. Let me show you something." I stood up and lifted the black locomotive and carriage cars off the train track. "The Minotaur," I said. "Unusual name for a train, don't you think? I'm going to set these cars aside for a minute. Do me a favor—grab that little water tower from the side of the track."

"This one? What do you need—this is odd. It's stuck. It's stuck solid. I can't lift it."

"Try the switching station."

"It's fastened down also. How odd!"

"Try that little horse."

"I can't budge it."

"How about that little row of tulips?"

"Dash, every single item is fixed solidly into place. What's the meaning of this?"

"It means that Mr. Wintour didn't want anything to fall off if the platform changed position suddenly."

"Surely you don't mean—?"

"I certainly do."

We heard a frantic banging at the door. "You in there!" came Crain's voice. "Why is this door closed? I've brought Dr. Blanton! Mr. Hardeen? Let us in, please!"

"We'd better hurry," I said. I loosened the butterfly bolts that appeared to anchor the wooden pedestal to the floor. "I hope I'm right about this, Harry. Come over here and give me a hand."

Harry joined me at the edge of the train platform. "Now push up at this end—put your shoulder into it, Harry! Give it everything you have!"

Harry and I strained and grunted for a moment or two. Then we heard a peculiar creaking noise as the entire platform lifted upward. "Impossible!" Harry cried.

"Not at all. The whole thing—the pedestal, the train set-up, even the tiny little wooden tulips—it's nothing more than the hatch of a giant trap door. No one would ever think of looking for an opening here, because the train set appears too unwieldy to move."

Harry shook his head, his eyes glowing with admiration. "It's astonishing! With the trap door open, the train platform is tilted completely onto its side. But everything stays as it was—the track, the water tower, the horse—everything! It's the perfect camouflage!"

"And when the trap door drops back into place, you'd never know that anything had ever been disturbed." I reached out to touch the tiny figure of a station master, who now stood in a horizontal stance as though walking up a sheer wall.

Harry peered into the opening in the floor. A crude wooden ladder led down into a deep black chasm. We couldn't see the bottom. "It's enormous! The hole must be six feet square! Where does it go? Why would anyone build such a thing?"

The banging at the doors was getting louder. The ladderback chair I had wedged in place began to give way. "Grab that lantern off the desk," I said. "We're going down there."

"But—what's down there?"

"Something you won't believe. Something that will make the Blois collection look like a Delmarvelo Magic Set."

"But—"

"Hurry up, Harry. I want to be out of here before Crain and Blanton burst in."

Harry darted to Wintour's desk and snatched up a large oil lamp. "Move, Harry! Down the ladder!" He sprang onto the top rung and made his way downward into the blackness. I grabbed a circular ring on the inside of the open hatch and followed him down, pulling the trap door shut behind us. I heard the doors of the study burst open just as the hatch dropped into place.

Harry and I stayed motionless for several moments, clinging to the top of the ladder as our eyes adjusted to the gloom. To our surprise, we could still hear muffled noise and movement from Wintour's study, even though the sturdy trap door was sealed in place. Above our heads, tiny pinpricks of illumination showed through the windows and doors of the model train station, admitting sound and light.

"Mr. Hardeen? Mr. Houdini?" Henry Crain's voice reached us as if from a great distance, though he must have been standing no more than ten feet away. "Where are you?"

"Where could they have gone?" came Dr. Blanton's voice.

"Phillips? Did you see them go out?"

"No, sir," said the butler.

"They couldn't have left," Crain said with considerable exasperation. "The door was jammed shut from the inside!"

"Perhaps we should ring for the police," said the doctor. "This is the most extraordinary thing since—"

"Yes," agreed Crain. "I'll ring for the police."

I nudged Harry's shoulder with my foot and signalled him to continue downward. We descended cautiously, our progress illuminated only by the feeble glow of the oil desk lamp. Neither one of us spoke until we had descended some twenty feet.

"So this is how the murderer got in and out," Harry said in a hushed voice, his eyes fixed on the blackness stretching below us.

"Apparently," I said.

"But this hole is immense! Who built it? And why?"

"Obviously Mr. Wintour built it himself. As to why, if my guess is correct, we'll know soon enough. Can you tell how much further down we have to go?"

Harry fished a coin from his pocket and let it drop into the blackness. We heard it clatter against something metal. "Not much more," he said. "Dash?"

"Yes, Harry?"

"You've changed your mind about who killed Mr. Wintour, haven't you? You don't think Evan Harrington did it, do you?"

"Fred Gittles, you mean? I think he's in it up to his eyes. But Jake Stein told us that there were two killers at work, and I guess the old man knew what he was talking about." My hands flailed in the dark for a moment as I nearly lost my grip on one of the rungs. "Fred Gittles never met Branford Wintour in his life. Wintour was killed by someone he knew. And whoever that man was, he's the one who hired Gittles to kill Josef and Frieda Graff."

"But who? Who killed Mr. Wintour? I can't have been— Dash! I'm at the bottom! What's down here? This lamp is practically worthless! I can't see anything!"

I let go of the ladder as my foot touched dirt flooring. "Stick close, Harry. If we get lost down here we may never find our way out. Perhaps our eyes will adjust in a moment or—"

I saw a brilliant flare of light as something hard slammed against the back of my head. I felt myself fall, but I don't recall landing.

I don't know how much time passed. I regained consciousness by slow degrees, gradually becoming aware of a vast, dark cavern lit by tall oil torches. Harry lay motionless in the shadows a few feet behind me, and it was only when I saw his restraints—he was wrapped in a virtual cocoon of metal chains and leather straps—that I realized that I was also completely trammelled. I tried to move my hands, but there was no slack. Cold metal bit into my arms with even the slightest movement. "Harry?" I called.

"Your brother isn't awake yet," said a voice from behind me. "I hear he's clever at getting out of things. That's not much use unless he's conscious, is it?"

"Who—?" I rolled over towards the sound.

"Nice to see you again, Mr. Hardeen," said Michael Hendricks. "And welcome to the Fifth Avenue subway station!"

~ 13 ~

BURIED ALIVE

"HARRY?" I SAID AGAIN.

"I believe your brother may be dead," said Mr. Hendricks, as if remarking on a sudden change of weather. "My associate seems to have hit him rather hard. I don't know that you've met Mr. Gittles, have you?" He indicated a short, powerfully built man standing behind him. "I expect you knew him as Harrington."

My face was pressed against a clod of hard earth. I strained to lift my head, but the movement sent a jolt of pain down my arms. Harry didn't seem to be moving at all. Behind him, I could see a tall stack of wooden packing cases, along with digging tools, haulage carts, and building materials. "What is this place?" I asked.

"I told you. The Fifth Avenue subway station. Or it will be, at any rate. We're going to build New York City's first underground public transportation system. See to Mr. Houdini, will you, Mr. Gittles?"

Gittles stepped forward and nudged Harry with his foot. When Harry didn't move, Gittles rolled him into a shallow trench behind one of the torches. Gittles moved toward me, waiting for Hendricks to give the next order.

"You're going to put omnibuses down here?" I asked, stalling for time.

"No, Mr. Hardeen. Trains. Big, beautiful Minotaur trains, all built by Daedalus Incorporated. That train in my study is no toy. It's a scale model of the first Minotaur underground train."

"You're going to build a full-size train and put it underground?"

"Don't play stupid, Mr. Hardeen. You're not as convincing as your brother. I know perfectly well that you've been nosing around. Mr. Gittles has been watching you day and night. When did you figure it out? When you were going through old Josef's files?"

I tried to shift position, hoping my head would clear. Tugging at my arms brought more pain, but no slack whatever. I was wrapped like a mummy. I doubted if even Harry could escape from these chains, assuming he was still alive. I squirmed onto my side, straining for a better view.

"Well, Mr. Hardeen?" Hendricks shined a lantern into my eyes.

I figured I'd better keep talking. "Sand," I said.

"Come again?" Hendricks took a step closer.

"You wrote up an order for sand. For the fire buckets. What sort of model train has real sand in the fire buckets?"

Hendricks considered the question. "Train enthusiasts have a great appreciation for that sort of detail, Mr. Hardeen. You know that perfectly well. We could have been planning to put real sand in the fire buckets."

"Half a ton of it?"

He gave out a barking laugh. "Very good! I'm surprised Josef never noticed!"

"He didn't know, then? About the underground train?"

"Josef? No, we let him think we were trying to take over the model train market. Of course we swore him to secrecy. Bran told him that our competitors were trying to steal our ideas, and that it would all go to pieces if he breathed a word of what we were doing."

"But it doesn't make sense! No toy train design would ever work on a real railroad! You can't have expected that it would haul passengers!"

"Of course not, Mr. Hardeen. The design is worthless. There is no train. But there soon will be."

"I don't understand."

Hendricks sat down on a wooden shipping crate. "It's very simple," he said. "Three weeks from tomorrow, Senator Platt is going to haul his lying, cheating politician's hide in front of the city control board and announce that he's taking bids for the development of the New York Underground Transportation Foundation. It's been an open secret for months now, ever since Boston got its system running. New York can't be second to Boston, so our trains will have to be even bigger and better. Platt has all the support he needs; he even has Tammany Hall behind him. But, of course, Boss Platt being what he is, he's already grooming one of his cronies for the job, complete with a hefty gratuity for himself. So what's an honest businessman to do?"

While Hendricks spoke, I could hear a faint rattling and clinking of chains behind me. *Harry*, I thought to myself. *He's alive and he's trying to escape.* I tugged again at my own restraints. Even Harry wouldn't be able to shake this metal cocoon easily. I figured he'd have a better chance if I could keep Hendricks talking. "I don't understand," I said. "If Senator Platt already has one of his own pals lined up, what's the point of all this?"

Hendricks stood up and swept his arm through the shadowy cavern. "I simply decided to start without him," he said. "As soon as the project is announced, I'm going to go before the press and tell them that my company, Daedalus Incorporated, has already launched construction of the underground railway, at a savings to the New York taxpayer of one million dollars."

"But this isn't any underground railway!"

"No? I have a working model of the Minotaur Express. I have a detailed blueprint of the entire rail network. I have all the necessary permits and documents. Once the press boys are done with him, Platt will have no choice but to award the contract to me."

"But your train is no good!" I cried.

"Yes, that's quite true. But by the time anyone realizes that, the contract will be all signed and sealed."

"You mean it's a con? A bait and switch?"

"Not at all, Mr. Hardeen. It's business. This project will generate millions and millions of dollars. My job is to get the license to build the train by any means necessary. Once I have the contract, they'd never dare to take it away from me. Platt and his minions will have too much political capital invested in our success. And if my initial projections won't quite hold water, and if I can't quite deliver on my original promises, that's simply politics as usual in this city."

The clanking noises from behind me were getting louder. I knew I had to keep him talking. "If you already have your phony model and plans, why did you bother to dig a tunnel?"

"That's the beauty of it, Mr. Hardeen. I didn't have to dig the tunnel. Bran did it for me. He had it done when he built the house. It's a brigand's entrance he ordered for his own amusement—doesn't run any farther than the stables out back. Only he and I knew about it."

"I don't follow you. If this is just a secret tunnel of some kind, what are all those packing crates and building materials doing here?"

"I would think that you'd be able to guess, young man. This is a stage set—a piece of elaborate scenery. I've dressed up the tunnel with a hundred feet of track, several crates of machine parts and a whole battery of work lights. It looks for all the world as if the diligent work crews of Daedalus Incorporated have been digging around the clock. And that's exactly what I'll tell all the city officials and journalists I'll be bringing down here. Why start digging on Broadway when we've already broken ground right here under Fifth Avenue?"

The rattling sounds increased sharply, though neither Hendricks nor Gittles appeared to notice. *Harry, pipe down*, I thought to myself. "But why did you kill Mr. Wintour? Surely he was in it from the beginning? The tunnel was on his property, and it must have been his idea to conceal the trap door with that train platform. The two of you were partners the whole time."

Hendricks mumbled something I didn't hear.

"I'm sorry?" I said, raising my voice to cover the sounds of Harry's struggle. "I didn't catch that."

"The Minotaur train was my idea," Hendricks said. "The planning, the timing, the execution. I worked out every last detail. But it was Bran's money. And so long as Bran was bankrolling the project, he dictated the terms. Eighty per cent of all future earnings were to go to him. Twenty for me. I was to be little more than an employee. Two years ago, before I lost my money, it would have been me in control of the operation. Now…" His voice trailed off, making the sounds of Harry's movements all the more conspicuous.

"That's it? You killed him for the money?"

"What else? I'm sorry if that disappoints you, Mr. Hardeen, but I'm hardly the first man who ever killed for money! Do you have any idea what sort of fortune is at stake here? Tens of millions! I'm going to make Rockefeller look like a rag-and-bone man! Good Lord, you and your brother were prepared to believe that Bran had been killed over a silly little Japanese toy! You can have your automatons, Mr. Hardeen. Me, I'll settle for becoming the richest man in New York."

"But why lay the blame on Mr. Graff? He didn't even know what you were planning!"

"Why?" Hendricks's voice rose to an angry pitch. "Because Bran saw fit to give him a three per cent share in Daedalus! And without so much as consulting me! All that man did was design the model—nothing more! I daresay you could have done it just as well yourself, Mr. Hardeen, and I doubt if you would have expected to be compensated with stock shares worth hundreds of thousands of dollars! And do you suppose this beneficence came out of Bran's share of the earnings? I assure you it did not. Bran was giving away my money hand over fist."

"I don't understand how you expected to get away with that.

Sooner or later Mr. Graff would have told the police about the secret dealings he had with you and Mr. Wintour. That would have brought the police right to your doorstep."

"Eventually, yes," Hendricks agreed. "But I sent him a message after his arrest. An expression of sympathy and concern, if you will. I told him to keep quiet about Daedalus—told him that our lawyers were working on his release, but that we couldn't risk tipping our hand on the very eve of our great triumph. He was happy enough to keep his mouth shut, especially when I told him I'd be needing a right-hand man—now that Bran was gone."

"Then you sent Mr. Gittles for him. For both of them."

"Yes. He handled it very cleverly, I thought."

"Was Mr. Gittles also responsible for the dart in Branford Wintour's neck?"

"No, Mr. Hardeen. I had to handle that myself. It wasn't difficult. Bran and I often used the tunnel to hide my comings and goings. It wouldn't have done for me to use the front door, not after what happened between him and my daughter. But he was a practical man, and so am I. The business relationship continued as before. I knew that Josef would leave *Le Fantôme* in Bran's study that afternoon. I scheduled a meeting with him shortly afterward. Bran couldn't wait to show off his prize. He started chattering away as soon as I came up through the tunnel. He had no way of knowing, of course, that I was the one who had engineered the sale in the first place, once I'd learned of *Le Fantôme*'s existence. Bran was positively thrilled. He jabbered on and on, showing me all the gears and weights, waxing rhapsodic about his hopes of acquiring the entire Blois collection. It was a simple matter to press the dart into his neck. He made a horrible noise as the poison did its work, but it was over quickly—thank God. It's a difficult thing to watch a friend die, Mr. Hardeen, no matter what the reason. That's why I'm sorry you had to get involved in all of this. You seem to be a bright young man. I could have used your help on the Minotaur. Can't be helped,

I'm afraid." He stepped forward and said something to Gittles, who gave a tight little nod.

"Well, goodbye, Mr. Hardeen," Hendricks said. "I'll take my leave now. I very much enjoyed your company the other day, and I'd prefer not to be here for this unpleasantness. As I said, it's a difficult thing to watch a friend die."

Hendricks turned and made his way down the tunnel, away from the ladder leading up to Branford Wintour's study. Gittles waited until the flickering light from the older man's lamp had receded. Then he turned to me and shook his head sadly. He stepped forward, reaching beneath his coat as he came. A long blade glinted in the torchlight. Crouching over me, Gittles spoke the first words I ever heard him say. "Nothing personal," he said. With that, he raised the blade high over his head.

That's when Harry returned from the dead. I heard him before I ever saw him. He sprang from the shadows with a wild cry, chains and straps hanging from his limbs, and plowed his head into Gittles's mid-section. The two men fell in a heap, rolling away from me into a pool of torchlight.

I pulled furiously at my constraints, desperate to get into the fight as Harry and Gittles got to their feet, warily circling one another. Gittles lashed out with the knife, but Harry jumped back and countered by swinging a length of chain at his attacker's head. Gittles let out a howl as the chain raked across his face, then made another thrust. Harry managed to ward off the blow with another swipe of the chain, and Gittles jumped back, readying for another thrust.

I could feel blood dripping down my arms as the restraints tore into my wrists. I tugged harder, blocking out the shock of pain that came with each movement. I now had a slight range of motion in my right arm—the chains were oiled with my blood—but every motion threatened to strip the flesh from my bones. I bit my lip and kept working.

Gittles lunged twice, slashing at Harry's eyes. My brother managed to parry, but lost his footing as he backed over a section of train track. Harry crashed to the ground, chains clattering off the metal track railings. Gittles vaulted forward, raising his knife for another plunge. Harry rolled onto his side, aiming a powerful kick at his opponent's knee. Gittles gave another shriek of pain and staggered backward into one of the work torches, which came crashing down onto his head. My brother leapt to his feet as the other man dropped the knife and frantically wiped oil and glass away from his eyes. Harry moved in for the kill, landing a solid right to the jaw and following it with a pair of vicious kidney punches. Gittles dropped to one knee, his face and hands still dripping with oil from the lamp. Harry cocked his arm. "Nothing personal," he said. Gittles tried to get his hands up but it was too late. Harry went over the top with a crushing straight, followed by a roundhouse that had his entire weight behind it. Gittles's head snapped back and his eyes swam. He went down hard and didn't move.

"Dash? Are you all right?"

"I'm fine. I just can't quite seem to shake these straps."

"Hold still. This won't take long." Harry opened his leather wallet and fished out a pick. "Hold still, I said." He worked at a small padlock that cinched a length of chain around my ankles. "You should be ashamed of yourself, Dash."

"Look, Harry, you're a better escape artist than I am. I admit it."

"That's not what I meant. For three days you insisted that we run to Lieutenant Murray every time we so much as drew a breath. But what did you do when you figured out the murderer's identity? You decided to apprehend him yourself. 'The police take a dim view of citizens who make arrests.' Wasn't that what you said to me?" The lock snapped open and Harry began unwinding the chains from my legs. "You're a fine one to talk, Dash."

"I couldn't be sure I was right," I said. "The whole thing seemed too outlandish. And I certainly hadn't anticipated that we'd find Hendricks in the tunnel—much less that Gittles would be with him. I—Harry! Behind you!"

I saw a glint of steel and a rush of movement from the shadows. Fred Gittles, knife raised high, sprang towards us.

"Harry!"

My brother turned and instinctively raised his hands. The blade sank into his forearm. Harry gave a strangled cry and drew back, a jet of blood soaking through his sleeve. I struggled to my feet, my hands still pinned behind my back. Harry clutched at his wound, leaving himself wide open to attack. Gittles reared up for another thrust.

I had one chance. I lowered my shoulder and drove it into Gittles's stomach, driving him back across the cavern. I heard the knife fall from his hands as the air rushed from his lungs, but he recovered quickly. He straightened up and tagged me with two hard jabs to the nose. With my arms strapped behind me, I had no way of defending myself. Gittles hammered me with a straight to the jaw. I staggered backward, but stayed on my feet.

He kept coming, snatching up a length of wooden planking from the ground. Harry was back on his feet now, but Gittles sent him sprawling with a hard smack across the forehead. He turned to me and hefted the plank like a baseball bat, readying for another swing.

It turned out to be a mistake. The edge of the plank caught the oil lamp we'd brought down from Mr. Wintour's desk. The glass globe shattered instantly, sending a shower of flame onto Gittles's oil-soaked clothing. His coat lit up like matchwood, with streaks of flame spreading quickly across his arms and legs. I watched helplessly as he flailed and thrashed, his screams filling the vast cavern.

Harry was there in an instant, knocking Gittles to the ground and slapping at the flames with his coat. A horrible, sickly smell filled the air as Harry tried to smother the fire, but his coat soon burst into flame. "Hold still!" Harry shouted. "Stop struggling!" He jumped up and grabbed a metal spade, desperately scooping up loose dirt and shoveling it onto the burning man. After a moment or two of furious labor, the last of the flames was extinguished.

Harry knelt down and brushed away a layer of dirt from what was left of Fred Gittles's face. It was a terrible sight, a patchwork of wet blisters and dark, cracked flaps of charred skin. A tortured, croaking sound escaped from the injured man's lips. "Thank you," he said. His head slumped to the side.

Harry said nothing as he released my hands from the remaining straps. Together we carried Fred Gittles down the tunnel to the wooden ladder. I went up first, working the metal ring to open the trap door as Harry followed behind with the injured man over his shoulder. In Branford Wintour's study, we found that Dr. Blanton and Henry Crain had been joined by Lieutenant Murray and a pair of uniformed patrolmen.

"What the hell—" Lieutenant Murray began at the sight of us emerging from the trap door. "What in God's—?"

"Dr. Blanton," I said. "This man is badly burned. He needs a hospital."

"What's happened?" the doctor cried. "What's going on here?"

I turned away from him. "Lieutenant," I said, "we need to get to the home of Michael Hendricks. Now."

"Hardeen, what's—?" He looked at my face and saw something there that made him stop. He turned to the uniformed officers. "Take the doc and get that man to a hospital," he said. "Hardeen, you and your brother come with me."

He led us outside to a waiting police wagon. Harry and I climbed in back while the lieutenant gave orders to the driver. As the wagon lurched forward, Lieutenant Murray dropped onto the seat opposite us. "You're sure you don't want the doctor first?"

I looked at Harry. He was filthy, his clothing was in shreds, there were streaks of black soot across his face, and he was clutching a bleeding wound on his forearm. I don't suppose I looked much better.

"Harry?" I said. He just shook his head.

No one spoke until we drew up in front of the Hendricks place. I reached back to help Harry down out of the wagon. "I'm fine, Dash," he said, shrugging off my hand. "Don't fuss over me."

We hurried up the front path and hammered at the door. Lieutenant Murray pushed past the butler and led us down the hall, throwing open the doors to the study without even breaking stride.

I don't know what I expected. Hendricks, sitting behind his desk, did not seem at all surprised to see that Harry and I were still alive. An expression of sadness and resignation washed over his face. He nodded at the lieutenant and set down the pen he had been holding. Pushing back his desk chair, he stood up and turned toward the bay window.

Harry saw it before I did. "Dash!" he shouted. "He has a pistol!"

Lieutenant Murray threw us both to the floor, shielding us with his body. His hand went to his belt, reaching for his own revolver. The gun hadn't even cleared its holster when we heard the shot.

Michael Hendricks slumped to the floor, a ghastly splash of red on the window behind him. I stumbled to the edge of the desk, feeling a wave of burning gorge rise in my throat. "It's finished, Dash," Harry said. "There's nothing more you could have done." I looked down at the body on the carpet and remembered what Hendricks had told me in the tunnel.

It's a difficult thing to watch a friend die—no matter what the reason.

14

THE JUSTLY-CELEBRATED
SELF-LIBERATOR

"YOU KNOW, HOUDINI," SAID LIEUTENANT MURRAY, "YOU'VE already received the citizen's commendation medal and a special proclamation from the mayor. That would be enough for most people."

"I am not like most people," my brother said.

The lieutenant nodded in vigorous agreement. "Yes," he said, "I guess we can agree on that."

Five days had passed. In that time, much had changed in our lives. The death of Michael Hendricks had set a remarkable series of events in motion, culminating in a four-hour emergency conference at the mansion of Mr. William Russell Grace, the former mayor. The governor, half a dozen state representatives, and the exalted Thomas Collier Platt were also in attendance, and a more grave and earnest assembly could hardly be imagined.

Harry and I were not included in this august gathering. Instead, we had been summoned to the Grace mansion and installed in a palatial antechamber to await the outcome of the deliberations. Lieutenant Murray was sequestered with us, and he spent the long vigil with a comically dainty tea cup clutched in his meaty paws, staring quizzically at a mysterious array of tiny bread wedges adorned with cucumber.

"You know," the lieutenant informed us, "they're in there cooking up a giant fish story. They won't let Michael Hendricks be the villain of this piece. Wouldn't look right. Wait and see."

"But Mr. Hendricks *was* the villain," Harry insisted, pinching one of the cucumber parcels between his thumb and forefinger. "I regret that he felt compelled to take his own life, but that is hardly an expiation for his sins."

"They'll make Gittles the villain," Lieutenant Murray said. "It's the only way Hendricks gets to keep his reputation."

"Seems to me there's more than enough guilt for both of them," I said. "How's Gittles doing, anyway?"

"Not so good. He may live; he may die. Once these fellows are done with him, he may prefer the latter. How are you two doing? You both went through the meat grinder back there."

"We are recovering nicely, thank you," said Harry. "Apart from the cut on my arm, I am feeling very little pain." He fingered the heavy bandages on his forearm. "The doctor tells me I was fortunate that the blade did not do more damage."

"You *were* lucky," Lieutenant Murray agreed. "Both of you. You could just as easily have been killed. That was a hell of a foolish stunt you pulled."

Harry and I didn't bother trying to defend our actions. The lieutenant's reproaches had been mild compared to those of Bess, who had unleashed a blast of white hot fury when we finally straggled home after our adventure in the tunnel. The anger soon gave way to hysteria, followed by a long period of moody silence. It would be some days before the atmosphere returned to normal on Sixty-ninth Street.

For me, the five days since Michael Hendricks's death had been a time of moody introspection. I had spent many long hours alone with my thoughts, either sitting in my room or taking long walks through the city. One of these walks found me standing outside the Hendricks mansion, where, on a sudden impulse, I decided to call in and pay my respects. I cannot say what I hoped to gain by this gesture. Perhaps I sought to ease my conscience. Perhaps I sought solace of a different kind. Katherine Hendricks had received me in a small drawing room on the ground floor, her lovely eyes ringed with heavy shadows. I offered a few clumsy words of condolence, then passed over the packet of letters I had retrieved from Branford Wintour's study. She accepted them without a word, and I turned to take my leave.

"Mr. Hardeen," she said quietly, as I paused with my hand upon the doorknob.

"Yes?"

"He was quite taken with you. My father."

"You are kind to say so."

"He told me as much. 'One need not be an English lord to cut a path in this world.' That was how he phrased it."

I said nothing. My throat had grown very tight.

"Of course, my own prospects are much changed now," she said evenly. "Much changed."

I nodded.

"Lord Wycliffe and I must wait a decent interval, of course. We shall make the announcement next spring, I should think."

My hand felt quite hot on the doorknob. "I wish you every happiness," I said. "I'll show myself out."

My last sight of her, as I closed the door behind me, saw her tossing the packet of letters onto the fire.

"Dash?" said Harry, recalling me to the present. "I believe the lieutenant asked you a question."

"I'm sorry?" I said, turning away from the window. "I was thinking of something else, I'm afraid."

"Never mind," Lieutenant Murray said. "Not important."

"He's been like this for days," Harry told the lieutenant. "Bess thinks he hit his head."

"My head is fine," I said. I gestured toward the closed doors where the council of city elders was taking place. "Can they really expect to hush the entire matter up?" I wondered. "You realize, Lieutenant, that my brother has never been one to suppress his own exploits."

"The public would be most interested—" Harry began.

"Tell me, Houdini," said the lieutenant. "Are your citizenship papers in order?"

The color drained from Harry's cheeks. "Don't be absurd!" he cried. "I'm as American as you are! I was born in Appleton, Wisconsin!"

"You're sure it wasn't Budapest?" He set down his tea cup as carefully as if it had been a hatching chick. "Look, Houdini, I don't give a tinker's damn whether you were born in Wisconsin or in Hungary or on the planet Jupiter. I'm just warning you. That's what they're going to use to keep you quiet." He sighed and looked at the closed doors. "These men always manage to get their way."

Matters developed much as the lieutenant had predicted. When the city worthies emerged from behind the closed doors, Harry and I were informed that certain information would be withheld from the general public so as to spare the Hendricks family any further distress. "I think poor Mrs. Hendricks has borne enough sorrow, don't you, gentlemen?" asked Mr. Grace. "Better for everyone if we keep this business to ourselves, wouldn't you agree?"

When it was clear that the Brothers Houdini were not prepared to argue, a climate of merry good fellowship prevailed—complete with whiskey and cigars and a series of ribald jokes from Mr. Platt. By the time the whiskey decanter had been drained and refilled three times, the company had grown extremely jovial indeed. I was enjoying a rubber of whist with a pair of aldermen and the junior senator when I happened to spy Harry across the smoke-filled room, deep in conversation with Mr. Grace. "That's the strangest request I've ever received, Mr. Houdini," I heard him say. "People usually want my help going the other way!" He clapped his arm across my brother's shoulders. "Let me see what I can fix up."

And so it came to pass that Harry got himself locked up in

the Sing-Sing State Prison after all, while a retinue of journalists awaited news of his success or failure in the warden's office. It was arranged that I should join him in this adventure as well, so that I might share in the expected publicity windfall. Now, locked away in separate cells facing one another across a gloomy expanse of prison corridor, I found myself regretting my decision to participate. First of all, I had not realized that I would be obliged to submit to the most rigorous and degrading medical body search that one could possibly imagine. Also, Harry and I were both stark naked. The guards had taken away all of our clothing, to forestall any possibility that we had tools concealed in them.

"Harry," I called, "can you hear me?" I leaned against the cell door and then quickly recoiled. The bars were freezing cold.

"Of course I can hear you, Dash."

"What are we doing here? You never did manage to break out of the lock-up at the precinct house. What makes you think you'll have any better luck here at Sing-Sing?"

"Call it a hunch," he answered. "I saw an opportunity and I seized it. We couldn't possibly ask for a better advertisement! Did you see how many newspapermen there were out there? Our names will be in every paper in town!"

"*Madman and Brother Locked Away at Own Request,*" I said, imagining the headline my friend Biggs was likely to supply. "*Best For All Concerned, Says Governor.*" I sat down on the metal bunk in my cell. "Good Lord, that's cold!" I cried, jumping up again. "Did they have to take away our clothing?"

"I'm afraid I insisted on it. I thought it would make our triumph more dramatic."

"But Harry, I don't see how you can possibly have concealed the lock-pick and reaching tool."

"I didn't."

"Pardon?"

"I don't have a lock-pick. I don't have a reaching tool."

I stepped to the door and gripped the bars. "Harry—"

"I learned a great deal down there in that tunnel beneath Mr. Wintour's house," Harry said. "I learned a great deal about treachery and deceit, and about what makes a man brave and what makes him foolish. I suppose Bess was right all along. I'm no hero, Dash. Josef and Frieda Graff are dead, and the world is no better for their passing. We might just as well have stayed at the dime museum."

"Harry, you know that's not—"

"There's one other thing I learned, Dash. I learned that appearances count for a great deal—perhaps more than the truth itself. Mr. Hendricks hoped to win a fortune by making it appear that he had done something he had not. I intend to do the same."

"What?"

"For weeks now I have been concentrating all my energy on how to escape from these cells. This was foolish. All that matters is to make it *appear* that I have escaped from the cell. I have Mr. Hendricks to thank for this."

"I'm not following you, Harry. This is no stage set. We're locked in a pair of cells at Sing-Sing. Either we escape or we don't. There's no room for window dressing."

"We're not locked in," said Harry.

"We're not?"

"No."

"Gee, Harry. These bars look pretty solid, and that lock seems awfully secure. Unless you're planning to bribe one of the guards, I really don't see how—"

"I would never bribe the guards. That would be dishonest."

"Then how do you propose to get out of here? You have no lock-pick, and even if you did, the lock is all the way down at the end of the corridor!"

"Do you remember when we used to play round robin, Dash? When we were boys in Appleton?"

"Harry, let me call the guard. You're clearly not yourself."

"Do you remember all those long afternoons I spent

throwing a ball against the side of our house? Throwing and catching, for hours and hours at a time?"

"Of course, Harry, but—"

I heard a ragged, coughing sound from Harry's cell. His hands went to his mouth.

"What do you have there, Harry?"

"An India rubber ball. I swallowed it forty minutes ago."

"Harry, what in God's name—?"

"Watch this, Dash." He leaned against the door of his cell and let his arms dangle through the bars. I could just see the little rubber ball clutched in his right hand.

"You see the lock?"

"Of course."

"How far away do you suppose it is?"

"I don't know. Ten feet?"

"Eleven and three-quarters. Keep your eyes on the lock, Dash." Harry drew his right hand back and sailed the rubber ball at the opposite wall. I heard a faint thudding noise as the ball bounced against the brick, caromed off the floor, and struck the metal padlock squarely in the middle. To my astonishment, the heavy padlock instantly popped open and dropped to the floor with a noisy clatter.

"Harry—how—?"

"It was never locked, Dash. When I asked the warden to let me examine it, I stuffed a packet of cotton wadding down into the opening. It was sufficient to hold the shackle-bar in place, but it prevented the lock mechanism from engaging. The padlock was never properly fastened. We were never truly locked in."

I stared at the open lock on the floor between us. "That's absolutely brilliant," I said. "Why didn't I think of it?"

"Because, Dash," said Harry, pulling open the door of his cell, "you have no imagination."

THE HARRY HOUDINI MYSTERIES

THE FLOATING LADY MURDER

DANIEL STASHOWER

TITAN BOOKS

1

OH, YOU WONDER!

AGAIN, THE DREAM.

A dark curtain lifted and he saw his brother, blue and lifeless, hanging upside down in the Chinese Water Torture Cell. Harry was bobbing gently in the grayish water, his hair pulsing like seaweed, his arms folded across his chest as though settled snugly into a coffin. He could see every detail. The dark mahogany and nickel-plated steel of the cabinet. The thick glass panels. The tiny clusters of air bubbles clinging to his brother's nose and lips. He could even hear the ominous strains of music rising from the orchestra pit. "Asleep in the Deep."

He would take a step closer, then, as the music started, and stretch out a hand as if to touch his brother's face. A terrible urgency would grip him as he knelt beside the front panel, peering through the clouded glass. Already he could hear the voices calling from behind, pulling him away.

A moment longer. That was all he required. In another moment, surely, his brother would open his eyes and give a sly wink. The blue-tinged lips would break into a smile as a stream of air escaped. Another moment. Just one more moment…

And then the ringing of the alarm. The dream always ended this way, leaving him confused and doleful. Perhaps next time, he thought.

The old man swung his legs over the side of the bed and

padded to a wash stand in the corner, trying to dispel the foggy residue of gloom. He chided himself as he made his way down the hall to bathe, and by the time he returned to his room to dress he began to feel better. Why did he let it trouble him so? He glanced at the calendar. That was it, he told himself. It seemed impossible, but another year had passed. He hoped that perhaps this year the anniversary might pass quietly. He sat down and began polishing his black wing-tips, just in case.

He had finished brushing his jacket and was considering a damp press for his collar when he heard the front door chime. He parted the curtains and peered down at the front stoop. A reporter. No mistaking it. The old man had known plenty of reporters in his time, and he recognized the type. Slouch hat, pencil behind the ear, well-thumbed note pad. In fact, it appeared to be the same man who had come out the previous year. What was his name? Matthews, was it? Yes, Matthews. Call me Jack. He'd brought another photographer with him, too.

He heard the chime again and listened for the sound of Mrs. Doggett's footsteps galumphing through from the kitchen. Mrs. Doggett kept a clean house and did not much care for this annual intrusion of cigarette-smoking newspapermen from the city. She would show Matthews and the photographer to the parlor with pursed lips and a furrowed brow. A moment later she would return with a tray of tea and Keepa cakes, clucking all the while.

The old man hurriedly fastened his collar and knotted his filetto silk tie, regarding himself in the hall mirror. He had selected his best coat—merino wool in a crow's foot pattern—but now he wondered if it might be showing a bit of wear. Were the pockets sagging? Were the shoulders riding a bit high? He ran a hand through his hair and centered his Windsor knot. He knew, at his age, that time spent preening was time wasted. Might as well go downstairs in his robe and slippers. Still, he had standards to maintain. In the old days, they called him "Dash."

The old man studied his reflection and wondered if there

would be time to go down the hall and splash on a bit of Lendell's toilet water. No, he thought, probably not. Already he could hear Mrs. Doggett coming to the foot of the stairs, calling up to him about the visitors in the parlor. He frowned over his cuffs and picked at a loose thread on his elbow. Ah, well. The show must go on.

They came every year, these reporters, on the anniversary of his brother's death. Just once he wished they might spare a question or two about his own career. Say, Mr. Hardeen, you were quite a celebrated performer yourself in those days, weren't you? You had a record-breaking run at the London Palladium, isn't that right? But no, it would be the same old shibboleth: Tell us about your brother, Mr. Hardeen. Tell us about Houdini.

The old man paused with his hand on the bannister and wondered what he would tell them this year. He had long since exhausted his supply of boyhood anecdotes— though "Ehrich of the Air" was always good for half a column or so. My brother would hang upside down from a makeshift trapeze in our yard, and he would pick up needles with his eyelashes! That one was a complete fabrication, but the reporters seemed to like it. Or maybe he could trot out that perennial favorite about the Belle Island Bridge leap in Detroit. The river had frozen over, but my brother refused to cancel the stunt. "But Harry!" I cried. "How are you going to do an underwater escape when the river is frozen over?" "That's simple," he replied, "we'll chop a hole in the ice…"

No, not this year. That one was beginning to wear a bit thin. Wasn't true, in any case. Not a word of it. Harry started putting that one about in 1906. Funny how things catch on.

The Floating Lady, perhaps. That one might be good for a column or two. Incredible story, really, if he decided to tell all of it. Certainly they would be familiar with the illusion. Was there anyone left in the world who hadn't seen the Floating Lady by now? They call it different names—Asrah, Levitation, Lighter Than Air—but the effect is always the same. A female assistant is placed under "hypnosis" and then made to float in mid-air. These days, of course, it's thought to be a bit old hat. Decades of endless repetition on the stage has robbed the effect of its power. They've even started to do it on television, where everything always looks like a cheap sideshow. But it was different back then, back when the Floating Lady was a prize worth having. That one effect in a magician's repertoire could guarantee years of work on the Orpheum or the Keith circuit. It could make a man's fortune.

See how she floats, as though on a gentle zephyr, borne aloft by the hypnotic force of animal magnetism. Please don't make a sound, ladies and gentlemen, for the slightest disturbance may break the spell...

The old man stopped outside the parlor door. But would he tell all of it? Would he tell them about Kellar? About the enchanting Francesca Moore? About Servais Le Roy and that astonishing hoop skirt? He hesitated, smoothing his lapels while he tried to arrange the details in his mind. Yes, he told himself, it could work. Besides, who would be harmed if he told the story now, after so many years? All he needed was a hook—a snappy curtain-raiser to catch their attention and hold it. He frowned over the loose thread at his elbow. Ah. Certainly. Very well, then.

You see, young man, Harry and I were present when that famous illusion was created. Oh, yes. No one has ever heard this story before, because it had a rather tragic outcome, I'm afraid. The first time it was performed—the first lady ever to float in mid-air—well, she died. The trick killed her. How? Well, that's a very strange thing.

And here the Great Hardeen would allow himself a dramatic pause. You see, young man, she drowned.

The old man smiled, squared his shoulders, and stepped forward to greet his interviewer.

I'm sorry, Mr. Matthews? Yes, that's what I said. She drowned. Yes. While doing the trick. While floating. Yes. In mid-air.

Pardon? You'd like to hear about it? Well, it's rather a long story, and you seemed so interested in that Belle Island Bridge leap, perhaps you'd prefer if we—no? Very well, but I must warn you that it's been many years since I've thought back on the Floating Lady, and it's possible that some of the details may have grown a bit muddled. Mr. Kellar made us both promise that we'd keep silent about the matter, out of respect for Miss Moore, so I've never had occasion to tell the story before. But it can hardly matter now, can it? They're all long gone. So far as I know, even Silent Felsden has never—pardon? My apologies. I suppose I'm getting a bit ahead of the story.

I seem to recall that the newspapers were in high dudgeon over the tragedy of the U.S.S. Maine, so it must have been January, or perhaps February, of 1898. Times had been pretty hard for Harry and myself. We'd had a brief burst of notoriety the previous year when we successfully escaped from Sing Sing prison, but it hadn't lasted long. Harry had yet to find regular work of any kind, and was a long way from achieving the worldwide fame he so desperately craved. My job in those days was to serve as Harry's advance man and booking agent. "You will sort through the various offers and opportunities as they present themselves," Harry had informed me, "and you will inspect each potential venue to determine whether it will be suitable for the Great Houdini." To be candid, there wasn't a whole lot of sorting and inspecting required. I don't recall that a single offer or opportunity ever "presented itself" in the manner that Harry imagined. I had to go out and beat the bushes. Much of my time was spent knocking on the doors of talent scouts, sitting in the waiting rooms of booking agents, and twisting the arms of theatrical managers. I can't say I was especially good at it. Every so often Harry pulled a week or so at one of the Dime Museums down around Union Square, and sometimes we'd do a month or two with the Welsh Brothers Circus, but on the whole we lived fairly close to the bone.

I was twenty-one years old at the time, and Harry was two years older. We were barely out of short pants in some respects, but when it came to show business, we felt like old hands. Worse, we were beginning to feel washed up. Strange as it may seem, in his youth Harry did far better as a magician and circus performer than he did as an escape artist. The "self-liberation" act had yet to find its audience, and Harry had not yet cultivated his genius for self-promotion. Whatever bookings came our way usually owed something to the bright sparkle of Harry's wife, Bess. There wasn't a theatrical manager alive whose icy heart failed to melt at the mere sight of Bess. I suppose you couldn't have called her a beauty in the conventional sense, but there was something about her that just stopped you right in your tracks. Trust me on this.

One of my duties as Harry's manager was to keep an eye on the notice columns of the New York Dramatic Mirror. That's where I saw Kellar's posting, and I suppose that's how all the trouble began. I read the Mirror religiously each morning with my tea and toast, trolling for tips and opportunities, and I would remain a faithful reader for many years—long after I no longer had the need. It was a marvelous paper, filled with column after column of news bits, booking information and "situation wanted" notices. I especially loved the back pages, where the call and response of daily business was played out in tiny snippets. Toupées manufactured, discretion assured. Stage gowns fitted, credit available. Voice culture lessons, the speaking voice thoroughly trained and developed. Stage dancing, positions secured. Over time, one could track the waxing and waning of a career or touring company. Edwin Thanhouser, Light Comedian, At Liberty. Grand Annual Tour of the Brilliant Comedienne Alma Chester, Supported by a Powerful Company of Recognized Artists in a Repertoire of Splendid Scenic Productions. Wanted by Mabel Paige: A Gentleman of Reputation to Work with her in a Sketch for Vaudeville.

Truth be told, it was seldom that I came across a notice that held any promise for Harry or myself. On that particular morning, however, it appeared that our prospects had suddenly brightened. There, on page 28, beneath a booking call for Proctor's Leland Opera House, was a thick, blocky headline reading: "Oh, You Wonder!" Beneath it were the words: "Opportunities with the Famous Magician Kellar." A photograph of the great man stared out at me, with the familiar egg-shaped bald head and clear, searching eyes.

I need hardly say that the name of Harry Kellar was as familiar to me as my own. Without question he was the most famous magician in America—and perhaps the entire world. Indeed, at that time there were many who ranked Kellar ahead of Bosco and Signor Blitz as the greatest conjuror of all history. His staging of an illusion entitled "The Witch, The Sailor, and The Enchanted Monkey" had been the sensation of the previous season, and the catch phrase "Oh, You Wonder!" had been on the lips of every member of his vast audiences.

My heart quickened as I read the small print beneath the photograph. "Staff required for '98-'99 Season," it read. "Apply Dudley McAdow, Mgr., 131 B'way." I folded the paper into thirds and reached for my coat and trilby. Our troubles were over, I told myself. I felt certain Harry would be overjoyed by this news.

With my heart aglow at the prospect of steady employment, I hurried to my mother's flat on East Sixty-ninth Street. In those days, Harry and Bess lodged with Mother as a matter of economy, while I kept a room at Mrs. Arthur's boarding house seven blocks away. Finances being what they were, it would probably have been better for all concerned if I had stayed at home as well, but I could not bring myself to do so. I felt that a man of twenty-one ought to be cutting the apron strings and making his own way in the world, though my brother held quite a different view. Also, I fancied myself as something of a dashing rake at the time, and I feared that living at home might place unwelcome restrictions on my social life. That particular concern, I regret to say, was unwarranted. Apart from the occasional night of theater with my friend Biggs, and a periodic hand of whist with fellow lodgers at

Mrs. Arthur's, my social calendar was not overburdened. I spent a great deal of time at the library.

I arrived at East Sixty-ninth Street to find my mother hovering over the stove as always, preparing the cabbages and carrots for a goulash. The air was heavy with paprika.

"My darling Theodore!" Mother called as I came through the kitchen door. "Sit! Sit! I will bring you a plate! You could use a little something on your stomach!"

It was a familiar greeting. In my carnal days I often had occasion to work with a 412-pound man named Hector Armadale. Hector was a delightful fellow and a wonderful storyteller, and it was always my hope that I would find an opportunity to bring him home to my mother, just to see if she would insist that this professional fat man could "use a little something on his stomach."

"Good morning, Mama," I said, setting my hat on the sideboard. "Thank you, but I won't take anything to eat just now. I have already had my breakfast." I nodded at my sister-in-law, who was stirring a pot of heavy porridge oats. "Good morning, Bess."

"Good morning, Dash," she said, giving me a peck on the cheek. "Why are you so bright and eager this morning?"

"I come bearing the promise of steady employment," I replied, brandishing the Mirror. "There might be something here for all three of us!"

"Thank heaven," she said, wiping her hands on her apron. "Mama and I have been taking in extra sewing, but—"

"I know, I know," I said. "But this could be the solution to all our worries, if only he can be made to see it that way. Where is the justly celebrated self-liberator, by the way?"

"You mean the all-eclipsing sensation of the stage? The man whom the Milwaukee Sentinel described as the 'most captivating entertainer in living memory'?"

"That's the one."

"He's still in the bath."

"He's running a bit late this morning," I said, pulling out a chair from the kitchen table. "Normally the smell of Mama's porridge is enough to—"

"Actually, Dash, you might want to go check on him."

"Pardon?"

"He—he's in training. He's been in there an awfully long time."

"Oh." I stood up again. "I'll just go and make sure he's still with us."

"Yes, run along, Theodore," Mother said. "Tell your brother his breakfast is getting cold."

"Among other things," Bess said.

I hurried down the center hall to the water closet and gave a quick rap on the door. Receiving no answer, I turned the knob and stepped inside.

As Bess had indicated, Harry was having a long bath, as one might have expected from one so fastidious in his personal grooming. What might have struck the casual observer as odd, however, was that my brother was entirely submerged beneath the waterline, and there were large chunks of ice floating on the surface.

I should perhaps explain that it was not unusual for my brother to bathe in ice water. He had recently hit upon the idea of leaping from bridges—fully tied and manacled—in order to win free publicity for himself. It was his hope that a regimen of cold immersions would inure him to the shock of the frigid river waters. At the same time, these long sessions in the family bathtub gave him an opportunity to build up his lung power.

I glanced at my Elgin pocket watch and waited as two minutes ticked past. How long would Harry stay down? How long had he been down before I arrived? I perched on the edge of the tub and stared down at my brother. His eyes were closed, his hands were clasped across his stomach and his expression was entirely peaceful. A tiny trickle of air bubbles escaped from the corner of his mouth. I looked again at my watch. Three minutes.

I took off my jacket and unfastened my shift cuff. Reaching down, I dipped my hand in the water and tapped my brother on the shoulder. Harry opened his eyes and let out a watery cry of delight, sending up a rush of air bubbles. "Dash!" he cried, breaking the surface abruptly. "Did you see me? I believe that may have been a new record!"

"Harry, you need to be a bit more careful," I said, noting the bluish tinge of his lips. "How long have you been in there?"

"Oh, not long," he said carelessly. "But that was certainly one of my better sessions. I believe I might have stayed down there another minute or two if you hadn't startled me. It's a question of mind control, really." He rose dripping from the tub and reached for a towel. "I've been reading the most fascinating little monograph about the fakirs of India. It seems that they can suppress their breathing altogether when the conditions are right. What did they call it? Kakta? Kafta? Never mind. I understood what they were driving at. It has to do with the power of the mind." He vigorously towelled himself dry and slipped on a robe. "It seems that if one can learn to focus the mind's energy upon a single—say, Dash, what are you doing in here, anyway?"

"I'm the only talent agent in New York who makes house calls," I said, thrusting the Mirror notice at him. "Cast your eyes on that!"

"A job?" Harry asked. "At last! I was beginning to think I'd never—" He snatched up the paper and scanned the item. "What?" he cried, his features darkening. "Impossible! It won't do at all!"

"But—why—?"

"I wouldn't even consider such a thing!" He tossed the paper aside. "The very idea is preposterous!"

"But Harry—?" I picked up the paper and looked again at the Kellar notice, wondering if there had been some mistake.

"Not at present, in any event. That sort of thing might do for you, Dash, but the Great Houdini must look elsewhere."

I followed him down the hall to his bedroom, where he persisted in giving voice to his ill opinion as he dressed in his familiar black suit, starched white shirt and red bow tie. The peroration continued as he led me back along the corridor to the kitchen. We arrived just as mother was serving up a steaming bowl of porridge oats, a dish I have never been able to tolerate. I noted with rising alarm that a place had now been set for me.

"Sit down, boys," Mother said, pouring out a fresh pot of tea. "It will be cold soon."

"Mama," I said weakly. "I told you that I'd already had breakfast at Mrs. Arthur's."

"And did Mrs. Arthur give you a nice cup of wheat grass tea?" Mother asked sweetly.

"No, but—"

"Was there a slice or two of brown toast?"

"No, but I—"

"And does Mrs. Arthur give you fresh cream with your porridge?"

"No, of course not, but—"

"Then you haven't had breakfast." Mama touched the back of my chair and beamed at me. It was a smile that would brook no resistance. "Sit, Theodore," she said.

With a sigh, I shrugged my shoulders and took my seat. Harry was already tucking a napkin under his chin. "Why do you fight it, Dash?" he asked, amused by my evident discomfort. "You can't possibly expect to do a full day of work without one of Mama's breakfasts."

"I've already done a day's work," I replied. "You're just too pig-headed to acknowledge it. You just aren't—" I broke off as Mother leaned in to fill my tea cup. "Thank you, Mama. You just aren't prepared to be reasonable, Harry."

"What's this all about, Dash?" asked Bess, who had now taken her place next to Harry. "You never did show me the notice."

I passed across the newspaper I had rescued from the floor. "'Staff required,'" she read. "Why, that's wonderful! Harry, whatever is the matter with you? Mr. Kellar's magic show is the finest in the world! It's perfect for us! He travels for months at a time, often to exotic foreign countries! Australia! China! Russia! Can you imagine? There might be as much as a full year of steady work for us. Perhaps more!"

"That's what I've been trying to tell him," I said. "He won't hear of it."

"I just don't think it's quite the right opportunity for us," my brother said, staring down into his tea cup.

"Harry," I said with considerable heat, "you and I are only one step removed from taking up our old positions at the tie factory. It's the only steady work we've had in months. Is that what you want? Do you want to be a tie cutter for the rest of your life?"

"No, Dash, but neither can I throw myself at every job you find in your newspaper. You'll have me working as a carnal busker next. Besides, I think that Mr. Kellar's day has passed."

"Indeed?" Bess folded back the newspaper and began to read. "'Mr. Kellar has been entertaining in Philadelphia, New York, and Chicago for the past three seasons. He perplexed the natives of Philadelphia for 323 consecutive performances at the Temple Theater; he amused New York for 179 consecutive performances at the Comedy Theater on Broadway; and at the Grand Opera House in Chicago he found it worth his while, last summer, to give 103 consecutive performances before bringing the run to a close over the strenuous objections of the management.'"

"Sounds like a career in trouble," I said with lifted eyebrows. "The poor man can probably barely keep body and soul together."

"Eat your porridge," said Harry.

"'Mr. Kellar's fame is scarcely less luminous upon distant shores,'" Bess continued. "'In recent years he has appeared before Queen Victoria at Balmoral Castle, Emperor Napoleon at the Palace of St. Cloud, the Czar of Russia at the Winter Palace of St. Petersburg, and Dom Pedro II of Brazil at the Imperial Palace of Rio de Janeiro.'"

"That's absurd!" cried Harry. "Napoleon has been dead for more than fifty years!"

"I believe it may have been a reference to Napoleon III," I said.

"Oh. Well, it's misleading, in any case."

"'The principal appeal of Mr. Kellar's entertainment consists of the rare and startling phenomena to which his own original and collective brain has given existence,'" Bess resumed. "'His work seemingly sets at naught all natural laws. It is replete with mysticisms and those occult deeds ordinarily ascribed to the redoubtable Prince of Darkness. Yet everything is simply done, and Mr. Kellar frankly disclaims any supernatural agencies. There is no entertainment similar to it in the country, nor is there any word in the English language which can properly describe it. It is entirely sui generis.'"

"What?" asked Harry.

"Sui generis," I said. "Means 'in a class by itself.'"

"Why doesn't he just say so!" Harry reached for a slice of toast. "Sui generis, indeed."

"'Mr. Kellar is as entirely different from the work of the commonplace magician as the electric light outshines its coal-oil predecessors,'" Bess continued. "'His phenomena are unique, amusing, and full of utter impossibilities developed from his own inner consciousness. The man himself is a marvel. He has traversed every part of the civilized as well as the uncivilized globe. He speaks with ease all the modern languages, and half a dozen besides of Asiatic and African dialects. He charms you by a grace of manner that is bewitching; he entrances by the subtle power which he so greatly possesses, and mystifies and bewilders you by the deftness and dexterity with which he executes his remarkable feats. He is simply a marvel beyond the comprehension of the ordinary mortal.'"

Bess neatly folded the newspaper and placed it beside her plate. "Mr. Kellar would seem to have a very spirited press agent," she said.

"Or perhaps an energetic younger brother," I suggested.

"His day has passed," Harry repeated. "The man is still performing The Enchanted Fishery! I ask you!"

"Harry," said Bess, placing her hands flat on the table. "Out with it. Opportunities like this one don't come along every day."

Harry picked up his teaspoon and polished it with his napkin. "Bess," he said to the spoon, "you must defer to my experience in these matters. My long years upon the boards have given me a certain amount of expertise when it comes to—"

"Harry," Bess said again. "Out with it."

My brother stirred his tea, carefully avoiding her eye.

Bess simply folded her arms and waited him out. It didn't take long. Harry stirred his tea for another minute or so, whistling a carefree tune and trying to appear unconcerned. Still avoiding Bess's eye, he began to hum and rap his fingers on the table. Then he gave a heavy sigh and his resolve crumpled. The truth was that my brother could withstand a long submersion in icy bathwater far better than his wife's disapprobation.

"You don't understand, Bess!" he cried in a sudden rush. "It isn't fitting! The Great Houdini is no mere stagehand! The Great Houdini is not a simple lackey to be ordered about at the whim of Mr. Harry Kellar! I am an artist! I am an original! I am the man whom the Milwaukee Sentinel called the 'most captivating entertainer in living memory'! I will not beg for scraps from the table of Mr. Harry Kellar!"

Bess looked over at me and nodded. At least now the cards were on the table. "Harry," she said in a much softer voice, "think of the experience. Think of the contacts. It could be the break you've been needing."

"It is impossible," he insisted. "Besides, he is a mere magician! I am an escape artist! I am the world's foremost self-liberator!"

"Harry," I said, pushing away my bowl of porridge. "So far as we know, you're the only self-liberator on the face of the earth. We've been over this before. No one knows quite what to make of your act. Sure, you've had some good notices, but it's hard to build a career on a few scattered successes. The Kellar show could give us all some seasoning."

"Seasoning!" he snorted. "Mama, do you hear that! Dash thinks I need seasoning!"

"Is that right, dear?" asked Mother, who had little time for idle chat when there was a goulash on the stove.

"Seasoning! As though I were a pepper roast!"

By way of a reply, Mother nudged my porridge bowl back in front of me. "Eat, Theodore," she commanded.

"Seasoning!" Harry said again. "Imagine!"

I lifted my tea cup and watched to see what my sister-in-law would do. She was a woman of many talents—an excellent singer, a graceful dancer, and perhaps the finest magician's assistant ever to carry a dove pan or clatter box. But of all her gifts, by far the greatest was her remarkable ability to manage my brother's various moods and tempers. I watched as she carefully assessed her husband's latest display of pique and considered her options. After a moment, she picked up a slice of brown toast from her plate and nibbled at a corner. "I suppose you're right, Harry," she said, dabbing at her lips with her napkin.

Harry lifted his eyebrows, clearly surprised. "Indeed I am," he said quietly.

"He is?" I asked.

"Certainly," Bess said. "After all, Harry has a certain reputation to consider. It wouldn't do for a man of his considerable renown to be seen as a mere assistant. What was it your father used to say? About a man and his reputation?"

"He said that a man's reputation is his greatest treasure," Harry declared.

"Indeed." Bess took a sip of tea. "Quite right. We won't discuss the matter any further."

I regarded her with some fascination.

"Best not to say another word on the matter." She gazed

serenely into her teacup. "And yet…" she added, as though a new thought had struck her, but then she thought better of it and let her voice trail off.

"What is it, Bess?" Harry asked.

"Oh, it's nothing. Let's not speak of it."

"No, tell me, Bess," Harry insisted. "We must have no secrets between us."

"Well," she said, with considerable reluctance, "it's just that I've read so much about Mr. Kellar, and I seem to recall—no, let's not speak of it. I'm sure you know best, Harry."

"Bess." Harry reached across and took her hands. "Please tell me what you are thinking. Although you lack a man's training and experience, I believe that you possess a certain—a certain naive wisdom that is always refreshing. Please, tell me what troubles you so."

My sister-in-law gave a demure sigh. She may have even fluttered her lashes. "Very well," she said. "When Mr. Kellar was a young man, he served as an assistant to a very well-known magician, did he not?"

"He did," Harry confirmed. "The Wizard of Kalliffa."

"But it wouldn't be quite accurate to describe their relationship as that of master and apprentice, would it? They were really more like father and son, were they not?"

"Yes, indeed," said Harry, warming to the subject. "The Wizard came to regard Kellar as his heir."

"I see," said Bess. "So in many ways, Mr. Kellar's career has served as the continuation of a great magical pedigree. A form of show business royalty, you could say."

"I suppose so," Harry allowed.

"Yes. A pedigree. I find myself wondering, could it be that Mr. Kellar has reached the stage of his own life where he finds himself ready to pass the mantle to some worthy newcomer? Is it possible that he is looking about for some eager and talented young man who shows himself willing to work hard and honor the great traditions of the craft?"

Harry put down his spoon and regarded Bess with narrowed eyes.

"And wouldn't it be a shame," she continued, "if Harry Houdini, who is easily the brightest light of his generation, should miss this opportunity because he was too proud to answer a simple newspaper notice?"

"Bess—"

"Tell me, Harry, how did the young Harry Kellar first come to the attention of the Wizard of Kalliffa?"

Harry turned his head away from us, as though he had caught sight of something fascinating in the wallpaper. "He answered a notice in the newspaper," he said softly.

"'Staff required,'" said Bess. "That's all the notice says. It seems foolish that we should not even trouble to see what positions Mr. Kellar is looking to fill. We have no other engagements at present, and no other calls upon our attention. Wouldn't it be simple enough to present ourselves at the theater and see what opportunity awaits?"

Harry turned back toward us. "There may be something in what you say."

"A man must keep an open mind in this day and age, Harry. Wasn't that another of your father's lessons?"

"Yes," he agreed, gathering conviction. "Indeed it was."

"Well, then," said Bess. "It's decided."

As it happens, I can't recall my father ever having said anything about keeping an open mind, and it must be said that open mindedness was not his greatest strength. At that stage, however, as Harry became caught up in his wife's reasoning, she could just as easily have convinced him that our father had desired us to colonize the ocean floor.

"Dash, we shall call at the theater this afternoon!" Harry cried, springing to his feet. "We shall show him the substitution trunk! Mr. Kellar will be positively dazzled! Why, I shouldn't be surprised if he places us at the head of one of his touring companies! After all, a talent such as mine doesn't come along every day! Mr. Kellar would be wise to have me as a colleague, rather than a competitor! Come along, Dash, we must get the trunk out of the store room!"

Bess poured herself another cup of tea, then looked up to find me staring at her with frank admiration. "Dash," she said with a smile, "you've hardly touched your porridge."

She may have lacked a man's training and experience, but— as Harry had suggested—she possessed a certain naive wisdom that was always refreshing.

ABOUT THE AUTHOR

DANIEL STASHOWER IS A NOVELIST AND MAGICIAN. HIS WORKS include: *Elephants in the Distance*, *The Beautiful Cigar Girl*, the Sherlock Holmes novel, *The Ectoplasmic Man*, and the Edgar-Award-winning Sir Arthur Conan Doyle biography, *Teller of Tales*. He is also the co-editor of two Sherlock Holmes anthologies, *The Ghosts of Baker Street* and *Sherlock Holmes in America*, and the annotated collection *Arthur Conan Doyle: A Life in Letters*.

SÉANCE FOR A VAMPIRE
by Fred Saberhagen

THE SEVENTH BULLET
by Daniel D. Victor

THE WHITECHAPEL HORRORS
by Edward B. Hanna

DR. JEKYLL AND MR. HOLMES
by Loren D. Estleman

THE ANGEL OF THE OPERA
By Sam Siciliano

THE GIANT RAT OF SUMATRA
by Richard L. Boyer

THE PEERLESS PEER
by Philip José Farmer

THE STAR OF INDIA
by Carole Buggé

THE TITANIC TRAGEDY
by William Seil

WWW.TITANBOOKS.COM